WHITE SPIRITUAL BOY

WILLIAM DE BERG

Order this book online at www.trafford.com
or email orders@trafford.com

Most Trafford titles are also available at major online book retailers.

Print information available on the last page.

ISBN: 978-1-4907-7044-4 (sc)
ISBN: 978-1-4907-7046-8 (hc)
ISBN: 978-1-4907-7045-1 (e)

Library of Congress Control Number: 2016902843

Trafford rev. 03/03/2016

www.trafford.com
North America & international
toll-free: 1 888 232 4444 (USA & Canada)
fax: 812 355 4082

"Early in June 1945, when U.S. tanks were less than twenty miles from Bambang, the 175 chief engineers of those vaults were given a farewell party 220 feet underground in a complex known as Tunnel-8, stacked wall-to-wall with row after row of gold bars. As the evening progressed, they drank great quantities of sake, sang patriotic songs and shouted Banzai ('long life') over and over. At midnight, General Yamashita and the princes slipped out, and dynamite charges were set off in the access tunnels, entombing the engineers . . . Those who did not kill themselves ritually would gradually suffocate, surrounded by gold bars." —Sterling & Peggy Seagraves, *Gold Warriors: America's Secret Discovery of Yamashita's Gold*, p. 1

"The supranational sovereignty of an intellectual elite and world bankers is surely preferable to the national auto-determination practiced in past centuries." – David Rockefeller, 1991 Bilderberger meeting

"I believe that banking institutions are more dangerous to our liberties than standing armies." – Thomas Jefferson

"It is well enough that people of the nation do not understand our banking and money system, for if they did, I believe there would be a revolution before tomorrow morning." – Henry Ford

"The 'Golden Rule' is 'He who controls the gold . . . makes the rules.'" – David Wilcock, *Financial Tyranny*

"Map of Luzon"

"Map of Luzon"

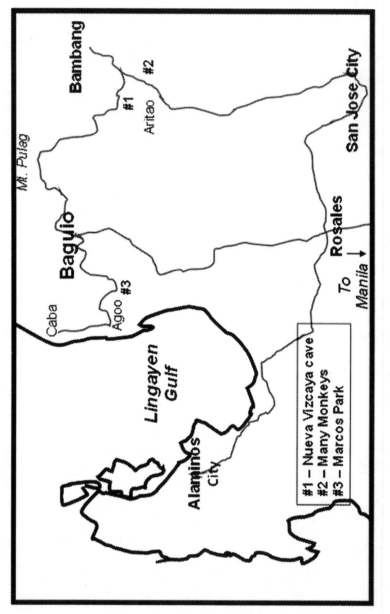

Northern Luzon towns and sites

#1 – Nueva Vizcaya cave
#2 – Many Monkeys
#3 – Marcos Park

CHAPTER
1

The call came at five forty-five on a Thursday morning in late April. After several rings, Rachel Echon roused herself from her bizarre out-of-body dream in which she was flying after her late husband. She listened intently as the voice message came through, not planning to pick up the phone at such an early-morning hour.

"Hi, Rachel, this is Craig from Imperial. I'm in New York for a few days and need to talk to you in person. Please give me a call at 292-245-2587. Thanks."

Craig from Imperial . . . what was this about and why was he calling so early in the damn morning?

She tried to get back to sleep, but she started obsessing over the purpose of the call, just as the early-morning traffic noise on Division Avenue started to pick up. She resigned herself that she would simply suck up her lost hour of sleep and down an extra coffee to make it through the day. She checked the number on the call—it was "292" instead of the usual "812", the extension used by Craig Brooke and his other marketing associates at Imperial Publishing, imploring her to invest in this website banner ad or that book fair or some new trade magazine ad. This call, probably from a cell phone, was clearly something different, as signaled by the veiled sense of urgency.

As she lay in bed, Rachel's thoughts went to the book and its progression from being a curiosity to her, then her rival for her late husband's focus, and finally almost a curse. *Maybe I should have just let it die after his death. But how could I have done that—it was almost the total sum of what he had been able to give to the world.*

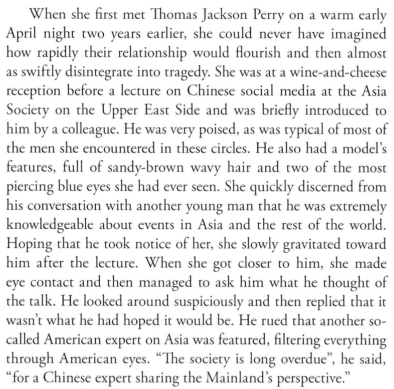

When she first met Thomas Jackson Perry on a warm early April night two years earlier, she could never have imagined how rapidly their relationship would flourish and then almost as swiftly disintegrate into tragedy. She was at a wine-and-cheese reception before a lecture on Chinese social media at the Asia Society on the Upper East Side and was briefly introduced to him by a colleague. He was very poised, as was typical of most of the men she encountered in these circles. He also had a model's features, full of sandy-brown wavy hair and two of the most piercing blue eyes she had ever seen. She quickly discerned from his conversation with another young man that he was extremely knowledgeable about events in Asia and the rest of the world. Hoping that he took notice of her, she slowly gravitated toward him after the lecture. When she got closer to him, she made eye contact and then managed to ask him what he thought of the talk. He looked around suspiciously and then replied that it wasn't what he had hoped it would be. He rued that another so-called American expert on Asia was featured, filtering everything through American eyes. "The society is long overdue", he said, "for a Chinese expert sharing the Mainland's perspective."

Before Rachel could reply, he added, "You know, we Americans never get to hear what others across the globe really think of us. And our media and politicians make sure that we don't encounter such truths in other public arenas."

"And how do *you* claim to know the 'truths' of the world?" Rachel countered.

"Let's put it this way—I have a unique vantage point on Asia . . . and America. But I'm probably sounding pretty pretentious. I'm sure you have a unique vantage point of your own, which I'd love to hear about." He paused, then looked her over more closely and then smiled. "I know a nice wine bar a couple of blocks from here. If you don't have plans, perhaps you'd care to join me?"

"I might, if you'd first be willing to tell me your name."

"Oh, sorry. Jackson Perry. And you?"

"Rachel . . . Rachel Echon."

Perry said goodbye to a couple of his acquaintances, then joined Rachel, who had come by herself to the talk. At the wine bar, Jackson ordered a hummus crostini and a small chorizo pizza and a chardonnay for Rachel and a malbec for him.

"So where are you from, Rachel?"

"Pacific Group."

"Ah, so that explains your interest in Asia. But, there's more, isn't there. Your father's side is from the Philippines, right?"

Rachel was surprised. "Well, *that* was a good read. But, you'd never guess the rest of my background."

"Oh, some European, that's all I'd surmise—with your hazel eyes and freckles."

Rachel slightly blushed. *Are my freckles noticeable even in this dark light?*

"Yes, my maternal grandfather came from light-haired Germans and my grandmother from a dark-haired Russian-Mexican family—both children of Jewish refugees. And, there's some additional Spanish ancestry on my paternal side."

"Oh, so you're a bit of a mongrel, are you? I'd say the mixture in your case turned out striking."

Rachel smiled but felt a little uncomfortable and decided to redirect the conversation. "So Jackson—"

"It's actually Thomas Jackson, but I prefer the middle name."

"Okay, Thomas *Jackson* Perry. That doesn't sound like a mongrel name."

"Hardly. We Perrys are real bluebloods, coming over on what was probably the second or third boat after the Mayflower . . . or perhaps some pirate ship chasing after it." Rachel laughed a little as he continued. "For as long as anyone can remember, we've been straight arrows—straight from Andover to Yale to the navy."

Rachel smiled again despite the sarcasm in his voice. "So you were in the navy, too?"

"No . . . at least not yet. I'm sort of the black sheep—more like the blond sheep—of the family. I decided to go to Asia after I graduated."

"Just to hang out?"

"No, I was on a Fulbright fellowship, and I stayed another year afterward improving my Mandarin and trying to start a little trading company. In the end, my Mandarin turned out a lot more successful than the company. I take it you've spent some time in Asia as well?"

"Yes, I was in China for a semester on an exchange program, when I was majoring in Asian studies, and then I went back again for a year in Taiwan, to teach English."

"So the Pacific Group is hiring English teachers these days?"

She smiled but was again a little irritated. "No, I went on for a master's degree in Asian studies at Columbia and then was hired straight off by the firm. I've been working there ever since."

He put his hand on his chin and managed a faint smile as he gazed at her with his azure eyes. Little did she realize at that moment how that mesmerizing stare presaged his descent into a psychotic death spiral.

Rachel tried again to deflect his focus on her. "I know Perry is a common name, but I was wondering if you're related to George Perry, the former secretary of the treasury."

"George Oliver Perry is my father," he said curtly.

"And . . ."

"And we don't get along very well." Rachel was a bit taken aback, but before she could say anything, Jackson continued. "But, then again, I don't get along with too many rich and powerful men my father's age. Fortunately, I do get along every now and then with beautiful and intelligent women your age—if they don't think I'm too intense. Do you think I am?"

Rachel smiled but was too intrigued to heed his warning sign. "No, actually, I find it a bit of a turn-on."

He smiled more broadly this time. "What I find a turn-on is how incredibly fit and lithe you are. Were you ever a dancer, by chance?

"Another good guess. I took dance lessons through much of elementary school, but I wanted to join some of my friends on a local soccer club and I pestered my parents to allow me to play with them. I played all the way through high school and then through my freshman year in college, until I developed some nagging injuries and realized I wasn't good enough to ever start for the varsity. So I went back to studying modern dance and performing a bit the rest of my college years."

"And where was that?"

"A little place straight up I-91 from New Haven that used to beat your Yalies up regularly."

"Maybe in women's soccer, girl, but not in football!"

They both laughed. She quickly became smitten with him and wanted to know and experience more of him and to find out, underneath his polish, what the source of that unnerving intensity and brilliance was.

It turned out that Perry lived within a few miles of her in Brooklyn, and he hailed a cab for both of them. He called her early the next week and invited her to go sailing on the Long Island Sound the following weekend. She accepted and spent all of a beautiful and breezy early spring Sunday on his skiff. Although Rachel had taken a course in sailing shortly after she started working in New York and had been a member of several crews early on, she was a little rusty at managing the sails. Perry refreshed her on a few techniques and helped her with the jib as she struggled in tacking upwind. They made good time on their downwind return to the marina and smiled languidly at each other as they absorbed the gentle winds and encroaching sunset. Afterward, he took her to a small Italian restaurant in Queens where they ordered cannelloni and bruschetta and salads. Perry was far more relaxed than on their first encounter, and they talked more of music and movies than of politics. Afterward, he caressed her gently as he saw her into her apartment.

The next weekend he invited her to his apartment for a special southwestern casserole dinner, and he downloaded a movie she had expressed an interest in the previous weekend. His thoughtfulness made her feel special, more than any of her previous boyfriends had. Although she had been in a couple of monogamous relationships since college, she found it hard to find lasting romance in the city. She had a classic Eurasian beauty and could radiate her femininity on occasion, but she was nowhere near as flirtatious or extraverted as her college friend Frankie was, which worked against her in a city where single women decidedly outnumbered single men, especially in Manhattan where she worked. The men she did date for a while were smart and good-looking, but they were more interested in their careers than in her. Jackson Perry seemed different, though, and she quickly became enamored. That night and most of the next day, they made love, with him dominating. Two weeks later, he told her he was in love with her, that he needed her, and that he knew from the start that she was the one for him. She wanted to believe all of it, except she had a nagging feeling that she didn't really know all that much about him. So she began to press him on the details of his family life.

He revealed, somewhat agitatedly, that his parents' marriage started to unravel within a few years after their wedding and the birth of his older brother Robert. Jackson figured he was a last-ditch effort to save the marriage, but his mother became steadily more depressed after his birth, eventually requiring electroconvulsive shock. He relished the moments when she would cuddle with him and sing nursery songs to him, but they started to become less and less frequent as he got older. Robert was far enough along on the road in identifying with his father, but Jackson was too young and vulnerable to absorb his mother's mood swings, heightened by her increasing reliance on alcohol and sleeping pills. One day, when he was only five years old, he came into his mother's bedroom and she couldn't be awakened and he started screaming in the empty house. He finally managed to phone his father, but it was too late—not only for his mother, but for Jackson ever to again feel secure with anyone.

He was too young to blame his father for his mother's death, but his father's critical bent and preoccupation with his business interests led Jackson to withdraw into a world of fantasy, some of it dark. When his father did remarry, Jackson found his new wife Patricia to be less interested in her stepsons than in basking in her own role as the wife of George Oliver Perry, while striving to keep her youthful figure intact.

Rachel imagined her now-intense Jackson as a young boy, beset with all of his loneliness and tragedy, and she felt a greater tenderness toward him. But she still wanted him to share more and refused to move in with him until he introduced her to at least his brother, with whom he still had a positive relationship. Robert was six years older and was already midway through Yale as Jackson was just leaving home for Andover. After graduation, Robert spent five years in the navy, so almost a decade went by with only sporadic contact with his younger brother. But Robert still had an attachment to Jackson, and he and his wife Ashley were pleased to invite Jackson and Rachel to dinner at their home in Scarsdale a few months after they started dating. Rachel relished the opportunity to see Jackson playing the uncle to their two adorable little twins, then four years, and his fondness for the girls sealed the deal for Rachel, who agreed to move in with him less than four months after their first date.

Jackson suggested they dispense with a wedding, but Rachel's traditional side insisted that they get married in a ceremony with friends and family in attendance, even if it was only a small gathering. Jackson eventually broke down and visited her parents in Austin to announce their engagement privately and then even allowed his father and Patricia to invite them to the Perry mansion for a small engagement dinner. They finally agreed that they would have a small ceremony and reception at the Perry family estate in Newport in mid-October, with only about one hundred guests in attendance, mostly family but also a smattering of Jackson's and Rachel's friends from college and work. George Perry was fine with the intimate setting because he had already hosted a grand wedding for Robert and Ashley several years earlier at the New York Yacht Club. Nor did he care about his new daughter-in-law's modest background, since Jackson wasn't the one he counted on to run the family's financial empire.

After a romantic honeymoon in the Galapagos, the first few months after the wedding passed harmoniously, with Rachel continuing to commute to the Pacific Group in midtown, where she mainly analyzed business opportunities and emerging social trends in China. Jackson, meanwhile, continued his adjunct teaching at the Brooklyn campus of Long Island University as well as his work on a book dedicated to revealing the "truth" about the events of September 11, 2001, and the powerful elites behind it, known as the Bilderbergers.[1] Jackson didn't actually need to work—the trust he received on his twenty-first birthday could have lasted several lifetimes given the modest lifestyle he led—but he was a talented writer and had an astounding memory and grasp of historical facts and events. Even after Jackson started obsessing about what she was later to term "The Book," she had no idea what it was doing to him. He would show her drafts of various chapters and they seemed to her all pretty rational and believable. When at first she was a little skeptical about the "no-planes" theory, he patiently sat down with her and explained the flaws in the composite video footages of the planes hitting the towers. He also pointed out how Tower Seven fell long after the planes hit the other buildings and for no apparent structural reason other than controlled demolition. It didn't take long before she concurred that the official government conspiracy theory was totally preposterous—how could a bunch of amateur jihadist pilots directed out of a cave in Afghanistan manage to evade the most sophisticated air defense system in the world and then fly some of the most complex aircraft in the world with impossible speed and precision into the strongest buildings ever built by humans and bring them down with free-fall speed?[2] But the notion that elements of her own government planned and executed the murderous hoax, and that all of the leading journalists in America conspired to sell it to the public, never consumed Rachel viscerally the way it did Jackson.

---

[1] For an introduction to the Bilderbergers, see Daniel Estulin's *The True Story of the Bilderberg Group* (TrineDay, 2009).

[2] For a general introduction to the massive number of contradictions to the "official conspiracy" theory of September 11, see David Ray Griffin's *9/11 Ten Years Later: When State Crimes Against Democracy Succeed* (Olive Branch Press, 2011); the documentary *Zero: An Investigation into 9/11*, http://www.youtube.com/watch?v=UFx1WaK54Vo; or an even more provocative and entertaining account by "Ace Baker" entitled *911—The Great American PsyOpera*:
http://www.youtube.com/user/CollinAlexander?feature=mhee

She could see things changing in Jackson, but she couldn't fathom the true depth of his exploding paranoia. At first, his beliefs had an almost puerile rebelliousness about them, with him wielding the sword of truth and justice against the powerful elites out to control the world. But as he began to personify the elites in the face of his father, the stress began to build. He delved more and more into various conspiracies and began to stay up later and later, with Rachel sometimes waking up in the middle of the night only to see him through the half-opened bedroom door staring at his computer. He started to read about Satanism among the political elites and how Satanic rings lured young boys and girls into pedophile nets that went all the way to the highest officials in the government, including vice presidents, senators and congressmen of both parties.[3] He began to freak out at the notion that his own father, as one of the leaders of the financial elite, could be part of those rings.

The mixture of his conspiracy research and paranoid disposition proved devastating. Most individuals who explore the dark conspiracy world can retrace their path and climb the rope back up over the lip of the cave and return to the light of "normal" existence. But there are a few like Jackson who keep exploring new caverns and passageways in order to find a nonexistent bottom and end up sinking ever deeper into the subterranean world of their mind. There were no more relaxing summer days on the skiff, no more theater visits, no more romantic dinners. His few friends became the objects of his suspicions, and not long thereafter he became totally estranged from them. He obsessed about Satanists and the Central Intelligence Agency and all sorts of powerful secret cabals and

---

[3]   The most famous of the pedophile rings involving the rich and powerful in the United States was the one centered in Omaha, Nebraska, described in detail in John de Camp's *The Franklin Cover-up: Child Abuse, Satanism and Murder in Nebraska* (2nd Ed.) (ATW, Inc., 2011), and Nick Bryant's *The Franklin Scandal: A Story of Child Abuse, Power Brokers, and Betrayal* (TrineDay, 2009).

started fretting that they were monitoring the websites he was searching and probing his correspondence and even accessing the chapters of his book. When they would drive somewhere, he would be constantly looking back to see if anyone was following, and when they'd return he would start checking all over the house for signs that someone had planted something. Eventually, he started spewing his florid paranoid rants in front of his classes, and then his teaching contracts were terminated.

Rachel had taken an abnormal psychology course at Dartmouth, but it hardly prepared her for the love of her life's descent into the maelstrom of schizophrenia. She tried to rationalize what was going on around her and pretended it somehow would soon end. But even on the increasingly rare occasions when Jackson would make love to her, he might be calmer the next morning but raging again when she came home from work. As he became more and more controlling, her days at the Pacific Group days became a refuge for her. But even there he would sometimes call her, and her work was affected as she kept postponing important Asian trips so he wouldn't be alone without her. She sought out help but Jackson refused to take his meds, and when she started slipping the antipsychotics in his food, he became suspicious and made her switch the plates around before he would eat. Rachel herself stopped wanting to eat, her stomach churning throughout the day.

Rachel knew she needed to leave, but she loved Jackson, or at least the man she once knew. Then it happened—a few weeks after their first anniversary, which Jackson barely acknowledged, he became enraged and started to accuse her of working for the all-powerful elites and even purchased a gun. Rachel became so alarmed that she moved into hiding in a hotel in New Jersey, not wanting to stay with friends and put them in jeopardy. She didn't know how long she would stay there, but after a couple of days she received the dreaded call at work. They had found Jackson's body in his skiff floating in the sound, with a gun and a pool of dried blood next to his head. She rushed home to see if there was a note and indeed there was one, resting on the bed. It was full of dense and bizarre handwriting, but scattered amidst the cryptic messages about God and Satan and the CIA and thought waves were the words "RACHEL . . . I . . . LOVE . . . YOU." And on top of the note was a flash drive containing the final, complete manuscript of his book.

Rachel broke down and began to sob uncontrollably. After regaining her composure, she quickly decided to do the only thing she could for Jackson—to protect that which ended up destroying him. She remembered what Frankie had told her once—if you ever wanted to hide anything, place it in your tampon or vibrator. So she replaced the battery in her vibrator with the flash drive. It proved to be a very propitious decision, because when she arrived back at the apartment later that day, she found that it had been ransacked and the computer stolen, but all of the valuables left behind. The vibrator with the valuable flash drive inside was left untouched.

At that moment, a sickening thought seized her. *Perhaps there was more truth in his tortured paranoia than I had ever wanted to believe.*

Rachel knew that somehow it had gotten out that Jackson was writing an expose on the masterminds of 911, and obviously someone connected to them didn't want it published. Perhaps it was even his father, if he was afraid the book might be published under the Perry name. In time, after she started to recover emotionally, she decided she would give to the world, for better or worse, the only major work Jackson had contributed to it. She used a pseudonym that played on a common conspiracy group's name and arranged to contact Imperial, who she gathered from the Internet was the leading publisher of independent books. She created an anonymous email account and made sure she never used her own computer but only those in public spaces such as libraries and Internet cafes. Within two months, the book had gone through editing and was at the marketing stage, which is when Craig Brooke got involved and started presenting various media venues and options to promote the book, all coming with costs. Rachel decided on a minimum marketing strategy and to let the book catch on as it may; she owed Jackson a forum for his ideas but not necessarily a best seller.

And, now, less than three months after its publication, Craig Brooke strangely shows up in New York, wanting to meet with her.

All of the names she dealt with at Imperial, like Paul Morrison, Alexandra Carson, Jason Thompson, and, presumably, Craig Brooke, were obviously Anglicized pseudonyms to make the publisher more palatable to prospective Western authors. She knew from the accents that Imperial had outsourced most of its operations to the Philippines, but it didn't matter to her. What did matter was why Brooke would venture across the Pacific to meet with her. While she conceded that he could have been meeting at company headquarters or even attending a book fair nearby, she was suspicious about the tone of the message. Had Imperial received threats from the book's publication, or had her role in its publication somehow been revealed against her wishes so that she herself was now in danger?

All that day, she fretted over the implications of the call, but she finally decided to contact Brooke later that night. He thanked her for returning his call and quickly delved into its purpose.

"First of all, Rachel, I want to alleviate any concerns of yours that you might be in any sort of danger. As far as I am aware, Imperial hasn't received any threats from its publication."

"That's good to hear."

"And, though we can talk about it later if you care to, I didn't call about any further marketing plans for the book."

"That's even better."

Brooke paused momentarily. "But I do need to talk to you about a venture potentially involving you that—and I'm not trying to sound too grandiose—could have a big impact on the lives of huge numbers of people around the world."

Rachel strained to keep from laughing. "And you're going to tell me that you can't reveal any of this matter over the phone because you'd have to kill me, right?"

"No, it's not like that. But please, I do need to talk to you in person. Are you free to meet for dinner tomorrow night?"

Rachel didn't respond right away. *I know I should back out right now, but there's something about his voice. Is it because he seems so earnest . . . or is it something else?*

"I could be. Where do you want to meet?"

"I'll send you a message tomorrow morning."

"This all sounds pretty cryptic—"

"That's because it is."

Rachel paused. "Okay, I'll look for it. But first, tell me how you got hold of my home phone number."

"I have my ways."

The next morning Rachel approached her office building on Fifty-First Street and Lexington, expecting to head straight for her desk and open her email and see Brooke's message. Instead, she was approached at the entrance by an older man who passed a note to her. The note told her to meet Brooke at seven-thirty that evening at Payag, a modern Filipino restaurant just off Queens Boulevard in Woodside—his treat.

CHAPTER

2

Rachel decided to stop briefly at a happy hour with some work colleagues near Central Park before taking a cab to the Filipino restaurant. She imagined Brooke to be a younger version of her father, but when she arrived at the restaurant she was quite surprised to find waiting at the entrance a tall, slender man with high cheekbones, hazel eyes slightly darker than her own, stylishly cropped hair, and a neatly trimmed beard. One other thing stood out—his gold earrings and dragon necklace chain atop his white turtleneck and blue blazer. She guessed him to be in his early thirties, at most.

He immediately reached out to her as he greeted her and then led her to a small table near the back. After helping her to her seat, he spoke to her in a refined, faintly Filipino-accented voice. "It's a great pleasure to meet you in person, Rachel. I think you'll like this place—I've been told it has the finest Filipino cuisine in all of New York. Have you been here before?"

"No, I haven't. And even though I'm half-Filipino, I really don't know too much about Filipino dishes. So perhaps you can recommend something for me."

He quickly pointed to the chicken adobo and the sizzling *sisig* and suggested she'd enjoy either one. Seeing as the latter mixed pig's head and liver, Rachel selected the chicken dish. Brooke then ordered some *lambanog* to go with the meal and insisted she try a glass. After she tasted it and nodded approvingly, he smiled at her.

"So you're probably wondering if I'm yet going to hit you up for some more marketing for the book, right?"

Rachel smiled. "No, I believed you when you said there was something else on your mind. But for sure, the book's had very little impact thus far . . . sort of strange, really, because I thought it was really well-researched and written."

"So you didn't write it, did you?"

Rachel smiled at his perceptiveness. "No . . . and I'm not telling you who did. But I would be curious as to why it's not selling at all."

"Book sales are a complex thing. But it doesn't surprise me, given that you're not out there in public and the book's pretty controversial."

"So what do you think about it? Do you think it's a credible account, what with the massive footnoting and other documentation?"

"I found it very convincing in most of its discussion of the events leading up to and taking place on September 11th. I just don't believe your author grasped the real reason for the Trade Center and Pentagon attacks."

Sensing Rachel was expecting more, Brooke continued on. "The towers were brought down because they contained a trove of records of illicit financial dealings—hundreds of billions in what is known as black ops financing—that were about to be exposed."

Rachel was intrigued but skeptical. "Really?" she replied. "So you're saying the whole idea to shock the American people into a bunch of wars and to collect billions in insurance payments from the fall of the buildings wasn't reason enough?"

"Reason enough perhaps for the act, but not for the timing."

"How so?"

"There were over two hundred billion in debt obligations set to clear the next day—September 12ᵗʰ—most of which were being handled by Cantor Fitzgerald, the largest tenant in Tower One and the one to suffer the greatest number of deaths. Most of this debt was arranged through the Bank of New York, which wasn't physically affected but was nevertheless given the funds to cover its huge obligations the next day by your Federal Reserve. Of course, the Fed justified its release of funds in order to quickly restore financial-system stability in the aftermath of the attacks, although no other bank was so generously treated."

"But I don't see how this relates to my government's role, or supposedly that of the Bilderbergers."

"Because these massive debt obligations were what we call 'black' ones, incurred clandestinely by a cabal of high financial and governmental officials—including the first President Bush— as part of 'Project Hammer', an effort to destroy not only the remnants of the old Soviet Union but the very heart of the Russian economic system that would replace it."[4]

"How's come I've never heard of this Hammer stuff?"

"Most people haven't, except in Russia. It was used to bribe hundreds of key officials, steal Russia's considerable gold reserves, take over key oil and gas industries, and basically destroy the ruble as a viable currency. All of this was done with Hammer money, which was handled outside of congressional and regulatory oversight."

"Why were the bankers involved in all of this?"

---

[4]   See Guy Razer for a detailed research on "Project Hammer" and its relationship to the events of September 11: www.scribd.com/doc/4866520/Collateral-Damage-911-Covert-Ops-Funding-Targeted See E.P. Heidner and Deanna Spingola for two additional accounts of Hammer and other shadowy financial dealings surrounding the events of September 11:
http://www.israelshamir.net/Contributors/Collateral_Damage_Part_II_26122008.pdf; http://arcticcompass.blogspot.com/2010/02/vvvvvvvvvvvvv.html

Brooke smiled. "Rachel, you've read your own book, haven't you? The bankers and other Bilderbergers are about control—of basically everything and everyone, regardless of where they reside on this planet. At that time, Russia was a major threat to their empire, having virtually no foreign debt, lots of gold and other resources, and large holdings of Western currency. All of that wealth was outside the Bilderbergers' control, until it was taken away by the most comprehensive program ever undertaken to bribe and extort the elite of a major power. Russia's economy went into a free fall as a result, with industrial production cut in half from 1990 to 2000 and its overall gross domestic product reduced by forty percent.[5] In the end, most of Russia's key industries were owned by oligarchs underwritten by Western banks. That's why Putin called the breakup of the Soviet Union one of great tragedies of the twentieth century."[6]

Rachel started shaking her head. "You're overreaching, Craig. My government didn't need to bring down the towers just to get rid of Bank of New York's obligations—just look at all the trillions of Fed funds transferred clandestinely to all of the banks beginning in 2008."[7]

---

[5]   The economic collapse of Russia after the breakup of the former Soviet Union is detailed in Geraldo Bracho and Julio Lopez's "The economic collapse of Russia":
        http://www.networkideas.org/featart/nov2005/economic_collapse.pdf

[6]   Although Russian President Vladimir Putin is often misquoted as saying the breakup of the Soviet Union was "the greatest geopolitical tragedy of the twentieth century," his actual 2005 words were that the Soviet breakup "was a major geopolitical disaster of the century":
        http://www.politifact.com/punditfact/statements/2014/mar/06/john-bolton/did-vladimir-putin-call-breakup-ussr-greatest-geop

[7]   The first-ever audit of the Federal Reserve reported in 2012 that the Fed secretly loaned an astounding 16 trillion to major financial institutions in the United States and Europe:
        http://www.sanders.senate.gov/imo/media/doc/GAO%20Fed%20Investigation.pdf
        (refer to Table 8). The entire amount of secret bailouts provided to

"Okay then, what about the fall of Tower Seven, which definitely wasn't hit, and the attack on the Pentagon, which also wasn't hit by a plane, as you well know.[8] According to official accounts, the supposed flight path of American Airlines 77 passed right on by the White House, the Capitol Building, and the Pentagon offices of the highest-ranking generals and civilians of the Department of Defense to hit a small, obscure portion of the Pentagon. Do you know what was in that sector?"

"You tell me."

"The southwest corner of the Pentagon contained the Office of Naval Intelligence, which at the time was monitoring Project Hammer and a whole lot of other illicit financial operations projects linked to it. As with key sections of the Twin Towers prior to September 11th, that corner had undergone 'renovations' over the previous months—by the same company that was then hired on a no-bid contract to clean up the debris from the Twin Towers![9] Did you know that the Office of Naval Intelligence had thirty-nine of its forty members located in that sector die that day—about a third of the total deaths in the Pentagon? And that Tower Seven, as well as Tower Six, both brought down by demolitions, had many of the other governmental agencies snooping into Project Hammer?"[10]

---

institutions may have actually run as high as 29 trillion dollars: http://www.ritholtz.com/blog/2011/12/bailout-total-29-616-trillion-dollars

[8] An immediate report by an onsite CNN reporter definitively ruled out that a plane had hit the Pentagon (https://www.youtube.com/watch?v=7BNqgNvUhRQ), and not one of the Pentagon's 80 security cameras showed a plane hitting it. For additional refutation of the official account of the Pentagon attack, see http://www.citizeninvestigationteam.com/videos/national-security-alert

[9] For a discussion of the role of the British firm AMEC in the Pentagon renovations, see http://digwithin.net/2012/06/15/from-renovation-to-revolution-was-the-pentagon-attacked-from-within

[10] Razer, *op cit.*

Part of Rachel was intrigued and even impressed at all of Brooks' new information, but she was also beginning to get uncomfortable and hoping the food would come soon. *I've been here with Jackson. These conspiracy theories, however valid, end up having no finish line. Why did I even ask him about the book?*

Just then, the waiter appeared along with the wondrous sight and smell of the chicken adobo. She tasted the dish, slowly savoring each bite.

Brooke poured some more lambanog in her glass. "I hope you like the chicken adobo. I recommended it because it's from the central Luzon area, where your Filipino side originates."

Her suspicions become aroused again. "Oh, really," she replied, "so how did you know where my family's from?"

Brooke smiled, trying to calm her, sensing she was becoming perturbed. "It's because Echon is a much more common name in that region than elsewhere in the Philippines."

Rachel was embarrassed. Brooke, for whatever reason, showed her how little she knew of her father's country of origin. She had visited there only three times—once as a little girl and once as a young teenager, and once when she was teaching in Taiwan. Her father rarely talked about his childhood and almost never cooked at home, which is why she had so little knowledge of his homeland, or its cuisine.

"I see. And, I was beginning to worry that you had been investigating me, such as where I grew up—"

"Austin, Texas."

"And where my father and mother worked—"

"Design engineer at Texas Instruments, professor of comparative literature at UT-Austin."

"Or where I went to college—"

"Dartmouth, class of '13."

Rachel stared warily at him. "So, what's this all about, Craig Brooke . . . if that's even your name."

"It's my real name. But, as you suspect, I haven't been on the level with you. In fact, I asked you to dinner because I have a favor I would like to ask of you—a *very big favor*."

Rachel initially showed no reaction, concealing her combination of curiosity and suspicion, but then she was surprised by Brooke's next question.

Pointing to Rachel's Rolex, Brooke asked. "I noticed your beautiful watch—is it twenty-four karat?"

"Yes. But why do you ask?"

"Just admiring it. So what makes it valuable for you?"

Rachel replied curtly, "It was a gift from my late husband."

Brooke stared at her, then turned away. "I'm very sorry, Rachel—"

"Don't worry about it. But, in case you're wondering, it was that book you published of his that ended up driving him mad—and me into widowhood." After Brooke remained impassive, she said, "Please keep going."

"Okay, so why else is it valuable to you?"

"Maybe because it's gold? Really, what are you getting at?"

"That's what I'm getting at—*gold!* Have you ever wondered why gold is so valuable, both as jewelry and as a currency?"

"Well, I'm not sure exactly." She tried to remember some properties of gold from her high school chemistry class. "Isn't it because it's pretty rare and one of the densest elements on Earth?"

"That's partly right. There are almost one hundred natural elements found on Earth, but most of them are either dangerously radioactive or highly reactive—metals like sodium and potassium, which blow up in water—or so light you could barely contain them in your pocket, like the gases. There are only a few transition metals like osmium, iridium, palladium, rhodium, ruthenium, silver, platinum, and gold that have all the desired properties for a good currency. But the first five are either way too rare or were discovered in the 1800s, or far too late to be historically valuable to humans. So that leaves gold, silver, and platinum."[11]

"Platinum's worth even more than gold, isn't it?"

"It is. But platinum requires higher temperatures to melt into jewelry and coins than would ordinarily have been attainable in ancient times. Plus, it's too rare to be used widely as coinage."

"And silver tarnishes too easily, as every housewife who has silverware and a silver tea set well knows."

Brooke smiled. "That's right, Rachel. So that leaves gold in a class of its own. Gold's been used as coinage since the early Greeks. It's driven much of human history—from the Roman conquests of foreign lands, to the collapse of European commerce after the fall of the Roman empire, to the Spanish conquest of the Western Hemisphere.[12] But there's a problem with gold as well."

"What's that?"

"Gold really isn't that rare, despite the general misconception, promulgated by the financial elite."

"And why do they do that?"

"Because they want to make it difficult for anyone else to own it."

"And how do you know this?"

Brooke looked at his watch. "Look, it's a little past eight-thirty now," he said as he glanced around the restaurant. "I assume this place closes around ten. Are you willing to stay till then?"

"If it means you getting to the point of all of this, perhaps."

"Good. Rachel, the reason I know so much about gold is the same as why I know a lot about you. I don't mean to sound

[11] For a discussion on why gold became by far the most valuable monetary instrument in history, see http://www.npr.org/blogs/money/2011/02/15/131430755/a-chemist-explains-why-gold-beat-out-lithium-osmium-einsteinium

[12] See http://www2.econ.iastate.edu/classes/econ355/choi/golds.htm

presumptuous, but I'm connected to people who know lots of things about others . . . and the world."

His grandiosity started to bother her. *Why do I end up hearing out men like Jackson and now Brooke. At least I'm not involved with him—yet.*

"Let me ask you this," Brooke continued, "what would you need to start a worldwide currency to compete with the dollar and euro?"

Rachel wasn't sure if it was the long day or the longer workweek or the happy hour or the lambanog or all three, but her mind was starting to fade and she tried hard to muster an intelligent response. "Well, first off, I would need something to back it with."

Brooke became more animated. "Exactly. And what would you need to back it with, for nations to use it, for it to be easily convertible, and the common man or woman to trust it?"

Rachel dutifully replied, "Gold?"

"And if you're a big financier out to control the world, what do you want to keep out the hands of other nations?"

"Gold again?"

"Exactly. And—"

Rachel started laughing, which temporarily halted Brooke's rhetorical questioning.

"I'm sorry, but your rant about gold brought back memories of when I was a little girl and how at family gatherings my grandfather used to often get into political arguments with my Uncle Marvin, who used to rail at this or that about the government. Once, after Uncle Marvin's complaint about the U.S. Government's abandoning the gold standard, my grandfather asked whether it would be better to own all of the gold—sort of like King Midas—or all of the food. You've got to remember that my grandfather started out as grocer before focusing on seafood. When Uncle Marvin replied 'All the gold, of course,' my grandfather then asked him, 'What good is all of your gold if I have all of the food?' And after my uncle's reply that he could buy my grandfather's food, he then countered with 'But, what if I don't want to sell it you?' And then my uncle would say something to the effect that he could pay troops with his gold to steal his food, but my grandfather would counter again 'What if I hid it from them?' And the back-and-forth went on for a while longer, never really resolving. But everyone thought it was cute that a little girl like me always took my zahdee's side, because he was so much fun to be around!"

"Well, your grandfather might have been decent, hardworking, and fun to be around, but his argument was sadly disproven in the 1930s, when Stalin looted all of the grain from the Ukrainian kulaks and shot anyone who resisted, leaving many of the rest to starve.[13] You might be surprised how many modern-day 'King Midases' there are—including most of the leaders of the Western financial system."

Rachel shook her head to indicate disbelief. "So you're saying our financial leaders are trying to wrest control of all the gold in the world?"

"No, they did that a long time ago; now, they're trying to hang on to it. Let me explain—between 1930 and 1960, a massive amount of gold flowed from private individuals and nations around the world to the western banking system, led by your Federal Reserve. By the end of World War II, the Fed controlled an estimated sixty percent of all the world's gold.[14] Most of this gold was either stolen or coerced or otherwise obtained under false pretenses. As a consequence, the U.S. dollar began to completely dominate world financial transactions."

Rachel tried to cover up a slight yawn. *It's been such a long day and with the happy hour and lambanog, I don't know how much more of this financial stuff I can process—especially when I*

---

[13] For a review of the Ukrainian famine of the early 1930s, known as the "Holomodor," see http://en.wikipedia.org/wiki/Holodomor

[14] See Glen Yeadon & John Hawkins, *The Nazi Hydra in America: Suppressed History of a Century,* (Progressive Press, 2008), p. 349.

don't know where it's all leading. Brooke sensed that Rachel was losing attention, so he tried to stir her. "Aren't you going to ask me how it was all done?"

"Okay, how was it all done?" she replied playfully.

"It started with your government's confiscation of all private gold in 1933 and was followed by a multitude of transfers, both legal and illegal, from around the world that created secret funds like the 'Black Eagle Trust'.[15] The 1933 gold confiscation, allegedly to shore up the dollar and to help exit the Great Depression, didn't result in a lot of gold transferred—probably not more than a few hundred tons—but it took your country once and for all off the gold standard. And, it set the stage for fabulous transfers all over the world in the 1930s, particularly from China."

"China? Why would it give up its gold?"

"Because a lot of wealthy individuals and government leaders in China had no confidence that China could fend off Japan, which had already taken over Korea and Manchuria and had plundered most of the wealth of those regions. The biggest transfers occurred in 1934, and the Chinese were offered

---

[15] No official documentation exists, or at least been released, concerning the "Black Eagle Trust"—named for the gold of the Nazis, whose symbol was the eagle overlying the swastika. Supposedly, it was created in 1944 at Bretton Woods as part of the new postwar financial order and initially managed by Henry Stimson and John McCloy, both powerful members of the Council on Foreign Relations (the leading intellectual arm of the Bilderbergers). A source quoted by the Seagraves states that the Nazi gold constituted about 11,200 metric tons (Sterling & Peggy Seagraves, *Gold Warriors: America's Secret Recovery of Yamashita's Gold,* (2nd Ed.) (Verso, 2005). Other accounts of the formation of the Black Eagle Trust include Yeadon & Hawkins, 2008, *op cit.,* pp. 342-358, and David Guyatt, *The Spoils of War:* http://www.bibliotecapleyades.net/sociopolitica/esp_sociopol_fed05e.htm. Eventually, the Black Eagle Trust is alleged to have housed most of the secret gold absconded during and after the Second World War.

special Federal Reserve certificates—now all worthless, but that's another story."[16]

"So, how much gold arrived from China?"

"Accounts range from twenty thousand to over one hundred thousand metric tons—over five trillion dollars at today's prices. Of course, no one knows exactly how much, because the first thing you realize when one starts investigating gold trading is that it is one of the most opaque—some would say 'occult'—worlds imaginable. But we do have hints that there was a massive amount of wealth transferred. For one, newspaper accounts reveal how in 1934 over six million in gold bars—we're speaking of 1934 dollars here—were transferred *in a single* day to the New York Federal Reserve.[17] Some of that was coming from Europe and other nations besides China, in anticipation of World War II. By 1936, your bullion depository at Fort Knox was constructed and by World War II it *officially* held over twenty thousand tons.[18] Why build such a large, fortified building for a couple of hundred tons confiscated from your own citizens, which could have easily fit into a small study? Do you realize that official estimates of all of the gold mined since the beginning of time are only about one hundred and seventy thousand metric tons? But the official estimates are way off—unofficial estimates put the true total at well over *one million* tons—with most of it coming from Asia." [19]

---

[16] See David Wilcock, *Financial Tyranny: Defeating the Greatest Cover-up of All Time* (Chap. 4): http://www.divinecosmos.com/start-here/davids-blog/1023-financial-tyranny (available as FinancialTyranny.pdf)

[17] See Wilcock, *FinancialTyranny.pdf,* for newspaper accounts of daily gold transfers to the United States in the 1930s.

[18] According to the economist Dr. Martin Larsen, the United States Federal Reserve purchased over 18,000 metric tons of gold between 1934 and 1941 (Seagraves & Seagraves, 2005, *op cit.*, p. 261).

[19] For a discussion of the "official" estimates and challenges to it, see http://www.bbc.com/news/magazine-21969100. Many experts, including Phoenix Powers and David Guyatt, claim the total gold

"Why Asia?"

"Because gold has been historically very important—and plentiful—in Asia. There were massive gold deposits in Southeast Asia that were being tapped long before Westerners arrived in the Americas. Marco Polo relayed stories of the 'land of gold'— Zipangu, or ancient Japan—where the palaces had roofs and floors made of gold. And did you know that the ancient name for modern-day Thailand —Suvarnabhumi—also means 'land of gold'?"[20]

"Really?" Rachel asked, perking up. "Now, that's interesting. I had no idea."

"Gold was everywhere!" he continued in an animated voice. "You could pick it out of streams and hillsides, almost pure. It was refined down to anything from coins and jewelry to solid-gold Buddhas weighing thousands of kilos.[21] And then, to top it off, for over a thousand years, gold found its way to Asia in return for the spices and perfumes and silks that were sent westward to Europe. Prior to World War II, Shanghai boasted the world's largest gold exchange, and even today the most productive gold mines and untapped gold deposits in the world

---

produced is well over one million tons. The biggest discrepancy with official estimates is the amount mined before 1850 and the amount mined since in several nations of Asia, including China. Indeed, the fact that officially 5% of the gold was produced in Asia, where the vast majority of the human population has resided throughout history, makes the face validity of the 170,000-ton figure seem rather ludicrous (see Seagraves & Seagraves, 2005, *op cit.*, pp. 9-10).

[20]   See http://web-japan.org/nipponia/nipponia45/en/feature/feature01. html and
http://cmualumniusa.org/siamthai.htm.   In   fact,   the   Bangkok International Airport in Thailand is known today as Svarnabhumi.

[21]   The largest golden Buddha in the world weighs 5.5 metric tons and is located in the temple of Wat Traimit, Bangkok: http://en.wikipedia.org/wiki/Golden_Buddha_%28statue%29

are in Southeast Asia, primarily Indonesia and Borneo.[22] This all set the stage for 'Golden Lily.'"

"Golden Lily? That sounds like the name of a saloon in Nevada!"

Brooke smiled briefly before continuing in a serious tone. "'Golden Lily' was originally the name of a poem by Emperor Hirohito, but it became the moniker for one of the most horrific campaigns in the history of humankind. Basically, it amounted to a very efficient strategy of mass rape and plunder of every nation the Japanese took over during World War II. The Japanese were determined to control the resources of the nations they conquered, to support their war machine, but even those resources couldn't cover the costs of the military operations. So they ruthlessly set about stealing every ounce of wealth in sight, entering government depositories, banks, homes, temples, and pagodas to remove all of the coins and jewels, gold being the most prized of these. They even stole toilets, wiring, paintings, flooring, anything that had value, and moved them into large warehouses before shipping them off. The Japanese made the Nazis with all of their thievery look like small-time crooks."[23]

"So, where did it all end up—in Japan?"

"Lots of it did. But when the Japanese took over Southeast Asia, there was a problem. They couldn't easily transport the loot over the mountains to China, so they shipped it by sea to Manila, where it was intended for reshipment to Japan. But by late 1943, American submarines controlled the waters between the Philippines and Japan and it became too dangerous to move the treasure, even though some got through on fake hospital ships.[24] So the Japanese decided to bury the treasure, most of it

---

[22]   For example, the Grassberg mine in Indonesia is the top gold-producing mine in the world: http://www.mining.com/web/worlds-top-10-gold-deposits

[23]   The single-best account of the Golden Lily treasure and its history is contained in Seagraves & Seagraves, 2005, *op. cit.*

[24]   Seagraves & Seagraves, 2005, *op cit.*, p. 203.

in the north of Luzon, some of it elsewhere, like Indonesia. They were hopeful that they could eventually keep the Philippines as part of a postwar agreement, not realizing that unconditional surrender terms were in store for them. The general in charge when the last sites were dug was Tomoyuki Yamashita, which is why the entire treasure became known as Yamashita's gold, even though most of the sites were dug before Yamashita arrived in Manila, under the direction of Hirohito's brother, Prince Chichibu."

"I once saw a special on Yamashita's gold. Some people don't believe it's real because so little of it has supposedly been discovered."

"Oh, it's real all right—there's a ton of documentation on it, or I should say documentation on well over one hundred thousand tons of it. Lots of it was buried in the countryside in caves, but some of it was buried in elaborate tunnels around Manila and other big cities, and some under hospitals and schools and military installations like occupied Fort Bonifacio, Clark Air Base, and the Subic Bay naval base. But as the Americans were approaching, the Japanese started to get desperate, burying it wherever convenient. One of the oddest stories was that of a senior Japanese naval officer, who was stuck with a bunch of gold bars near the end of the war and had to quickly bury them. He and some other officers were watching a movie on Corregidor Island at the mouth of Manila Bay when a bomb exploded nearby, leaving a crater. The officer immediately seized the opportunity to deposit the gold in the crater and quickly filled in the hole. But a few minutes later, American paratroopers arrived and killed the Japanese officer and all of his men."[25]

"Now, that would make for a great movie . . . or book!" Rachel looked at her gold watch. It was almost nine-thirty and the restaurant would be closing soon. After the waiter brought

---

[25]   Seagraves & Seagraves, 2005, *op cit.*, pp. 209-210.

coffee and the dessert Brooke had ordered—banana *lumpia* in a coconut caramel sauce—Rachel voiced her lingering suspicious. "Look, Craig, I'm not sure why you invited me here tonight and drew up the dossier on me. If all of what you say is real, and I'm not sure it is, then it's likely that all of the treasures would have already been discovered by now. What's all this got to do with me?"

Brooke tilted his head toward her and said quietly, almost in a whisper, "Because most of Yamashita's gold *hasn't* been recovered! There were reputedly some one hundred and seventy-five known sites, but only a fraction have been found and had their gold removed—perhaps less than a quarter, most of them smaller ones. Less than a dozen of the largest sites—designated '777' by the Japanese—have been discovered, with one '777' reputedly having contained *over twenty thousand metric tons in gold bars!*[26] Some experts believe there may be hundreds of thousands of metric tons of Golden Lily treasure yet to be found . . . just in buried gold, let alone the other gems and other precious metals.[27] But it's not so easy to recover."

"Why's that?"

"First, there are two sets of maps—one set is geographical, in white, which shows *where* the sites are. The other set—the red one—contains coded engineering drawings that depict *how* to extract the actual treasure.[28] The group I represent has the most complete set of white maps currently available, but the remaining white maps are not all in one place. Some of the originals were

[26] Seagraves & Seagraves, 2005, *op cit.*, p. 177-183, for a description of the recoveries at the Thereas-2 site.

[27] See Phoenix Powers, *The Great Gold Swindle: Yamashita's Gold* (Lulu. com, 2012), p. 163.

[28] According to Seagraves & Seagraves, 2005, *op cit.*, there were actually three sets of maps—white for geographical location, blue for official engineering, and red for specially coded engineering maps. For a discussion of the maps and their significance, see Seagraves & Seagraves, 2005, *op cit.*, p. 162.

evidently destroyed, and copies ended up in other countries. The Japanese have some maps, but many of the Japanese involved were executed or killed by the war's end. The Japanese weren't allowed to explore the sites officially after the war, although a couple of rural sites were opened when Japanese businessmen were ostensibly developing some remote Luzon regions for resorts. As for the red maps, they are believed to have ended up eventually in the hands of Robert Curtis, an American smelter who was hired by then-President Marcos to recover and refine the Lily gold. Curtis supposedly took secret photographs of them before smuggling them out in a piece of furniture he shipped off to America. The red maps describe the site entrances, booby traps, and bomb placements, coded as turtles. They also show depths, coded by clock faces, and the locations of poison gas canisters, false walls, even overhead sand traps, coded by slanted arrows. They also have clues as to which direction to read the map, in some cases requiring a mirror. The Japanese clearly did not want anyone accessing the treasures and made it extremely dangerous to do so without the required knowledge."

"And you're looking for those red maps, presumably those of Curtis?"

"Exactly . . . but Curtis no longer owns them. My colleagues tell me he was shaken down by American intelligence officials, who passed them off to the Bilderberger financial cabal. But the engineering maps are pretty much useless without our white maps, and vice versa."

"So, what would you do if a trade was arranged and you— and they—each had combined sets. Would you split the loot? And if so, what good would that do?"

Brooke smiled. "No one knows what would happen. We're more than willing to split the treasures, but I can't speak for the Bilderbergers. Our assumption is that they will, at least initially."

"Why's that?"

"Have you ever heard of the 'prisoner's dilemma'? It's used a lot in negotiation research."

"I vaguely remember something about it in a social psychology class I had in college."

"Then, let me refresh your memory of it. In the prisoner's dilemma, two people are thrown into prison, and there are three outcomes. The best collective outcome is if neither side cooperates with the authorities—but this requires trust on the part of both parties. The least advantageous outcome overall is if both end up snitching on each other. The final outcome is the most interesting—if only one side cooperates, it gets off almost scot-free whereas the side that doesn't ends up in the worst shape. That's analogous to the conundrum facing the Bilderberger cabal."[29]

"How so?"

"If they don't deal with us, one outcome is that the gold stays in the ground. They benefit in that we don't end up with the gold to compete with the euro and dollar. But, the cabal also loses out because without the gold, they'll forfeit some of the ability to control even their own fiat currencies in the future . . . in addition to other things."

"Like what?"

"Like black ops. Most of the Yamashita gold discovered by Marcos and his cronies eventually went into coffers of the big New York, London, and Swiss banks, never to be seen again. But a lot of the Yamashita gold ended up being used by the Americans to thwart the advance of communism throughout Asia after World War II, in Japan and elsewhere, just as the recovered Nazi gold was used to fund covert anticommunist activity in Europe after the war. This pattern was repeated with Sukarno's gold, Gaddafi's gold, South African gold, Ukrainian gold, and, of course, the Russian gold I already mentioned.[30] The

---

[29] For a discussion of the "prisoner's dilemma," see http://en.wikipedia.org/wiki/Prisoner's_dilemma

[30] David Guyatt quotes a source who claims that Sukarno's gold, some it in Swiss banks and some in secret locations in Indonesia, totals over $100 trillion U.S. dollars (see Guyatt, *The Secret Gold Treaty, op cit.,*

irony of it is that Marcos' gold—some of which was extorted from him just before the CIA escorted him from Malacañang Palace in 1986 after whipping up the so-called 'people power' revolt that put Cory Aquino into the presidency[31]—was allegedly used to help underwrite the funding of Project Hammer, which ended up stealing all of the Russian gold."[32]

As Brooke paused, he could see Rachel's eyes focused on him and her mouth slightly upturned, suggesting her slightly bemused continuing interest. "The worst outcome for them if they don't deal, Rachel, is that we could recover the gold on our own. The Western financial cabal could then no longer prevent

---

Section 4.1). The Russian gold reserves, which disappeared after the fall of the Soviet Union, were estimated to contain around 3000 metric tons:
http://www.greenenergyinvestors.com/index.php?showtopic=4679
The gold of the Libyan government, which accumulated under Col. Muammar Gaddafi but disappeared after his overthrow by NATO-led rebels in October of 2011, was estimated at 150 metric tons, partly intended for the creation of an African Monetary Fund:
The South African gold reserves were allegedly moved out of the country just before the African National Congress took over in 1994 (see David Guyatt, *Project Hammer: Covert Finance, The Parallel Economy & Elite Actions*, http://www.bibliotecapleyades.net/sociopolitica/projecthammer/hammersummary.html
Accounts of the theft of Libyan and Ukrainian gold are described in: http://www.24hgold.com/english/contributor.aspx?article=40301209 08G10020&contributor=Charleston+Voice and http://www.examiner.com/article/rumors-abound-of-gold-theft-by-u-s-from-ukrainian-vaults

[31] According to David Guyatt, *Spoils of War, op cit.,* Footnote 40, documentation exists that Bilderberger guru Henry Kissinger demanded payment of nearly 63,000 tons of gold from Marcos in 1986, but Marcos initially refused, possibly contributing to his removal from power. The gold was eventually loaded onto barges and sent to the United States Subic Bay naval base north of Manila. The role of the U.S. in removing what was once an old ally from power remains controversial: http://www.larouchepub.com/other/2004/site_packages/econ_hitmen/3150philipp_coup.html

[32] See footnote #4.

the emergence of gold-backed alternative currencies, which would deal a severe, possibly fatal blow to their own currencies."

"And what's the probability that could happen?"

Brooke smiled. "There's a lot of danger in exploring without the red maps, but modern mining and advanced imaging technologies have made it more of a possibility. In fact, there is a site in the Cordillera Range near Bambang that my group is about to pry open, as a test case. What's important is not how many sites we might get into on our own, but rather how many the Western cabal *thinks* we can empty without them. If they begin to fear we can pull it off on our own, they'll be more likely, at least initially, to choose to cooperate with us. It's not the most lucrative option necessarily, but it's the safest."

"And if they cooperate . . . and later don't?"

"Then we have to be prepared for their usual stuff."

"You mean assassinations and coups, don't you? Things that they've been pretty good at over the years."

"Yes, but the world's changed. For one, there are a lot of powerful players these days, and we have our antennas all over the Philippines now. And after all of their mischief, their sordid playbook is worn pretty thin these days."

"But even if you deal, you haven't told me how you're going to hold on to what you salvage from the sites. Do you really think you can outwit the Bilderbergers?"

"That's our problem, not yours." Brooke then motioned to the waiter for the bill and asked the waiter if he could pay him with a gold Krugerrand. The waiter stared at the coin and then picked it up, saying he would have to check with the owner before accepting.

After the waiter left, Rachel petulantly asked "What was that all about, Craig? Are you trying to show me how convertible gold is as a currency? I don't think you'll have any luck."

Brooke smiled and then pulled out a rolled-up manila folder from the inner pocket of his jacket and extended it toward Rachel. "Rachel, since we're out of time here tonight, I'm going to leave you with this background paper that will help explain a little more of what we just talked about." He paused. "Because you remember I said I was going to ask a big favor of you, right?"

"I do."

"My friends would like to contact the men who run the West's financial system and who we believe to be in control of the red maps, but it's difficult to do so while remaining discreet."

"So, you want me to contact them for you—me, a lowly foreign policy analyst?" she said sarcastically.

"You may be a lowly analyst, but we believe you have special access to the current leader of the Bilderberger financial cabal."

"Who's that?"

"George Oliver Perry."

Rachel blanched at the sound of her father-in-law's name, then looked away, worriedly. She knew George Perry was powerfully situated and remembered when, on one of her few visits to the Perry estate at Chappaqua, she saw what looked like the chairman of the Federal Reserve talking with Perry in the sitting room. *But could he really be the head of the whole group . . . or are they totally mistaken?*

Her thoughts were immediately interrupted by the waiter, who came back with the gold coin Brooke had offered him. The waiter stiffly announced that the owner would accept the coin, but only with a fifty percent discount. Brooke nodded his assent and the waiter went to return with his change.

Rachel was unnerved—and upset. "So, you're losing, what with the price of gold at fifteen hundred an ounce and the bill around fifty dollars, *seven hundred dollars* . . . just to prove a point that anyone with a measuring cup and a scale can tell if it's real or not and treat it as currency!"

Brooke smiled as he arose from the table, "Not quite seven hundred, Rachel . . . you forgot to figure in the tip."

As they left the restaurant, Brooke offered Rachel a ride home. She was still a little peeved, but she was tired and there was no direct bus service between Woodside Avenue and her apartment in Williamsburg and a cab might mean a fair wait time, so she reluctantly accepted his offer. She was surprised to see him approach a late-model Lexus IS convertible—definitely not a typical rental car. Although the air temperature was in the mid-fifties, the breeze against her face was invigorating as the car accelerated toward the Brooklyn-Queens Expressway.

Once underway, she asked him a question that had been on her mind since she first saw him. "Craig, I hope you don't mind me saying this, but you surprised me when I first met you. I guess I was expecting you to look . . . somewhat different."

He laughed. "You mean more Filipino-looking, right?" After a brief pause, he asked her, "Have you ever heard of the white rajahs?"

"No, should I have?"

"Well, you know a lot about Asia, so I thought you might have heard of them. It doesn't matter, though—all you need to know is that I'm descended from their line."

Rachel's interest was piqued. "So, please tell me about them . . . and you."

"Back in the 1800s, my distant relative, James Brooke, was born to an Englishman in India, but he had Asia in his blood. When he put together a sufficient fortune as a young man, he bought a fortified trading ship that travelled throughout the straits of Malacca and the northern coast off Borneo. Once, when there was trouble off Borneo, he and his ship helped out the sultan of Brunei stop some marauding pirates. As a token of his gratitude, the sultan gave him the title to part of central Sarawak and a few other smaller regions, making him the 'rajah,' or king. James and his nephew Charles expanded the territory to what resembles the province of Sarawak's present-day boundaries. It remained in my family until after World War II, when Charles' son Vyner —the last white rajah—ceded the territory to the British, against the constitution of Sarawak, which guaranteed self-rule, and over the heated protests of his nephew Anthony—my grandfather—who was denied his right to be the next rajah.[33] In 1963, Sarawak became part of the Malaysian Federation—again, without popular consent."[34]

"So, your name really *is* Craig Brooke. But aren't most of the Anglo names at Imperial—"

"Contrived? Yes, that's for marketing purposes, as you can imagine."

"But, judging from your faint Filipino accent, you must have grown up in the Philippines."

"I wasn't born there, but most of my time has been spent in and around the islands, although I did spend a few years at Cambridge—sort of a family tradition."

"I won't ask you how you ended up at Imperial, but I *am* interested in why you have such a personal interest in Yamashita's gold."

"It's pretty simple. Some of the Golden Lily treasure buried in the Philippines was stolen not only from the state coffers in Kuching[35] but also from my family's estate in Sarawak, and we want it back. Even though my family ruled Sarawak much more benignly than the typical English colonial and spread the wealth around quite a bit, we were still able to obtain a considerable wealth from rubber and palm oil plantations. Much of it was

---

[33] Craig Brooke is fictional but Anthony Brooke and the Brooke dynasty in Sarawak—as well as their conflicting views of the British takeover of Sarawak—are not: http://www.dailymail.co.uk/news/article-1367066/The-White-Rajahs-The-extraordinary-story-Victorian-adventurer-subjugated-vast-swathe-Borneo.html For a discussion of the opposition to the 1946 cession, see http://en.wikipedia.org/wiki/Anti-cession_movement_of_Sarawak

[34] For a current view of the validity of the 1963 cession of Sarawak to Malaysia, see http://www.themalaysianinsider.com/malaysia/article/malaysia-agreement-1963-invalid-claims-sarawak-ngo

[35] Kuching is the capital of Sarawak.

converted into gold, as was typical in Asia. Some additional gold came from the nearby mines."[36]

"So, you represent your family's interests, primarily."

"No, I represent lots of families in East and Southeast Asia, from China to Indonesia. Some had their riches eviscerated by Golden Lily, others have been unable to redeem their gold certificates given them in the 1930s by the United States, and still others have had later gold-backed certificates voided by Western banks. I presume you've never heard of the 'White Dragon Family,' or have you?"

"No, is that something real?"

"It is . . . but it's not really a family but representatives of a group of wealthy Asian families who share one thing in common—they've all had their wealth absconded by the Western financial cabal via plunder and deception.[37] All have agreed that most of any recovered wealth will be shared with the people of Asia. They find it appalling that Asian nations from Myanmar to Indonesia remain some of the poorest on earth, despite their historical riches that amazed the early Europeans. All of our misfortune, grievances, settlement efforts, and goals

---

[36] Sarawak and Sabah, the only two Malaysian provinces located on the island of Borneo, have produced most of Malaysia's mineral wealth in gold and oil (http://www.goldmadesimplenews.com/mining/tests-suggest-that-new-sarawak-gold-mine-may-be-one-of-the-richest-7884) but have remained Malaysia's poorest provinces (http://www.malaysia-today.net/the-roots-of-poverty-in-sabah-sarawak-in-malaysia-exposed) and are increasingly pushing for independence: http://www.themalaymailonline.com/what-you-think/article/sabah-sarawak-50-years-in-malaysia-plagued-by-bad-politics-joe-fernadez

[37] The White Dragon Society/Family is supposedly the name of a wealthy Asian group that opposes the Western financial establishment, as initially described by Benjamin Fulford:
http://www.bibliotecapleyades.net/sociopolitica/sociopol_fulford99.htm
Whether the White Dragon Society actually exists or not is unclear, but it was the claimant in an actual lawsuit filed in New York City in 2012 (see footnote #53).

are in that document I gave you—minus the names of our people, of course."

As they neared her apartment block, she was about to point out where to turn but then realized he already knew where she lived.

"So, Rachel, here's what I propose—read the paper carefully to gain a little more background and to see if you might be interested in helping us out. If so, you'll have to stop by on your next Asian trip and visit Luzon and meet some of the 'Family'. If you're still in at that point—and we fully understand if you don't want to be—we'll give you a copy of one of our white maps. If your father-in-law is interested, you'll exchange it for a red map and get it back to us. When's your next trip to Asia for the Pacific Group?"

"Next month. I'm leaving on the fifteenth for the AsiaPacific Trade Fair in Singapore."

"Good. In that case, I recommend you leave a couple of days on the return to stop by Manila, ostensibly for the purposes of visiting your family. We'll drive you to Rosales, where your father's family lives—"

"Actually, most of my closest relatives, at least the younger ones, now live in Alaminos City."

He smiled and said, "So there, I don't know everything about you." Then, in a more serious tone, he added, "After you visit with your relatives, we'll drive up the mountains to Baguio to meet the Family and then cross the mountains on the road to Bambang, where we're about to explore the new Lily site I mentioned. Hopefully, you can enter it and see for yourself that it's all for real."

Rachel pondered the itinerary and then the whole operation, which was difficult to fathom. "But Craig, how do you know George—"

"He'll be interested, believe me."

"You didn't let me finish. I was going to ask how do you know he's the head of it all? I mean, I know he's involved with the Council on Foreign Relations and all, but—"

"Read the document, Rachel, and decide for yourself. But *please don't show or talk about it to anyone.*" He added, "The Family is certain that George Perry is the person who will be able to deal." Then he handed her the encryption code for communicating with him on the Internet and to set up the Manila meeting.

As they arrived at Rachel's apartment, Brooke gazed at Rachel for a moment and his eyes seemed to soften. "I know tonight may have seemed strange, but I promise you'll know all of what's going on soon. And Rachel, whether you know it or not, you may be a key to unraveling the stranglehold of the financial system that's trapped billions in debt and poverty around the world."

Rachel couldn't quite decipher his stare, despite its strange effect on her. He then offered a firm handshake and got out and watched her as she climbed the stairs to her first-floor town home. Rachel was surprised that he wasn't more effusive. Despite his lack of a wedding ring and no sign of being gay, his mannerisms seemed devoid of sexual interest, more like those of a big brother or business partner. And despite his refined good looks, intelligence, and obvious wealth, she didn't feel any sexual stirrings at that moment, either. Perhaps it was because it was too soon after Jackson's death, or perhaps it was because of the risks the proposed mission entailed. *Or perhaps it's because he reminds me too much of Jackson and his conspiracy theories and historical wrongs and other intense quirks that were once so captivating before they unraveled into madness.*

But she had barely closed her front door after waving to Brooke and seeing him drive off when an intense, almost suffocating loneliness swept over her.

CHAPTER

3

Rachel waited until the next weekend to open the document. On a warm Saturday afternoon, she sat down on a chair on her small back patio next to a rhododendron bush in bloom and started reading it.

The text, actually more of a manifesto, was fewer than fifty pages in length but replete with historical facts and financial details, including information about specific transactions and accounts. It contained a summary of evidence for Brooke's main tenet that East and Southeast Asia were once the richest regions on earth, with an estimated eighty-five percent of the world's gold in its possession. Then came the European conquests beginning with the Spanish and Portuguese in the sixteenth century and continuing on with the Dutch and British and French thereafter. World War II resulted in a massive transfer of wealth to the West, first by means of the voluntary Chinese gold transfers after the Japanese takeover of Manchuria in 1931, followed the Golden Lily operation and its usurpation by American financial and intelligence groups, and then the postwar Western intimidation of Sukarno and others to relinquish their gold. In the end, Southeast Asia, despite its historical riches, was mired in poverty, lacking control over its vast mineral resources and dependent on Western lending institutions like the World Bank for economic and infrastructure development.

Rachel had no idea if Brooke wrote the document or was merely an emissary of the group, referred to as the White Dragon Family throughout the text. The White Dragon Family was described as mainly comprised of Asians who either owned, were trustees for, or otherwise had claims to the gold transferred or stolen prior to, during, and immediately after World War II. The members came primarily from China, Indonesia, and the Philippines, but Vietnam, Cambodia, Malaysia, Taiwan, and Thailand were also represented, although no specific individuals were listed by name.

The document revealed that much of the massive gold wealth was exchanged for gold certificates or placed in gold collateral accounts, technically redeemable. Rachel read the amounts on the certificates and accounts and was astounded by their value—into the tens of trillions in some instances. She thought there might be some mistake, but then she remembered Brooke's discussion about the hundreds of thousands of metric tons of gold allegedly stolen during Golden Lily alone and realized that, given the current price of gold at nearly fifty million American dollars per metric ton, this could easily equal upward of fifty trillion dollars when factoring in interest. Some of the collateral gold accounts seemed pretty straightforward, as in the Sukarno Trusts. These were the accounts created when Sukarno transferred huge quantities of Indonesian gold—originally intended as the backing for a new lending agency for developing nations, independent of the West—to Swiss banks under pressure from Western intelligence.[38] Needless to say,

---

[38]   Guyatt, 2012, *op cit.*, (Section 4.1) quotes a source that estimates the value of the gold and gem stash once controlled by President Sukarno of Indonesia as $270 trillion in 1964 U.S. dollars. Some of the alleged wealth dated back centuries, from the era in which Indonesia was a major Asian trading hub, while some reputedly came from Japanese

his exchange did not protect Sukarno and he was eventually overthrown in arguably the bloodiest coup in world history.[39] But other accounts had strange names such as "White Spiritual Boy" and "Spiritual Wonder Boy," [40] which were possibly code names for accounts linked to Don Severino Garcia Diaz Santa Romana, a wealthy Filipino businessman and confidante of President Ferdinand Marcos, who ended up with some of the first of the Golden Lily stashes. "Santy," as he was typically referred to, reputedly had many aliases, including that of a Catholic priest. He was linked to many intelligence arms, including that of the Vatican, and he was allegedly present during the torture of Major Kojima, a Japanese officer who was an aide-de-camp to General Yamashita late in the war.[41] Under

---

exchanges for Indonesian oil (Seagraves & Seagraves, 2005, *op cit.*, p. 353), while still other parts of it came from indigenous production.

[39] The coup against the Indonesian Communist Party in 1965 killed officially around a half million but by some estimates as many as three million Indonesians: http://en.wikipedia.org/wiki/Indonesian_killings_of_1965%E2%80%9366. Many historians point to the deep complicity of the United States and other Western nations in the coup: www.globalresearch.ca/historian-says-us-backed-efficacious-terror-in-1965-indonesian-massacre/14254 After the coup, Sukarno was stripped of his powers although he continued as Indonesian president for two more years.

[40] These accounts were reported by former Wall Street Journal correspondent Benjamin Fulford: http://alcuinbramerton.blogspot.com/2012/01/white-spiritual-boy-off-ledger-black.html. There is no independent evidence that they are real. An intriguing discussion of the purported gold collateral accounts and the White Dragon Family is contained in an interview with Neil Keenan and his team: http://sgtreport.com/2015/05/a-new-monetary-system-is-coming-controlled-economic-collapse

[41] The Seagraves are convinced on the basis of their sources and documentation that the mysterious Santa Romana was an agent of the Vatican (Seagraves & Seagraves, 2005, *op cit.*, p. 245). It is strange that, despite massive evidence to the contrary, the Philippines government has officially denied that Santa Romana ever existed!

torture by Edwin Lansdale and other American intelligence officials after the Japanese surrender, Kojima revealed the locations of the last several of the Golden Lily sites, constructed just before the American liberation of the Philippines in 1945.[42]

As Brooke had intimated, the Dragons' thesis described how a large portion of the Asian gold ended up as "black gold" in the hands of the Western governments and financial institutions. The "black gold" was off the regular financial books and often used to fund covert operations aimed at eliminating perceived threats to Western control, such as the assassination of leftist politicians and sympathizers during postwar Japan, the overthrow of leftist Central American governments, and the destabilization of the post-communist government of Russia in the early 1990s.[43]

Using several high-profile examples, the Dragons further claimed that even when authenticated certificates existed, the Western banks and governments that ostensibly "possessed" the gold never intended to honor them, either in gold or currency. Rachel then proceeded to read over some of the major fiascos involving attempts to obtain collateral gold repayments. One of the most famous was that of Paul Johnston in 1995, an Australian banker who was arrested for merely asking to *store* a gold certificate for seven hundred and forty metric tons. Johnston was representing Edison Damanik, supposedly the trustee of PTY Galaxy Trust, an Indonesian firm that had ties to the Marcos fortune. Johnston eventually spent a year in prison after officials at the Union Bank of Switzerland ruled the certificates fake, even *before* they had examined them.[44] A subsequent case involved members of the wealthy Laurel clan of the Philippines, who tried to cash one hundred billion in 1934 Federal Reserve notes (known as "Morgenthau" bonds after

---

42   Seagraves & Seagraves, 2005, *op cit.*, p. 89

43   Seagraves & Seagraves, 2005, *op cit.*, epilogue.

44   Guyatt, *Secret Gold Treaty, op cit.*, Introduction.

the American Treasury Secretary at the time) in Chicago in 2002; their case was summarily dismissed before any significant testimony even occurred.[45] Then, there was the attempt in the following year to cash a twenty-five-million-dollar portion of a much larger batch of certificates at the Royal Bank of Canada in Toronto. Graham Halksworth, an English forensic scientist, and Michael Slamaj, a former Yugoslav intelligence agent, were convicted of conspiring to defraud the Canadian government.[46] In a rather bizarre twist to the story, Slamaj claimed to have received millions in bonds from a Mindanao tribe, which claimed to have discovered boxes containing hundreds of millions in 1934 Morgenthau certificates in a remote dry riverbed. These were purportedly lost by a B-29 plane that crashed in the jungles of Mindanao in the late 1940s en route to China from the United States carrying bonds for General Chiang Kai-Shek, who had transferred much of his remaining gold after World War II in anticipation of a communist takeover of the mainland. The next major case making international headlines occurred in Chiasso, on the Swiss-Italian border.[47] Two Japanese nationals tried to bring one hundred and thirty-four billion dollars in 1934 gold certificates to Switzerland, most of it in five-hundred-million-dollar notes in a suitcase with a false bottom, but border guards confiscated the certificates. It was followed up in the same year by a one-and-a-half-trillion seizure in Spain and a six-trillion-bond seizure in Switzerland in 2012 that also made headlines briefly.[48]

---

[45] The Laurel case is covered in detail in Seagraves & Seagraves, 2005, *op cit.*, chap.17.

[46] For a synopsis of the Halksworth verdict, see http://www.theguardian.com/uk/2003/sep/19/ukcrime.rebeccaallison#

[47] See http://en.wikipedia.org/wiki/Chiasso_financial_smuggling_case and, for arguments for their authenticity: http://www.marketskeptics.com/2009/07/everything-suggests-that-american-bonds.html

[48] See http://www.dailymail.co.uk/news/article-2102800/Fake-bonds-bank-vault-Italian-police-seize-6-TRILLION.html

The Dragon Family clearly believed the certificates seized in the alleged counterfeiting rings were real.[49] What most rankled the Family was that Western governments and banks in these cases brazenly repeated the false claim that only sixty thousand tons of gold had been mined in all of world history up to 1934, thereby "proving" the gold certificates could not have been genuine.[50] The Canadian government used that argument in the Halksworth trial and the United States Federal Reserve used it in allegedly offering Yohannes Riyadi—a supposed heir to Indochinese wealth—only five hundred million American dollars on certificates worth fifteen trillion dollars, despite the fact that the certificates had been accepted by the Royal Bank of Scotland.[51]

The Dragons' thesis concluded that Asians had to start playing by a different set of rules. It was clear the European and American courts would never honor their certificates, so the gold was essentially lost legally. A massive trillion-dollar lawsuit filed by the Dragon Family in New York against the U.S. Federal Reserve and other global financial entities to get back some of the wealth was meant to rattle the Bilderberger financial cabal and put it on notice, by threatening to pry open the massively illegal transactions that had hitherto remained opaque to the citizens of the West.[52] Although the Family knew that the lawsuit would basically go nowhere, amidst the crushing poverty of Asia were renewed stirrings of wealth, especially in China. China and other emerging economic players—Brazil, Russia, India, and South Africa, known as the BRICS—were starting to

---

[49]   See Seagraves & Seagraves, 2995, *op cit.*, pp. 262-264, for evidence of the authenticity of the 1934 bonds.

[50]   See http://www.rense.com/general43/whow.htm

[51]   See http://www.bibliotecapleyades.net/sociopolitica/sociopol_globalbanking190.htm and https://www.goldstockbull.com/articles/15-trillion-bond-fraud-to-prop-up-the-u-s-dollar

[52]   The Dragon Family lawsuit was filed by the reputable law firm of Bleakley, Platt and Schmidt, with Neil Keenan listed as plaintiff.

undercut the Western cabal's global monopoly on capital lending to developing nations.[53] But for any new currency to stick it to the West and its failing fiat currencies, it needed backing by gold, and lots of it.[54] And where would that gold come from? *The vast stashes remaining in Asia!*

The Family had a couple of big aces in its hand, the biggest being the white maps detailing the locations of the Golden Lily treasure. A large collection of them had been found in various locations throughout the island of Luzon and then stolen by Ferdinand Marcos, while a few additional maps were recreated from memory by individuals under torture by his henchmen. When he realized that he was about to be overthrown by the Americans in 1986, Marcos passed the white maps—over fifty in total—on to various wealthy Filipino elders in charge of the Marcos Trust, who then became allied with the Dragon Family. But the Dragons were still missing the critical engineering maps required to open the sites. Marcos' henchmen had discovered that a Luzon native, Ben Valmores, had them in his possession. Valmores as a boy had been the favorite servant of Japanese prince Takeda, Emperor Hirohito's cousin, for almost two years before the latter fled the Philippines in a submarine as the Americans recaptured the Philippines in 1945. Takeda not only spared Valmores' life when he escaped to Japan but left him a satchel containing the red engineering maps.[55] Eventually, Valmores' maps ended up in the hands of Robert Curtis, an American gold refiner hired by Marcos to help convert the Golden Lily bars into legitimate ones that could be sold on the international gold market. Fearing for his life, Curtis double-crossed Marcos, smuggling out photographs of the red maps in some furniture he had bought and then burning the originals in

---

53   See http://rt.com/business/173008-brics-bank-currency-pool

54   "Fiat" comes from the Latin "let it be done"; a "fiat currency" is created by a governmental entity and is divorced from any commodity backing.

55   See Seagraves & Seagraves, 2005, *op cit.*, pp. 70-82.

a *hibachi* on the balcony of his Manila hotel's conference room.[56] The Family was now interested in dealing for those maps, which their various sources had indicated were in the hands of the American financial cabal, which had stolen them from Curtis after his escape from the Philippines.

The document reiterated what Brooke had mentioned to Rachel at their dinner: the Bilderberger cabal did not have an immediate need for the gold as it had absconded with most of the world's known gold and successfully prevented its being a threat to the Western fiat currencies for over seven decades. Left unchallenged, the Western financial cabal would be willing to let the massive underground wealth remain undisturbed, at least for the time being. If, however, the cabal became convinced that the Dragon Family had the capability of going it alone, which they were prepared to do, it would almost certainly agree to deal. Even if the Dragons only managed to split the Golden Lily wealth with the cabal, its members had all pledged that most of it would end up in the hands of the people of Asia, massively invigorating their economies and even those of the rest of the developing world. The recovered wealth would usher in a new golden era for Asia, both literally and proverbially, leading Asia out of its perennial poverty and dependence on the Western financial system.

The key would be to act discreetly, with the Family hinting at its hand without stirring up publicity and revealing its organization. It was well known that the Western financial cabal was very difficult to approach—its leaders were much harder to contact than even the president of the United States.[57] But there were inside ways to get the message to them, starting with

---

[56] See Seagraves & Seagraves, 2005, *op cit.*, p. 182.

[57] General Erle Cocke was a key figure in many of the black ops financial dealings, as stated in a deathbed confession/deposition in April of 2000. In it, he claimed it was easier to see the president of the United States than John Reed, the head of Citibank (Seagraves & Seagraves, 2005, *op cit.*, p. 271).

George Oliver Perry, who as the former longtime chairman of the Council on Foreign Relations, was the titular head of the Bilderberger cabal. If the Bilderberger cabal wasn't willing to deal secretly, the Dragon Family had the means of ratcheting up the pressure, although the text concluded without revealing what that additional pressure would be.

After reading the entire document, Rachel still didn't know what to make of all of its contents. What if White Spiritual Boy, the White Dragon Family, the 1934 Morgenthau bonds, even most of the Golden Lily stuff, were all just part of a huge hoax, perpetuated to rattle things up and extort a few billions here and there from Western banks and governments?

Real or not, Rachel realized that she was going to be the bait—or more precisely, the barb holding the bait, which could be worse—that would be dangled in front of the most powerful men in America, one of whom happened to be her father-in-law. *Or is he my ex-father-in-law, if suicide figures the same as a divorce?*

Rachel knew that she needed more advice on this one. Fortunately, her most trusted and knowledgeable source on this matter would be her close sorority friend, Karen, who just happened to be throwing a birthday bash that very night for her boyfriend Jacques, a party to which Rachel had been invited and would now most definitely attend.

CHAPTER

4

By the time she arrived at the party, Jacques Delacroix had already had downed a couple of Jack Daniels and was in high spirits, surrounded by male colleagues from work talking about the upcoming America's Cup. "Don't underestimate the magique of the *Riviera Royale*," he crowed about the top French yachting syndicate. "I assure you that the next cup will be hosted on the Cote d'Azur—in fact, I've already rented all of us a house in Provence for the occasion!" That led to a chorus of "Vive, La France!" by his laughing pals as they lifted their beer bottles and vodka and bourbon glasses in a hearty cheer.

Rachel slipped in unnoticed and quickly searched for Karen, who was in the kitchen. After Karen turned around and saw her, she smiled and said, "Hey there, Rach, glad you could make it."

After a quick hug, Rachel offered her help with the hors d'oeuvres, but Karen indicated everything was under control. "What I do need you to do is help entertain those playboys out there. Fortunately, Jacques isn't like them most of the time. Especially watch out for Henri, the tall one, and don't let him get you anywhere near the water unless you want to be totally grossed out by his Speedos." Rachel chimed in with an "Eeeww!" as they both broke out in laughter.

Karen Marie Kruchak was, along with Frankie Stewart, one of Rachel's two closest friends, part of a threesome that hung out together for the better part of four years in Hanover, mostly at Delta Gamma, with all three managing to end up working in New York. Unlike Frankie, Karen didn't come from money and was much more circumspect, but like Frankie she was brimming with confidence, mainly stemming from her amazing intellect. Karen was one of the top students at Dartmouth, graduating summa cum laude with a major in economics and a minor in math. Rachel and Karen grew to be friends while in freshman women's soccer, but with her tall and rugged frame, Karen was definitely the better striker; in fact, she was headed for varsity until she broke her ankle in several points and had little choice but to try the one sport requiring no serious leg action—women's crew. After hitting the weights for almost a full year and braving the icy Connecticut River winds for months, Karen with her newly broadened shoulders and upper arms clinched a spot with the varsity eights her sophomore year, in the process acquiring her nickname "Krew." Karen and Rachel started hanging out together from the beginning, and it was Karen who enticed Rachel to rush and pledge for Delta Gamma, one of the few sororities on campus that served alcohol due to its lack of a national affiliation. Rachel would always be grateful for the many hours during the spring semester of her freshman year when Karen walked her through her calculus problems, patiently explaining all of the derivative solutions.

Despite her academic strengths, Karen also was funny and prankish, and she became famous around campus for an event in the winter of her junior year. It was customary for sororities to host a fraternity one weekend a year, and Karen encouraged her other Delta Gams to invite the brothers from Theta Delta Chi. Theta Delt was also known as the "Boom-Boom" lodge because of a murder that occurred there in 1920 after one of its brothers stole a whiskey bottle from a bootlegging operation elsewhere on campus and was shot twice in the chest at close range in retaliation. It housed over a quarter of the Big Green varsity football team, and Karen got to know so many of them while spending long hours in the weight room that they unofficially adopted her as their "sister". Karen had the idea of hosting a Super Bowl–themed mixer with the Boom-Boom Lodge the night before the actual event, with most of the girls dressing in their favorite National Football League team jerseys. Karen wore her Chicago Bears jersey, but Rachel decided to wear her old Austin Westlake jersey since Austin didn't have a professional football franchise and Rachel didn't follow football much in any case. A half-dozen or so girls wore skimpy NFL cheerleader outfits, with Frankie dressed in a red, white, and blue Patriots cheerleader outfit. One girl knew a triplet drag trio from Boston, who came up to Hanover to provide the opening act, dressed in Dartmouth cheerleader costumes and doing a bawdy rendition of some well-known Dartmouth fight songs. The Boom-Boom boys, already full of various denominations of alcohol, roared in laughter and even had a bunch of selfies taken with the drag queens. The night never degenerated into total lewdness and the gay community on campus mostly thought it was all good fun. But the nervous Dartmouth administration—always bemoaning the gap between the college's lofty academics and its weekend Greek debaucheries—called Delta Gamma to task and Karen took the fall in a feigned apology to the dean.

After Dartmouth, Karen went back home to Chicago and joined up with Teach for America, where she taught math at a high school in Lincoln Square before becoming totally disillusioned with the urban American educational system. She then went to work for the World Bank in Washington, DC, for a two-year stint as a junior analyst before getting her MBA from New York University and joining BNY Mellon as an investment banker in New York City. When Karen first met Jacques, a Manhattan bullion trader, Rachel didn't think the relationship would last. Jacques loved fast cars and faster women, whereas Karen was smart and sturdy, despite her attractive, even stylish, appearance when she set her mind to it. But it turned out that Jacques had a serious side as well, being nothing short of a genius when it came to financial markets. Jacques and Karen together probably knew more about high finance than any young couple around, and they also enjoyed the same pastimes—skiing in the winter in Vermont and the Poconos and sailing in the summer, mostly up and down the sound. Karen became an avid weekend companion to Jacques on his ten-meter sailboat, and she accompanied him on several expeditions up and down the East Coast. Once, Rachel and Jackson accompanied them up the Sound to Nantucket, one of the few times they hung out with another couple in their short marriage. Even though they weren't married, Karen and Jacques had together invested in a two-bedroom townhome in Waterside Plaza, with a panoramic view of the East River and upper Manhattan. They snared it for just over seven hundred thousand on a short sale after the 2017 downturn, which their separate six-figure incomes could easily afford. Rachel was grateful that in the first several weeks following Jackson's death, Jacques and Karen let her sleep in their extra bedroom/study. While they worked, Rachel stayed home from work and slept and watched reruns of old movies on cable. Despite her long hours with BNY Mellon, Karen did most of the cooking, save for a few takeouts and a couple of times when Jacques prepared fondue or pasta.

After Jacques introduced Rachel to some of his friends at the party, she returned to Karen again and asked about Frankie. Karen said Frankie had hoped to stop by but backed out after a friend asked her on short notice to join him on a trip to Vegas. "You know, I've only seen Frankie a couple of times since last year, and she always seems to be dating a new boyfriend," Rachel offered. They both laughed when Karen added with a wink, "Yeah, she shows no signs of slowing down . . . more of laying down!"

Most of Jacques' friends were discussing sports, their upcoming vacations, and the latest rumors about stocks and commodities. As the evening wore on and all of the guests had imbibed a healthy volume of alcohol, some of them started to hit on Rachel, who deftly fended them off until one by one they started to leave. Rachel then sat down with Karen and opened up about the strange meeting with Craig Brooke the previous weekend. Karen was the only one of her friends who knew she had published Jackson's book under a pseudonym, and she also found it strange that Imperial had managed to track Rachel down. Karen was intrigued by her tale of the gold collateral accounts, the Chiasso and other arrests, and the overall outline of the occult financial system, which Rachel revealed to her without mentioning the source of that information—the document provided to her by Brooke.

"You know, I've only been in this business a few years, but it wouldn't surprise me if most of what your publisher says is true. Every now and then at work we get a whiff that something's about to happen and then a lot of funds are moved quickly. Obviously, there's a ton of insider information floating around, almost none of which leads to prosecution. And I'm aware of the basic facts about the Bilderbergers and their financial reach from your book."

Without going into too many specifics, Rachel broached the subject of the 1930s gold transfers, Yamashita's gold, and the Project Hammer efforts to destroy the ruble. Karen just gave a quizzical look at the end. "I just don't know, Rach . . . it all just seems so fantastic. Do you mind if I bring Jacques in on this when he sobers up? If there's something up with gold, he'll know about it."

"Thanks, Karen, I was hoping you might tell him about it. I just need a little more information before I plunge into anything."

Karen smiled. "So, Rachel, you're not planning to return to Brooklyn tonight, are you? I'd really prefer that you stay in the spare overnight, so we can catch up on things. In fact, I wish you'd move to our neck of the woods permanently. C'mon, you know you can easily afford it."

"Not really. I did get a little from his Jackson's life insurance, but I didn't take a penny from his inheritance—it would have been too painful to spend."

"So, what happened to it?"

"I put it in a trust. Someday I might give it all away, but I just haven't found the right groups to give to. I thought about giving some to some environmental groups or even some of the various 911 Truther Movements, but I decided against it for the time being. But, to set your mind at ease, I *am* looking to move to Manhattan and would love to be closer to you guys." Then she added, "I really appreciate your offer for tonight, but do you think Jacques will mind? After all, it *is* his birthday. And I imagine you have something special planned for him tonight."

"Hell no, not with all that alcohol on his breath! Rach, don't worry about Jacques' feelings—after that box of Cohibas you got him, you'll be in his good graces for a while."

"Okay, I'm in. But let me help you clean up a bit."

Karen smiled. "No problem. But afterward, with you staying here for the evening, we're going to do some real gossiping while we get smashed."

"You bet . . . just like at the olden days at Delta Gam."

Karen got in touch with Rachel a few weeks later, the Friday before Memorial Day. She mentioned she had come up with some things after researching around a bit and asked if Rachel wanted to stop by. They instead agreed to meet the next day for a late lunch in the city at an Italian pizzeria near Karen's condo. Despite it being a Saturday, Karen had already put in six hours at her firm, which was common in the investment banking world.

"Thanks for getting back to me, Karen. I'm surprised you were able to get into this stuff so quickly, what with your long hours."

"Yeah, I had to put in a few late nighters, but Jacques fortunately was a big help. But I've also been bogged down with some Dartmouth stuff, now that I'm class secretary."

"Yeah, I heard about that. Sorry I forgot to congratulate you."

"No worries. But you know, all of my other shit doesn't begin to compare with the stories Craig Brooke told you about, Rach. I know you've been doing some checking on your own, but as far as I can tell your friend, whoever he is, seems spot on with most of what he told you."

Rachel added, "At least his basic story about the white rajahs of Sarawak seems to check out. He's definitely a descendant of theirs—if he's who he says he is. I'm just not sure what he's doing working for an indie publisher in Cebu, though."

"I don't know about all that rajah crap, but I can tell you about some of the other stuff. Let's begin with the notion that there is a lot more gold out there than has been officially acknowledged. When I posed the 'one hundred and seventy thousand metric tons' figure to Jacques, he scoffed big time. According to him, the pre-1850s estimate of a few thousand or so metric tons of mined gold are laughable,[58] as it ignores the massive bullion wealth of Asia, South America, and Africa while Europe was still in the dark ages. Think about it, Rach—do you really think that all of the gold produced in the history of the world could fit into a couple of swimming pools?[59] Hell, some African king in the 1300s had some twelve thousand slaves and an army of camels carry a humongous cache of gold on

---

[58] See http://www.gold-eagle.com/article/worlds-cumulative-gold-and-silver-production

[59] The actual volume of official gold is about three Olympic-sized swimming pools: http://www.numbersleuth.org/worlds-gold

a religious pilgrimage to Mecca.[60] And, didn't the Inca king captured by Pizarro offer the conquistadores a huge room full of gold for his ransom? Which, by the way, didn't save his ass in the end.[61] C'mon, Rach, just the gold jewelry you, Frankie, and I have could fill half a wading pool!"

Rachel smiled. "Maybe yours and Frankie's, honey, but not mine!"

"Yeah, right. As if I'm too blind to see you're wearing twenty-four karats on your wrist!" Karen smiled wryly, then continued on. "The second indisputable fact is that there is indeed a 'shadow' financial system involving such notables over the years as Castle Bank, Nugan Hand, BCCI, even the Vatican Bank.[62] But what's even more disturbing is how much of the regular financial system is performing double-duty for the 'shadow' one."

"How so?"

"The fact of the matter is that the actions of our central banks—and, in particular, the Bank of International Settlements—are rarely, if ever, audited, allowing them to create, transfer, and clear funds without impunity. But I'll get to that later."

---

[60] http://en.wikipedia.org/wiki/Musa_I_of_Mali

[61] http://latinamericanhistory.about.com/od/theconquestofperu/p/The-Treasure-Of-The-Inca.htm

[62] Castle Bank (based in the Bahamas), Nugan Hand (based in Australia), and the Bank of International Credit and Commerce International (BCCI), with offices in London and Pakistan, were all CIA-linked banks used for black ops that all collapsed amidst scandal and even mysterious deaths in some cases. See http://wolfwhistle.the-eleven.com/archives/stories/BCCI1.html for a brief account. See Yeadon & Hawkins, 2008, *op cit.*, Chap. 8, for a discussion of the role of the Vatican Bank in laundering Nazi gold, and Seagraves & Seagraves, 2005, *op cit.*, p. 105, for a brief discussion of its role in illicit Asian gold transactions. For a more general discussion of its role in anticommunist activity after World War II, see David Guyatt, *Holy Smoke and Mirrors: The Vatican Connection:*
http://www.bibliotecapleyades.net/vatican/esp_vatican16.htm

"Okay, but what about some of Brooke's specific claims—say, the Asian gold certificates. You know, the ones that everyone seems to be cashing in."

"Yeah, it's pretty interesting that the United States government denies that they ever existed, at least in the massive dollar denominations folks are bringing in—up to five hundred million, in some cases. But a lot of them are coming forth, which seems pretty strange. There are a few recent cases that have really raised eyebrows, mostly involving the so-called Morgenthau bonds."

"The 1934 gold certificates issued with the signature of Henry Morgenthau, the Treasury Secretary. Are they real?"

"They're definitely real in principle. But what we don't know about are the specifics concerning which bonds were issued. I checked on the Chiasso and other incidents you mentioned—all made the headlines but only briefly, and all involved the 1934 bonds—at least ten trillion in certificates, maybe more."

"Those numbers are mind-boggling—surely, we're dealing with counterfeit funds."

"Maybe and maybe not, Rach. One assumes they're fake because of the fantastically large amounts and denominations. Plus, there were some misspellings and other simple mistakes in them, but those could have been made deliberately in 1934 for later denial purposes, or maybe just simple mistakes because these were obviously not regular, mass-produced certificates.[63] But the lithographing and validation documents were so amazing that some of the leading experts in the world have ruled at least some of them authentic; *and,* they were in official

---

[63] Another example of the use of deliberate mistakes were the "57" bonds, indirectly tied to funding of anti-leftist black operations in Japan after World War II. The United States colluded with the Japanese government to claim they were counterfeit and the latter refused to honor them formally, even though they were unquestionably legitimate (see Seagraves & Seagraves, chapter 9).

Federal Reserve boxes from that era.[64] Why not go for smaller amounts that might be expected to arouse less suspicion? And why are they always 1934 bonds? Counterfeit or not, someone was willing to buy the bonds, even at a steep discount, or else the bearers wouldn't have risked transporting them. Someone figured they would eventually be worth something."

Karen then looked Rachel directly in the eye and said in a slightly lowered voice, "Did you know that heirs to some of the most prominent Philippines gold accounts have never received a dime from their certificates—only a lot of stonewalling by the big New York and Swiss banks."

"Are you talking about the Laurel, Marcos, and Santa Romana accounts?"

"Yep. The latter being Don Severino Garcia Diaz Santa Romana, who went by numerous aliases, including Father Jose Antonio Diaz—"

"The priest who evidently tortured the hell out of some Major Kojima guy after World War II until he spilled the beans about the Yamashita treasure."

"Wouldn't surprise me. Of course, he wouldn't have been the first priest to run afoul of the scriptures, Rach."

"Coming from a Catholic girl!"

"Ex-Catholic girl. Anyway, 'Santy' was knee-deep in a lot of black-ops stuff. Some say he was a CIA agent, some think he was an agent for the Vatican, no one knows for sure.[65] But we do know he had bank accounts all over the world and lived the high life for decades."

"And when he died?"

"His fortune—allegedly worth over fifty billion—was willed to his common-law wife and daughter and some to his accountant. Much of it was stored in Citibank right here in New

---

[64] See http://www.asianews.it/news-en/Everything-suggests-that-the-American-bonds-seized-at-Chiasso-are-real-15648.html

[65] See footnote #42.

York City, and his heirs had impeccable documentation and even the famous attorney, Melvin Belli, working on their case. But Belli died shortly after the lawsuit was filed and Citibank stonewalled, eventually transferring the funds to offshore accounts. In the end, it never paid out a dime."[66]

"None of this makes any sense, Krew—unless there really *was* a lot of gold in Asia that was transferred before and after World War II to Western banks. If, as Brooke told me, there were over one hundred thousand tons of Chinese gold brought to the United States in 1934 alone, then those certificates at the original price of thirty-five dollars an ounce and four percent interest over the thirty-year maturity term could be worth hundreds of billions. If you then figure in today's price of gold, they could be worth tens of trillions! It would certainly have been an easy task to place that much on planes and ships in short order. Add in the Golden Lily gold transfers along with the legendary Sukarno gold shipments and we're probably talking in the hundreds of thousands of tons of gold—"

"Or more. Jacques thinks the total's *well over a million tons* . . . most originating from Asia."[67]

"But what hard evidence is there that any of Yamashita's gold or any of the other stuff actually existed—or still exists."

"Did Brooke bring up the case of Rogelio Roxas?"

"Not that I recall."

"Roger Roxas was a locksmith and amateur treasure hunter in Luzon, who got wind of a Golden Lily site from the son of a former Japanese soldier who was once an interpreter for Yamashita. Roxas searched for months until he finally found the entrance to a tunnel that led to an underground complex near the central hospital in Baguio—if I recall, that's not too far from where your relatives live. When he entered the first chamber, he

---

[66]   See Seagraves & Seagraves, 2005, *op cit.*, chap. 15 (for a discussion of the Santa Romana heirs' efforts to retrieve their wealth) and chap. 17 (for a discussion of the Laurel clan's efforts to retrieve its wealth).

[67]   See footnote #19.

found boxes of gold ingots and a golden Buddha, which took ten men to move out. Of course, word quickly spread and Roxas eventually was visited by Marcos' henchmen and he not only gave up the treasure but one of his eyes after being tortured. After Marcos was deposed and ended up in exile in Hawaii, Roxas eventually sued Marcos for the theft of the treasure, of which Roxas was legally entitled to thirty percent. By the time the case went to trial, in 1996, both Roxas and Marcos were long dead. After hearing the evidence, the jury awarded Roxas' estate over forty billion—*forty billion, from just one Lily site*—which at the time was the largest settlement in financial history. Although the award was later reduced on appeal to about twenty million in total—which by the way was never paid—the trial proved beyond a doubt that the Yamashita gold was real."[68]

"I just can't believe this whole international gold theft could be pulled off without the general public knowing about it. Somebody has to be driving the entire show—who the hell are they?"

"It's not hard to keep things from the public, Rach, when all of the mainstream media are part of the very group running the occult economy.[69] The first thing you have to realize is that

---

[68] See www.state.hi.us/jud/20606.htm There are a great many other pieces of evidence to prove the Yamashita gold real, including a document certified by Ferdinand Marcos in 1987 that 280,000 metric tons of recovered gold were turned over to him by Alberto Cacpal, who was granted permission by an earlier Filipino president to recover gold at Clark Air Force Base. (Seagraves & Seagraves, 2005, *op cit.*, p. 358). There was also an affidavit signed by 96 members of the Philippine Army's Sixteenth Infantry Division that claimed that over 60,000 tons of gold and other treasure were dug up for Marcos under the command of Gen. Fabian Ver in the 1970s and 1980s: http://www.bibliotecapleyades.net/sociopolitica/secretgoldtreaty/soldiersoffortune_appendix3.htm

[69] Almost all of the major national media in the United States are controlled by six corporations: http://www.businessinsider.com/these-6-corporations-control-90-of-the-media-in-america-2012-6

although there may be tens of thousands of corporations in the world, there is so much interlocking with the major financial centers of the West that the number of controlling entities is quite small—in fact, some researchers have shown that a little over one hundred corporate entities control over forty percent of the entire world's wealth.[70]

"Sounds like we need a global antitrust buster!"

"No kidding. It's like before Teddy Roosevelt came along in the early 1900s. During the late 1800s, we went from over four thousand firms in America to about three hundred trusts that controlled over forty percent of our manufacturing."[71]

"I thought we always learned that systems are supposed to disperse over time. Doesn't this concentration of wealth violate all that?"[72]

"Yeah, but entropy only occurs in isolated, random systems, Rach. There's nothing about laissez-faire capitalism that's random—starting with the word 'greed'!"

After they both chuckled, Karen continued. "And you know what ultimately directs the activity of those one hundred and forty-seven entities, don't you? The major financial institutions and central banks of the West."

"Presumably all under the control of our Federal Reserve . . . based on the mega-trillions secretly transferred from the Fed to the large American, British and German banks after the 2008 financial collapse. Am I right, Krew?"[73]

"You betcha. Can you believe it, Rach? The Fed is a privately owned rich man's bank that has the sole keys to our precious

[70] See Vitali S, Glattfelder JB, & Battiston S (2011). The network of global corporate control. *PLoS ONE* 6(10): e25995

[71] See Simon Johnson and James Kwak, *13 Bankers: The Wall Street Takeover and the Next Financial Meltdown.* (Pantheon, 2010).

[72] The Second Law of Thermodynamics, dating back to Carnot in 1824, argues that entropy will increase in an isolated system with increased energy.

[73] See footnote #7.

money![74] The Fed is the epicenter of the shadow financial system,[75] working with the Bank of International Settlements—"

"You mean the bank that was designed to manage the German reparation payments after World War I? Why would it still be around?"

Karen smiled. "It shouldn't be. It was supposed to be dissolved after World War II, but the British financiers objected.[76] Even the American representatives voted for its demise, but no one bothered to turn off the lights and the Fed continues to this day to be its controller—or, according to some accounts, its slave.[77] So figure this—an unelected and unaccountable body operating with almost total secrecy plays God with the world's financial system. Strange, isn't it?"[78]

"What I can't understand is why the Western financial cabal has been trying to corner the gold market all these years? I thought that kind of greed went out the door with King Midas."

"No way! Do you see any of these Midas wannabes giving up their homes in the Bahamas or Newport or the Riviera? The last rich guy to do that was the Buddha eons ago—if we can believe it. Rach, the rich don't see the world like you and me."

"How so?"

---

[74] The Federal Reserve, like many of its counterparts in other Western nations, is a private bank that operates independently of the United States government even as it controls the total amount and flow of the United States dollar.

[75] See Wilcock, 2012, *op cit.*, p. 19

[76] See http://en.wikipedia.org/wiki/Bretton_Woods_Conference

[77] See http://theeconomiccollapseblog.com/archives/who-controls-the-money-an-unelected-unaccountable-central-bank-of-the-world-secretly-does

[78] "Playing God with the world's financial system" is more than just a figurative statement. The Bank of International Settlements is housed in a large tower-shaped building in Switzerland known as the "Tower of Basel" and some view it more as a modern "Tower of Babel" in view of the bank's supranational orientation and its supposed attempt to control all of the planet's financial wealth.

"According to Jacques, who is privy to a lot of the inside gold transactions, the Western bankers claim that it's better to corral all of the gold and take it out of circulation. That's why the powers that be always tell you owning gold is a bad investment, to keep folks from owning it, even though the opposite is true: since 1972, gold has gone from thirty-five an ounce to *fifteen hundred an ounce*, one of the greatest investments in history! The elite's rationalization is that paper fiat currencies, free of a gold standard, allow for greater borrowing, investment, and economic progress—and, of course, more money lining their own pockets. I'm not saying it's right, but there is something to be said for placing our savings in banks that can lend it out rather than stuffing it under the bed or in a box under the house where the rats and mold can get to it. Jacques claimed even the Chinese were in on the plan to keep gold out of circulation—based on some so-called Secret Gold Treaty[79]—but recently they've gotten disillusioned with the machinations of the Western lending agencies. That's the main reason they helped bring about the BRICS currency—to undercut the dollar and euro."[80]

"So where do you think they keep all of the gold they stole, Krew—Fort Knox?"

"Hardly. According to Jacques, there's almost no commercial-grade gold left in there. He has high-placed friends who swear most of it is underneath big banks like J.P. Morgan and Chase in New York, with most of the rest in underground vaults in Switzerland."[81]

---

[79] The putative treaty between China and the Western nations led to David Guyatt's book title, "*The Secret Gold Treaty*"

[80] See footnote #54.

[81] The rumors over whether there is any gold remaining at Fort Knox are fueled by the refusal of the United States government since 1953 to allow an audit of its gold reserves located there and the recent failure to honor a request for repatriation of German gold: http://goldsilverworlds. com/physical-market/the-us-gold-in-fort-knox-is-secure-gone-or-irrelevant. There are several gold vaults below the large Western

Rachel struggled to absorb it all, but the complexity and opacity of the occult financial system were almost too much to fathom. After a few seconds, she turned to Karen and asked, "So what else did Jacques have to say?"

Karen stared at Rachel with a stern look. "Only that people who start poking around the black gold trade have a tendency to underperform the actuarial tables."

Rachel blanched, then looked down and away while remaining silent.

Karen was alarmed. "Rach, tell me you're not going to get involved in all of this fucking mess and end up way over your head—if you've still got one left." Then, after observing Rachel's blank stare, Karen placed her head down in her hands in exasperation. "So, when are you gonna start on this 'Midas Project'?"

Rachel placed her hand on Karen's. "Krew, I know I can trust you with a total secret. I'm leaving for a pre-planned Asian trip in three weeks. Then, I'm taking a few extra days off to go to the Philippines, ostensibly to visit some of my dad's relatives in Luzon—"

"But in actuality to hook up with your Craig Brooke in some wild-goose chase that involves Yamashita's gold or some other secret stuff."

Rachel half-smiled and nodded. "You're as good as ever at figuring things out, Krew."

---

banks of New York and London; one repository located five stories underground in New York City is reputedly longer than a football field: http://listverse.com/2013/04/03/10-highly-guarded-vaults.

CHAPTER

5

The next week, Rachel informed the Pacific Group that she would be taking an extra week of vacation after the AsiaPacific Trade Fair and Convention in Singapore to visit her family in the Philippines, which they assented to with hardly a suspicion.

At the convention, Rachel was expected to attend several of the main seminars and also to hang out at the Pacific Group's booth. The Pacific Group had two main arms: a nonprofit research institute and a for-profit trading company, the latter of which provided most of the income for the institute. Although primarily a research analyst, examining social trends in Asia in relation to business opportunities there, Rachel would often charge her time to the trading branch when consulting on more immediate business opportunities.

The annual AsiaPacific Trade Fair contained a mixture of topics on manufacturing (from industrial to high tech), finance (mostly focusing on exchange and interest rates), emerging media, and demographic and other socioeconomic and cultural trends. Rachel attended mostly the last group of panels and seminars, where discussions concerning the growing economic power of women as entrepreneurs and consumers captured her attention, which she planned to write about when she returned to the States. Rachel noticed big changes since her last Asia Pacific Convention, in that the American company exhibits, aside from Apple, were receiving a lot less interest while some of the Chinese companies—Tencent, Lenovo, and Xiaomi—were drawing big crowds. Despite President Obama's pledge to devote more resources to the Pacific region,[82] it was slowly slipping out of the American economic sphere, another topic Rachel planned to write about.

After the conference ended, Rachel caught a Philippine Airlines flight to Manila, where Craig Brooke greeted her upon arrival at the Ninoy Aquino International Airport. Because of the late hour, Brooke recommended she stay at the Marriott near the airport, courtesy of the Family, where he would pick her up the next morning before heading north.

The next morning, Rachel and Brooke, dressed in a white polo barong shirt, had a continental breakfast, along with an older Eurasian gentleman Brooke brought with him who did most of the conversing. The older man, who Brooke introduced as Don Ignacio Pariso, was very well-spoken and gracious toward Rachel, remarking on her Filipina beauty and ancestry and thanking her for her willingness to help the Family in its pursuit of justice. He mentioned that Craig was fully empowered by the Family to work with her and that if she needed anything during her stay, the Family would make sure she lacked for nothing. She would see for herself that Yamashita's gold was real and that it represented the former and hopefully future wealth of Asia. He also indicated that she would meet other high-ranking members of the Family in Baguio. He concluded that it was his hope that she would someday be able to tell her grandchildren of her noble role in restoring the wealth of Asia to its rightful citizens.

---

[82]   See   http://www.telegraph.co.uk/news/worldnews/
       barackobama/8895726/US-will-shift-focus-from-Middle-East-to-Asia-
       Pacific-Barack-Obama-declares.html

After the breakfast meeting, Brooke drove Rachel north on the South Luzon Expressway to downtown, where they had to exit the freeway until they joined up with the North Luzon Expressway at Quezon City. In the slow-moving traffic, she visually took in everything she could, from the jeepneys and crumbling shanties and litter-strewn streets of Ermita to the new high rises in the Makati District. Brooke was strangely quiet, focusing on the congestion in front. Only after they had passed the business district and turned onto Bonifacio Avenue did he open up.

"How much of this do you remember from the last time you came here?"

"A little bit. But it's been almost six years since I visited while I was teaching in Taiwan, and much of Manila, like everywhere else in Asia, has changed. It seems a little more chaotic."

Brooke nodded in assent. "Chaotic is a nice euphemism for all of the squalor. But there are some nice spots to the city. If we had more time, I would have taken you to the Baywalk off Roxas Avenue—no connection to the Roxas of Yamashita fame. Staring out on the bay from the city can be beautiful, especially at certain times of the day . . . and year."

Alluding to the stifling tropical air, she said, "But not at this time of year, right?"

Brooke smiled and Rachel stared at him. He was just as good-looking as in New York, but she felt more comfortable now, given his softer demeanor.

"What have you found most interesting in your glimpses thus far?"

"Actually, I find the jeepneys the most fascinating; they're so colorful, as they trundle along, overloaded with people. Definitely something I've never seen anywhere else in Asia."

"The jeepneys are a testament to Pinoy ingenuity. When the Americans left after World War II, they left behind a lot of old jeeps that used to ferry supplies and men about. Filipinos started decorating them and turning them into cheap taxis, and that tradition continues today." He paused. "You know, the Philippines, despite its natural beauty and resources, has had a cursed modern history. The Spaniards helped unify the islands, but then by the mid-1800s had begun to wear out their welcome and revolutionary fervor took hold. In the midst of the uprising against Spain, the Americans started warring with Spain and then received the Philippines as a spoil of war. But relations with the Americans quickly soured and a new, unsuccessful uprising against the Americans claimed hundreds of thousands of more lives.[83] The Japanese caused further misery with their occupation in 1942 and their brutal finale in April of 1945, in which over one hundred thousand civilians in Manila were massacred."[84]

Brooke continued. "After the war, the Americans kept effective control over the islands and eventually installed Marcos as their anti-communist puppet. I say installed, quote unquote, because the Philippines has officially been a democracy for most of the latter part of the twentieth century, but your government has always had an enormous covert presence here, pulling strings all over the place. Throughout all of the occupations and endemic corruption and political strife—not to mention horrific typhoons and volcanic eruptions—we Pinoys persevered but hardly prospered. We went from one of the richest nations in Asia after World War II to one of its poorest now, [85] and our population has exploded to over one hundred million. That explains the shantytowns that litter the Metro region, a small fraction of which you're seeing today."

Rachel didn't know what to add. She knew the basics of the island nation's modern history and was aware of its endemic poverty, with almost forty percent of the Filipino population

---

[83]   See http://www.historyguy.com/PhilipineAmericanwar.html#.VE2c5fnF_hs

[84]   See http://en.wikipedia.org/wiki/Manila_massacre

[85]   See http://www.globalsecurity.org/military/world/philippines/economy.htm

surviving on less than three dollars a day.[86] But she didn't want to dwell on the negatives but rather just take in the scenery and enjoy the prospect of meeting her relatives.

"Fortunately, Rachel, we're headed north, where the population is less dense, the poverty less suffocating, and the air a little crisper."

Rachel looked forward to meeting her Aunt Isabel and her cousins in Alaminos City but was a little more nervous about what to expect in Baguio. The plan was for Brooke to drop her off at Alaminos City on Saturday afternoon, where she would spend the rest of Saturday and all of Sunday with her aunt's family. Her family would then travel to Rosales on Monday morning, where she would visit with her grandmother at her father's family estate before being picked up by Brooke in mid-afternoon. He would then transport her on the drive up the mountains, where she would meet some of the Dragon Family for dinner. The next day she would visit the new Golden Lily site and determine for herself whether the whole thing was for real.

Rachel maintained her silence while staring intently out the window as the car sped north on the expressway, past the high rises and shanties of Quezon City and onto Angeles, adjacent to Clark Air Force Base. As they approached the base, once a bastion of American military power in the Philippines but now a free-trade zone, she could see looking to the west the grayish outline of Mount Pinatubo, whose eruption in 1991 devastated the region and led to the abandonment of the base. A year later, the giant U.S. Navy's port at Subic Bay, so active during the Vietnam era, was also turned over the Philippines. As Brooke turned onto the Subic-Clark-Tarlac Expressway, she couldn't help but again be reminded of the Philippines' historical difficulty in forging its own identity.

The traffic began to thin out as they approached Rosales, where the expressway ended. Once off the expressway, the visible

---

[86]   See http://data.worldbank.org/indicator/SI.POV.2DAY

contradictions of Filipino society—the modern low-rises versus the ramshackle shanties and unpaved streets—reared themselves again but on a smaller scale and in leafier surroundings than in Manila. *If I were poor in the Philippines, I'd rather be in a smaller place like Rosales at least than in Manila.* Her father's family was a prominent one from Rosales, but now only her grandmother and some great-aunts and great-uncles lived there along with their families. According to what she had been sketchily told, her father's brother, the eldest of the three children, was rebellious and became enamored with left-wing politics at the University of the Phillipines in Manila and was killed in some sort of accident. His death ultimately propelled her father to apply to universities outside the Philippines for engineering, eventually ending up at the University of Texas at Austin, where he met her mother. Only her Aunt Isabel continued to live in the region, but she had moved away to Alaminos City near the coast after marrying her husband, who managed a large hotel in the city. Alaminos was a popular tourist destination because of its proximity to One Hundred Islands National Park, a beautiful atoll of islands and reefs and beaches that jutted out into the Lingayen Gulf. Her aunt's family was the only one she regularly corresponded with, usually via Facebook but sometimes using email as well.

They arrived in Alaminos by mid-afternoon. Rachel was warmly greeted by her *tiya* and cousins in front of their two-story modern stucco house. Brooke left shortly after being introduced to her family and headed for Baguio. Rachel had brought T-shirts with New York logos for her cousins and a pair of pearl earrings for her aunt and a bottle of Chivas Regal for her uncle. Her tiya had prepared a traditional feast in Rachel's honor, with the *lechon* (whole-roasted pig) served with a spicy rice and a variety of vegetable dishes. Rachel was a little bemused at the pig—either they had forgotten about her Jewish side or they knew that she didn't keep kosher. She found the *dinardaraan* delicious, until afterward when she was told it contained pig entrails. Even after Rachel was satiated, Isabel implored her to eat more, saying she was *payatot,* although Rachel thought she looked overweight compared to her Filipina cousins. She marveled at how thin their figures could be given all the fried foods in the Luzon diet.

After dinner and a *halo-halo* for dessert and *basi* (sugarcane wine), her cousins badgered her with questions about New York and the latest trends in fashion and music. *To them, life in New York seems so glamorous, but if they only knew. Or perhaps they do but are too polite to mention anything about Jackson.*

The next day, after attending an early mass, her aunt arranged a boat trip to one of the islands and prepared a picnic lunch that included shrimp, arugula salad, *suman* (rice in coconut milk wrapped in banana leaves), and a fruit platter. When they were about to leave, Rachel realized that she hadn't brought a swimsuit with her, so she quickly darted into a beach store and purchased a bright salmon bikini that fit her curves and light-olive skin well. After a day of lounging and snorkeling and exploring an underwater cave, she briefly fell asleep on the way back to a restaurant on the water, where her uncle honored her with a toast before the food came. When they arrived back at the house, Isabel brought out some old photo albums and showed Rachel pictures of her father as a young boy along with the stories that accompanied them. It was clear from her soulful eyes that her aunt still missed her older brother, and she couldn't understand why he didn't visit more often. Rachel told her aunt she would work on her father, but that someday she and her girls should come to the states and stop by to see her in New York, which brought a smile to her tiya's face.

The next morning Rachel and her aunt and one of her cousins went to Rosales to visit her grandmother, who was wheelchair-bound in the family hacienda after having suffered a series of strokes and falls in her early eighties. Rachel's grandparents were once wealthy mestizo landowners near Rosales, but they had turned over most of their hacienda to a corporation when land reform policies went into effect, limiting their private holdings. The spacious white-stucco house in which Rachel's father grew up was now inhabited only by her grandmother and a couple of great-aunts from her grandmother's side. The pleas by Isabel for Rachel's *lola* to move permanently to Alaminos City were met with deaf ears, although her grandmother did spend a few extended stays with her aunt while she was still mobile. As on her previous trip five years before, Rachel noted how much less imposing the hacienda seemed than she had remembered it as a little girl on her first trip to the Philippines. She remembered her grandmother as a proud and refined and even stern woman from her previous visits to Luzon and also when her grandmother spent over six months visiting her in the States when Rachel was still in preschool. Now, however, her grandmother was very humbled by her condition and fearing death, and her demeanor toward Rachel was much more soft and tender. All of them sat for a brief lunch on the veranda, where the topic of what business Rachel had in Baguio afterward was barely mentioned. At her farewell, her grandmother took off her gold necklace and asked Rachel to give it to her father. Then, teary-eyed, she pleaded, "Please beg my Daniel to visit me one more time."

Brooke arrived mid-afternoon and decided to take Kennon Road out of Rosales, which scenically followed the boulder-strewn Bued River as it cut a gorge through canyons up the slopes of the Cordilleras into the southern entrance to Baguio City. Rachel took in the steep, verdant hillsides, punctuated with cascading waterfalls, while Brooke negotiated the seemingly endless hairpin turns, most of them lacking guardrails. Before long, they were in the mountains, and Rachel became nervous about what lay ahead.

"Can you tell me a little more about what to expect during the visit here?", she asked

"Well, we're going to a semiformal affair tonight—you did bring an evening dress, didn't you?"

"Yes, fortunately."

"With a sweater or shawl to cover, right?"

"No, I didn't realize I would need anything like that."

"The climate is different up here; it will get down to about twelve Celsius tonight." He tried to calm her. "Fortunately, I brought a black shawl for you to wear if you get cold, and tomorrow should be warmer. We'll be going into a cave, so hopefully you brought some hiking boots and comfortable jeans."

"I did."

"So, don't worry. . . you'll do fine."

Brooke could see that Rachel was still anxious, so he continued to reassure her. "Most of the attendees—six or seven of the couples—will be younger, basically our age. Only two will be older like Don Ignacio—one being the cousin of the former sultan of Sulu, who has come up from Manila, and another representing the Chinese branch of the Family. It will mostly be just relaxing conversation. Most of the younger crowd either work for the Family or are students at one of the Baguio universities. Although the dinner is officially in your honor, you won't be put on the spot—yet."

"What do you mean *in my honor*? You never told me this was going to be such a big deal."

"If I had, perhaps you wouldn't have come. But you shouldn't look a gift horse in the mouth—very few your age can claim to have been a guest of honor at such a gathering. Again. don't worry—I promise you're going to enjoy the evening. And, as they say, don't judge the book on the basis of its cover."

"Spoken like a true bookseller."

I beg your pardon—director of marketing for the largest independent book publisher in the world!"

Rachel smiled at him as she patted him on the shoulder. "No offense, Craig."

They arrived in Baguio at three-thirty in the afternoon, when it was starting to cloud over. She was aware of Baguio's high elevation—almost a mile above sea level—and its moniker as the "City of Pines," for the tall Benguet pine trees that covered its hillsides and carpeted the ground with soft needles and enveloped everything below with their scent. She was nevertheless surprised at how different Baguio looked from the other parts of Luzon that she had visited, with the houses, some more modest than others, rising straight up the mountainsides. Before dropping her off at the Baguio Burnham, Brooke drove her to a couple of places she hadn't expected. One was the Baguio General Hospital and the plot of land next to it (now built over), where Rogelio Roxas allegedly discovered the entrance to the Golden Lily site that contained the golden Buddha. Then, he drove past the summer residence ("The Mansion") of the president of the Philippines, currently unoccupied, and then finally to Camp John Hay and the American Ambassador's Residence. Although the Ambassador's Residence was still owned by the American government, the rest of camp had been turned into a tourist enclave. The residence was gated, but as they slowly passed by the outside of it, Brooke relayed the history of the camp and residence, a two-story white-stucco mansion that was built just after the turn of the century for the American governor to escape the summer heat of Manila, in the era before air-conditioning. Camp John Hay was historically important in that it was the site of the first Japanese bombing of the Philippines in World War II and also the final stop of the Japanese occupation, where General Yamashita handed over his swords to Brigadier General Wainwright in April of 1945. Legend has it that during the massive Luzon quake of 1990 that flattened dozens of buildings in Baguio and cut off the city for days, the painting of the Yamashita surrender ceremony not only remained intact but even perfectly centered.[87] In passing by the camp, all of the mystery of Yamashita's gold sprang to life in Rachel's mind, which was undoubtedly Brooke's intent.

Just as she was being dropped off at the hotel, Rachel started again worrying about whether she would be dressed properly and, somewhat embarrassingly, asked Brooke if he would take a look at her evening dress. She had brought a strapless, knee-length light-green silk cocktail dress. After seeing it, he assured her it would be just perfect for the occasion and told her he would meet her at six-thirty and then head to dinner.

As they drove from the hotel to the residence, the drizzle that had fallen for about an hour was letting up. The residence lay behind a gated entranceway that opened into a drive that climbed to the top of a ridge and another white-stucco mansion.

---

[87] See http://manila.usembassy.gov/wwwhamb1.html. After the surrender, Yamashita was imprisoned and eventually hanged in a war-crimes trial in Manila under the direction of U.S. General Douglas MacArthur. The trial was highly controversial and went all the way to the U.S. Supreme Court, where his conviction was upheld but with dissent. It set a precedent (never enforced against any Western general afterward) that a field commander can be executed for atrocities committed under his command but not with his knowledge or authorization—although the Japanese soldiers committing the worst atrocities in Manila at the end of the war were not effectively under his command. By most accounts, Yamashita was one of the most educated, capable and honorable of all of the Japanese generals: http://en.wikipedia.org/wiki/Tomoyuki_Yamashita. Yamashita is wrongly associated with Golden Lily, as he assumed command of Japanese troops in the Philippines near the end of the Japanese occupation, whereas the actual Golden Lily operation was initiated long before by Princes Chichibu and Takeda under the orders of Emperor Hirohito. In fact, Yamashita's execution served the purpose of silencing all of his personal knowledge of the Golden Lily operations and thereby helped protect the Japanese royals and also the purported American removal of the treasure. It is ironic that the very person responsible for executing Yamashita—Gen. MacArthur—became the controlling entity for much of "Yamashita's gold" after the war (see Seagraves & Seagraves, 2005, *op cit.*, chap. 8).

Brooke and Rachel entered the mansion together and were directed to the main sitting room, where she was introduced to each of the guests, about twenty in all. The elder Chinese gentleman, who introduced himself as Li Shiang, was the most gracious, complimenting her on her "combination of rare beauty and intelligence". Rachel was surprised, even a little amused, to see copies of a couple of her articles from the Pacific Group's newsletter and one from *Asian Entrepreneur Magazine*. She knew of Li Shiang from her research and was aware that some considered him one of the wealthiest men in Asia, although his investment company was privately held and most of its assets hidden.

Shiang motioned for Rachel to move toward the porch, which overlooked the valley, now obscured by the fog. After a few perfunctory exchanges in Mandarin, obviously a test of Rachel's proficiency, he said in a soft voice in English, "It is a great honor for you to have travelled such a long distance to help the Family, Rachel. I know Craig Brooke has filled you in a little about who we are and what our purposes entail, but you will learn so much more about our Dragon Family in your short time here. For instance, did you know that this building is not just a residence but houses the main administrative offices of the Family?"

"No, I wasn't aware of that. So is your official name the 'Dragon Family'?"

"Oh, no," Shiang laughed. "To outsiders, we are Luzon Financial Partners, but everyone working here knows our true identity—as do you."

Rachel then asked, "I am curious as to why you chose Baguio City to be your headquarters?"

"For one, Baguio is fairly prosperous and pleasant, very multicultural, with stunning views and a temperate climate. The views of the mountains are magnificent when it's not as overcast as tonight, and the surrounding pines give it a unique atmosphere. But, as you can imagine, there's more to it than that."

"Such as?"

"Baguio is very centrally located in latitude for the Family, which is dispersed from China and Taiwan in the north to Indochina and Indonesia to the south. It has excellent universities, which many of our children attend. And although it is not accessible by commercial airlines since the runway is too small, it handles business jets easily. Many of our members have business interests in Luzon, and there is a small export zone located here, as well as the larger Clark Freeport Zone a few hours away. Finally, as you already know, it is in the center of a lot of the Golden Lily treasure."

"But wouldn't it make more sense to be located in Manila?"

"Perhaps. But it is easier to stay below the radar in Baguio." He then added wryly, "This is not to say we don't benefit from the protection of certain elements of the government here, as well as other ones throughout the region."

Rachel was about to ask why but then she realized the obvious. The Dragon Family was comprised of wealthy, well-connected Asians, and the governments of East and Southeast Asia would clearly benefit from any success they might have in recovering the wealth that had been lost over the past century.

Shiang's cell phone rang, and he excused himself. Rachel was struck by the phone's gold case, which, if solid, meant it could have been worth thousands of dollars. Rachel then joined Brooke and some others in conversation about a new social media site that was catching on in Asia. When the last of the guests arrived, the group started to assemble around the main dining table, which was T-shaped, with Rachel sitting in the middle of the front table and flanked by the sultan's cousin and his wife on one side and Shiang and his wife on the other. Along the sides were most of the younger guests, and at the opposite end was Brooke, who Rachel noticed was observing her intently in his white suit jacket. The sultan's cousin gave the initial welcome and, being Islamic, recited a brief blessing in Arabic, which almost no one else in the room understood.

The meal started with a shrimp *sinigang*, moved onto a fruit and vegetable salad, and then led to a sizzling boneless *bangus* (milkfish), deep-fried beef, and *a kare-kareng manok* (chicken in annatto peanut sauce) as the main courses, all served with *suman*. She noticed there was no traditional pork dish, probably not because of her but because of the sultan's cousin and his wife. The meal concluded with a *turon* (plantain spring roll) and Filipino coffee. Most of her conversation was with the two men, although every now and then one of the wives would chime in.

After the desserts were consumed, Shiang motioned to Rachel to say a few words. She greeted them with a few words her grandmother had taught her in Tagalog and then went into English. She first created a laugh when she said that she would have eaten much more of the delicious food but didn't want to get stuck in the cave entrance the next day. She went on to state that, though she knew much more about some other Asian countries than the land of her father, she admired the great beauty of the Philippines as well as the warmth and spirit of her people. Then, using the precise words that Brooke had given her, she concluded in Tagalog with *"Ibinabahagi ko ang iyong mga layunin"* ["I share your purpose"]. She could see Brooke at the other end of the long table smiling and giving her a discreet thumbs-up.

Shiang then stood up to speak. He expressed how delighted he was that Rachel, as an expert on Asia, had agreed to visit Baguio and honor not only the Family but the Filipino people and, even more generally, the people of Asia. He relayed what everyone in the room knew—that the White Dragon Family represented all East Asians—indeed, all peoples fighting for justice in the world. He asked rhetorically how it was that Dragon members from several rival nations, representing different cultures and languages and religions, could work together to gain back what was stolen from them? The answer was that East Asians had historically always been more interested in peaceful trade with each other than with constant warring. It was only with the coming of the Western gunships over the last few centuries that serious conflict arose.[88] The critical event was the creation by the West of an imperialistic Japanese military power never previously seen in the region, one that during World War II massacred and raped and stole the wealth that had been accumulated over several millennia. Shiang emphasized that the stolen wealth belonged not just to the Dragon Family, most of whom were personally wealthy, but to the people of Asia, who were still beset with the colonial miseries of poverty and despair. The Dragon Family was making great progress toward rattling the Western financial elite, and it was only a matter of time before the latter would have to relinquish its gold and other wealth so the Family and its political partners could create a new financial order outside the clutches of the West. Shiang concluded with an exhortation for everyone to keep working tirelessly and loyally to achieve the Family's noble aims. At the conclusion of the speech, everyone rose to applaud the charismatic Shiang, who Rachel now realized must be a principal member, if not *the* leader, of the Family.

After his speech, Shiang and the sultan's cousin asked to retire to their residences, but they implored the remaining couples to remain and enjoy the evening, which was still young.

The younger couples quickly relaxed, with the men removing their coats and ties. After a few minutes of conversation, one of the young men took out his smart phone and started playing a popular dance song on its surprisingly loud speaker while he and

---

[88]   Indeed, Robert Kelly has pointed out that in the two hundred years prior to the Western presence, East Asia was at peace 99.5% of the time whereas Western Christendom was at peace only 39% of the time: http://asiansecurityblog.wordpress.com/2010/06/05/off-to-china-3-there-was-a-confucian-peace-after-all

a couple of the young women started dancing to it. Pretty soon more of the couples joined in, and eventually one young man motioned to Rachel to join him, which suited her fine since she was familiar with the same song from the dance class that she was currently attending. After a few minutes of dancing, some alcoholic drinks were passed around and the conversation livened up. A lot of the young women were pressing Rachel on the latest summer fashions and other trends in New York. To most of them, New York was as exotic as Baguio was to Rachel. Rachel noticed that Brooke was talking quietly with another man in a corner of the room; she figured he didn't know very many of the people at the dinner. Before she left, a lot of the young women wanted to take some selfies with Rachel, who motioned to Brooke to come over to take one with her as well.

About ten-thirty, Brooke announced that he and Rachel would have to leave for her hotel, since they would be rising early the next morning. As they were driving back to the hotel, Rachel had some questions for him.

"So, you were right—I did enjoy the evening and, God knows, I've never felt so honored in my life . . . and probably will never do so again, maybe even at my funeral!"

"Don't be so sure . . . if it all works out as planned."

"Okay, but tell me one thing. Is Shiang the leader of the Dragons? And was the purpose of the whole dinner to get his approval?"

"Shiang is by most accounts the wealthiest of the Dragons and certainly one of its most dynamic leaders. And yes, he was 'looking you over,' so to speak. But Li Shiang is not the major strategist—you will meet that person tomorrow night, after we visit the cave."

"And this other person will give me the specifics—the maps, the plans, and the final pitch?"

"All of those."

As Rachel was about to get out of the car, Brooke placed his hand in hers and added, "Rachel you did very well tonight. Just before he left, Shiang told me he was very pleased. But we have a big day tomorrow and it's a long ride across the mountains. Please be ready at six-thirty."

As he drove away, Rachel realized that the man who seemed so intimidating and unapproachable in New York was a mere lieutenant in the Dragon army. Although her feelings toward him had warmed, she was determined to find out still more about his background and ambitions.

CHAPTER

6

The sun rose early through the scattered fog. During a brief break in the fog, Rachel stared out from her balcony and could see the city as it spread out southwesterly toward the peaks of nearby Cabuyao and Santo Tomas, guarding the western entrance to Baguio. She turned directly south and viewed the willow trees surrounding the manmade lake in Burnham Park beneath her, home to a few early-morning joggers and walkers. Then, the sky darkened and a light rain began.

Brooke was right on time, driving a Toyota 4Runner in place of his rental car. He had some pastries and coffee for the trip over the mountains. The site they were visiting was just off the Benguet-Nueva Vizcaya Road, about fifteen kilometers southwest of Bambang, near the intersection of the mountain road with the Pan-Philippine National Highway just north of the town of Aritao. Although the site was only about one hundred kilometers east of Baguio, winding through the mountainous terrain would lengthen the trip to about three hours.

As the two-lane road curved back and forth, occasionally hugging the sides of steep ravines, Rachel took in the montane rainforest, punctuated by small enclaves of homes, the nicer two-story ones made of wood and the small shacks made of corrugated metal. Many of them hugged the road with parked cars periodically jutting into the road. Cars, vans, small trucks, bikes, and motorbikes comprised the weekday traffic, which gradually thinned as they drove eastward, with occasional stretches where no other cars were seen. She noted how traffic would slow and move to the right for passing cars, just as it used to do along the country roads of Texas when she was a little girl.

At one point the road almost brushed Pulag National Park and came within fifteen kilometers of Mount Pulag, the second-tallest peak in the Philippines at over three thousand meters, but it was obscured by trees and the mist. Shortly thereafter, they bypassed the large Ambuklao Hydroelectric Dam on the Agno, recently rehabilitated after the massive Luzon quake of 1990. Although only a small percentage of the Filipino population was situated in its adjacent provinces, the Cordillera region contained a substantial portion of the Philippines' wealth, mostly agricultural and mineral but also hydroelectric. Over sixty percent of the Philippines' temperate vegetables came from the region, as well as eighty percent of its gold. And the huge amounts of rainfall and steep elevations created a hydroelectric potential that was so vast that, by some estimates, the region was capable of providing over half of the Philippines' energy needs.[89] Mining and dams were not popular with the entrenched indigenous peoples, however, who constantly fought the large-scale projects that threatened their way of life.

As they descended toward Bambang, the clouds began to break and Rachel was able to see glimpses of the vast and fertile Cagayan Valley in front of her, as it extended eastward toward the Sierra Madre. As the elevation decreased, the pine forests started to mix with oak and laurel stands and eventually gave way to some tall lowland rainforest varieties. Due to the limestone overlay of the volcanic Cordillera base, the region was full of caves and caverns and tunnels, which afforded the

---

[89]   See http://en.wikipedia.org/wiki/Cordillera_Central_(Luzon)

Japanese many large sites in which to bury the massive Golden Lily treasure.

About one kilometer after they veered right at the bridge over the Santa Cruz River in their approach to the National Highway, Brooke's GPS-linked beeper on his smartphone went off. He slowed down and started searching to his left. He quickly spotted a small dirt road that, after a few kilometers, led to a highly concealed little opening covered in underbrush. After quickly removing the cover, Brooke got out of the 4Runner and moved a couple of small trees, still in their soil containers, that blocked the entrance to a little dirt road that was hidden from above by the overhanging canopy. Brooke then drove the SUV slowly though the opening before stopping again and motioning to Rachel to get out and help him move everything back into place. Nearby, some screeching macaques showed their displeasure at the new human presence. The entrance to the cave was a hundred meters or so beyond, and the road was barely wide enough for the 4Runner to pass through, brushing the ferns and orchids hanging from the branches above. Three men stood watch at the cave entrance. Brooke got out and started talking in Tagalog to what appeared to be the foreman of the group. He gently nodded and periodically interjected with a question while the other man talked and motioned with his fingers. Then, Brooke motioned to Rachel to join him and began describing the situation to her.

"Pepe says we're in luck . . . only yesterday did the methane levels drop low enough to go into the cave for the first time without a mask."

"Methane from what?"

Brooke paused. "From decomposition of the bodies."

Rachel blanched slightly but remained silent.

"I don't know if you did any research since my New York visit, but after the large Golden Lily sites were finished and the gold put in place, the Japanese would throw a big party for the workers and soldiers and engineers who worked on the site.

After they had drunk a lot of sake, the commanders—whether it be the emperor's brother Prince Chichibu or his cousin Prince Takeda or perhaps General Yamashita himself—would slip out and then the entranceway would be exploded to trap everyone inside, so the secret of the location would be secured. Then, the entrance would be covered in dirt so the forest could regrow around it."

Rachel was horrified. "And the bodies—they're still in place?"

"Yes . . . at least what's left of them."

Rachel grew noticeably paler and nauseated, and Brooke came over to hold her hand and calm her. After a minute or so, he struck up again. "Rachel, there are other bad things in that cave . . . giant spiders and even snakes. Most of the snakes are nonpoisonous, but if we come across a cobra infestation, we're out of there right away. Are you still in?"

No, I wish I were a thousand miles from here. But I'm not going to give you the satisfaction of knowing that.

"I'm still in . . . as long as you go first and play the snake music."

Brooke smiled. "Good . . . I always figured you were pretty tough deep down. But don't worry, there will be a team of us going in, with adequate lighting."

And then all five of them—Brooke, Rachel, Pepe, and the two other men—gathered at the entrance, wearing light-cotton long-sleeve shirts and caving helmets with LEDs. After traversing a tight passageway and a narrow and precipitous drop, they were suddenly in a large room that began to glisten. She was entranced by the sight of large piles of gold further on, until Brooke grabbed her arm gently and pointed to a space on the ground in front of her, where several skeletons were present. "Be careful," he whispered.

Aside from the gold and skeletons, the small stalagmites and stalactites reminded Rachel of the limestone caves she used to visit in the Hill Country of Texas with her parents and relatives.

The ground had small pools of standing water in places but was less flooded than might have been expected given the daily rains in the area, presumably due to the slope of the ground above, which diverted most of the water. Only when she got near to the first pile of gold did the truth of the Golden Lily legend begin to sink in. She estimated there were fifteen bars in each of twenty stacks, with each stack spreading ten rows deep. She did the quick calculations in her head—three thousand bars in total, in such a small area.

"How many ounces in each bar?' she asked.

Brooke replied, "If I remember correctly, there are over thirty troy ounces to each kilo, so each bar would contain about three hundred and seventy-five ounces total."

"Three hundred and seventy-five times three thousand . . . that's over a million ounces total. At fifteen hundred or so an ounce, that's—"

"Just under two billion dollars . . . *in this pile alone.*" Then, while she was unsuspecting, he snapped a photo with her and the gold pile on his smartphone and added kiddingly, "This will be for your grandkids someday."

Rachel was too entranced by all of the gold to appreciate Brooke's attempt at levity as she moved about the large room. She quickly counted the piles—eight in all. Not to mention at least a dozen large drums full of diamonds and other gems.

"So, we're talking about fifteen billion total!"

"But there's more, miss," Pepe chimed in. "See that wall? Our imaging shows a hidden door that may open to a larger room. Based on what we know of the Golden Lily numbering system, this was a '777' site—one of the largest. Others like it have been shown to contain more than twenty billion in gold and other minerals. And there's still more."

Pepe led Rachel and Brooke to a smaller side chamber. When he shined his flashlight in the center of the room, Rachel gasped. A den of snakes was crawling on what must have been at least a dozen skeletons, some of which had samurai swords next to them. And in the middle of it all was a glistening golden Buddha, at least a meter high, probably similar to the one that Roxas had found in Baguio and perhaps full of diamonds like his. Pepe motioned not to get too close. "This must have been where they spent their last few hours, next to the statue. Of course, the pit vipers weren't there at that moment."

"Pit vipers? How would they have gotten in?" Brooke asked.

"Probably through little cracks in rock that opened up after the explosives. I've never seen them before . . . there's not much here for them here except for a few small lizards. And now us, of course."

Pepe sensed that Rachel wasn't amused. Turning to her, he said, "Don't worry, miss, I hear they use the viper venom in wrinkle creams these days . . . not that you need it."

Brooke chuckled and then interjected, "How do you know so much about snakes, Pepe?"

"You probably didn't know I was majoring in biology and helping with some reptile research at the university here until I got my Christina pregnant . . . which meant I needed a real job all of a sudden."

Rachel asked Pepe if they were planning to remove the Buddha from the cave.

"It'll be the last thing, for sure. It will be hard to get it out of the entranceway, but we should be able to manage with ropes."

No one talked for about another minute. Rachel was taking in the entire experience. *Yes, it will be a good story for my grandchildren . . . if I ever have any.*

They slowly walked from pile to pile. Brooke picked up a bar from one of the piles that had about half of its bars missing. "Look at this one, Rachel . . . do you see the stamp?"

Rachel looked at what Brooke held close to her and could see what looked to be some lettering finely imprinted on one side of the bar, one of which resembled an italicized *S*.

Brooke came by and picked up another one with the same mark. "See, this came from the treasury of Sarawak in the

1800s . . . so do you mind if I take one as we leave? No one will miss a mere three hundred thousand American dollars."

Rachel was perplexed. "But I thought you—"

"Were going to give it all to the people?" Brooke laughed and gave Rachel a look of *You sure are gullible for an Asian scholar.* "Actually, Rachel, we're all going to take some bars out of here today. If each of the men take four bars and you can carry two, that's over two hundred kilos in all. I don't think I want to task the 4Runner with any more going up the mountain."

Rachel asked, "So you're just like that going to take them to Baguio?"

"Why not? That's where they're being stored . . . for the time being."

Rachel barely managed to make it through the large chamber to the entranceway under the weight of her two bars. *I can't believe I'm carrying over a million dollars worth of gold!* As they reached the vertical passage, Rachel glanced at the two skeletons to her left before handing the bars to Brooke and then climbing up the passageway. When they all were out, the bars were loaded into the 4Runner and the entranceway was again covered with brush. Then Pepe and the other two men began walking down the dirt road toward the main road and disappeared, while Rachel and Brooke waited next to the 4Runner.

"I can't believe you're leaving billions of dollars in gold back there. Aren't you worried about someone stealing it . . . or even robbing you of the millions in the SUV?"

Brooke smiled. "There's a lot more security than you think around the site, Rachel—infrared cameras, motion sensors, trip circuits, and the like. And those men—they didn't leave the premises altogether."

"And Pepe can be trusted?"

"Get in and see for yourself. We're going to go pick up Pepe down the road and have a little lunch with him. As for outsiders knowing about all of this, our biggest advantage is that we operate under the radar—in small movements and transports. We could bring in some large vehicles to remove everything quickly, but that would attract too much attention."

Sure enough, Pepe emerged from the underbrush as they approached the main road. He moved the small trees away to let the SUV through and then returned them to their previous state, concealing the main entranceway once more.

Pepe hopped in and directed Brooke about five kilometers down the road to a little clearing, where they saw his white pickup parked. Rachel and Brooke got out and sat on a rock underneath a large dipterocarp, while Pepe took out some sandwiches and fruit and water bottles.

Brooke opened the conversation. "So, Pepe, Rachel was wondering how we could leave billions of gold back there in the mine, entrusted to you and your men."

Pepe smiled. "I was wondering the same thing!"

"Seriously, try calming Rachel's worries."

Pepe turned toward Rachel. "I guess you know about the Dragon Family . . . or you wouldn't be here."

"I know a little, mostly based on what Craig has told me and what I found out last night."

"Then you should know two things—first, that we are secret, although some general information about us has started leaking out in the past year or so, and two, that we are committed. For half a millennium, the Europeans came in wave after wave to Asia, to strip it of its wealth. We weren't able to mount a collective resistance—if it wasn't their gunboats that destroyed us, then it was the sellouts of own rulers. Now we are about to achieve one of the great vindications in history . . . and I would trade that moment for a few gold bars?"

Pepe continued. "My father was a revolutionary, a leader of the indigenous tribes in the region during the struggle during the 1970s against Marcos and the landowners. When he was killed, I was barely two. *Tiyo* Benito—"

"The man you'll meet tonight," Brooke interjected.

Pepe continued. "Tiyo later adopted me and raised me after my mother died several years later, so to me he is even more than an uncle. He is a man of great honor and strength . . . and vision. He would tell me often of the rebellion and of my father's role in it. He always vowed that his death would be avenged and that justice would prevail, and that someday the Philippines would be free of Western economic domination. But when I was heading off to study, the struggle had subsided. As I mentioned, I was initially interested in biology, but my plans had to change and I ended up working in the mines, eventually becoming a foreman. Two years ago, Tiyo came to me and told me with my experience, I could be a big help to the Family, not disclosing the details. I didn't hesitate when he asked me to help open the cave, despite the dangers. Nor did those men, who are very loyal, mainly to me personally."

"Because you had once saved their lives, right?" Brooke interjected again.

Pepe nodded. "And because I am also their local tribal leader."

Rachel asked Pepe, "So how did you manage to open the cave without destroying it?"

"As Craig no doubt told you, we knew there was a site somewhere in the general vicinity. During the war, the Japanese would cross the mountains, but the road wasn't anything like this. Some of their geologists and engineers would scour the forest cave openings for underground storage sites, and this one proved very convenient because of its large chamber inside. Using some advanced imaging techniques, we were able to determine the outline of the cave and what must have been the entranceway. My men and I carefully dug out the opening, and after passing the entry, we used some robotic devices to check for booby traps and tripwires. Because we are working very slowly, mostly at night, it's taken awhile to open up the main passageways and chambers, but as I mentioned, there's still more to the site than we've uncovered. Of course, we could have moved much faster had we had the engineering maps."

"And how long do you think it will take to remove all of the gold?"

"The gold you saw should take about another month. But we know there's at least one more chamber . . . possibly two. All told, we may be looking at anywhere from two to four months."

"That seems like a long time for you to escape detection."

"Perhaps. But from what I've been told, the problem with some of the past recoveries is that they had too much visibility. Patience—and commitment—are the keys here."

Brooke looked up at the sky, with the sun directly overhead. "Unfortunately, patience is what we no longer have here today. It will take close to four hours to get back to Baguio, perhaps more as loaded down as we are."

Pepe then took out two big plastic containers of gasoline and emptied them into the 4Runner until its tank was full for the trip back, since they were a long way from a filling station. Then, Brooke thanked Pepe for his help and for the supplies, and he and Rachel climbed into the SUV. Just before they left, Pepe went up to Rachel's side and said, "Thank you, miss, for helping us. I've heard a lot of good things about you and your courage."

Rachel extended her hand to Pepe, but rather than clasp it, he kissed it. And then he stepped back and waved them off.

As Brooke had predicted, it took them longer on the return trip, mostly because of the extra weight they were carrying on the uphill climb. Rachel and Brooke stared ahead as they quickly passed the dirt road that led to the cave and then started winding up the mountain for several more kilometers. Finally, Rachel decided to break the silence. "Pepe's a good man, isn't he?"

"There are a lot of good men and women working for the Family, Rachel. But yes, he is one of the best and, because of his skills, most valuable. Because he's an Ilocano tribal leader, he also commands a lot of respect."

Rachel then asked, "What I can't understand is why the Japanese would have left the red maps here. Why didn't they take them back to Japan?"

"One can assume they were left here for insurance purposes. There's no telling what could have happened to the maps if they were in some ship or submarine sent back to Japan that sunk. Prince Takeda—known only as 'Kimsu' to the local servant-boy Valmores—evidently planned to return but never did. He told Ben, who he had great trust in, that he could do whatever he wanted with the maps, but only after twenty-five years. Only a few of the red maps would have been of any use to Ben, in any case, since he personally had visited only a couple of the sites."

"And how did the white maps come to be found?"

"They weren't all in the same location or even towns—some were found in churches, some in military installations, and such. A few were even recreated from memory—sometimes under torture—by some of the Japanese soldiers and other locals who were privy to the location of the original stashes. Without the red maps, they were basically useless and so they would periodically be offered for sale—or just outright stolen by Marcos and his men."

Rachel was silent for several seconds and delicately posed her next question, which had been nagging her from the moment she first set foot in the cave. "So, after the gold's all removed, what are you planning to do with the bodies?"

"You mean skeletons."

"Yes."

"We'll leave them where they are; there's no need to remove them. I know what you're thinking, but it's been over sixty years and no one has any illusion that the men would still be alive. So what's the point?"

Rachel didn't reply. After another few kilometers, she opened up again. "So those two skeletons near the entrance . . . do you think they were probably trying to escape in the end?"

"That's what I would surmise. They knew the direction of the entrance and may have been clawing at the dirt and rocks, but there was too much of it. There wouldn't have been much time, either—hours at most before their air ran out."

Rachel started feeling very tired, lulled in by the undulating road and drained not just from the physical exertion but also from the depressing thoughts of all of the men gasping for air in their final moments. Just before she fell asleep, she thought, *How horrific humans can be to each other; yet, this was just a small sliver of the horror that was wreaked during World War II and an even smaller sliver of the horrors throughout all of human history.*

When she awoke, they were only fifty kilometers from Baguio and the grade wasn't as steep. She felt she had slept for days, but it was actually only an hour and a half when she glanced at her watch. She could feel that the air was cooler now, and thick clouds had formed, presaging another downpour.

"You were really out of it, Rachel. We passed through a hard rain and it didn't even faze you. You were even snoring a bit . . . but it was a very sexy snore."

"Oh, stop it. I'm surprised I wasn't crying out in my sleep after what I saw today. Had you ever been to one of the sites before?"

"To be honest, no. But I had heard countless stories about them, so perhaps that's why it wasn't more shocking to me."

"So what will tonight be like, with Tiyo Benito?"

"We're going to meet in the hotel restaurant. It should be rather informal—no evening dress necessary. You'll find

Fernandez very easy to talk to. But don't be fooled . . . he's one of, if not *the* most impressive men I've ever met."

"And the brains behind the Dragon Family?"

"There are a lot of brains in the Family. But as I mentioned before, Don Benito is perhaps best viewed as our master strategist . . . and inspiration."

CHAPTER

7

It was five in the afternoon and raining when Brooke dropped Rachel off at the hotel. Because of her sleep, she was feeling wide awake but in need of some relaxation. She checked to see if she could still get a massage, but it was too late. So she decided to lounge in the jacuzzi bath in her deluxe room instead.

She turned on the Asian News Channel while she was dressing. In Asia, aside from some brewing typhoons, the biggest news concerned some large trade deals involving China and two of its neighbors—Myanmar and Vietnam. There was the usual turmoil from the Middle East but no news from the United States and only a single story from Europe. *How different events register in this part of the world—if only our leaders could truly experience the different vantage points of other nations.*

She arrived at the restaurant lobby to find Brooke, dressed in a white polo and khakis, chatting with a middle-aged gentleman who looked her father's age or slightly older and who introduced himself as Ben Fernandez. He was about the same height as Brooke and wore glasses and had a firm handshake and a very confident air. Although he had a slight Filipino accent, his mannerisms and pace could have passed for American.

"It's a pleasure to finally meet you, Rachel. I trust Craig here has hosted you well?"

Rachel glanced at Brooke and smiled. "Very well."

"Good. We wanted to make sure you feel very comfortable with the Family and have become more knowledgeable about our strategies and goals. Tonight is a very important one in our relationship."

Fernandez exchanged a few more pleasantries before ordering Rachel and Brooke a drink, but Rachel could tell he was the type who allotted only a certain amount of time for small talk.

Once they had sat down and ordered their meal, Fernandez started delving into an unexpected line of conversation. "Did you know I was good friends with your uncle Miguel, Rachel? I also knew your father, but we were not really friends in the same way."

Rachel was very surprised. *Is he going to bring Uncle Miguel to life? Isn't it strange that almost no one in my family ever talked about him over the years . . . except that he seemed to be killed in some accident or something when still in college.* "I had no idea there was a connection."

"Nor did I, until we started gathering the background information on you. Miguel and I went to school together, but I would visit your house now and then. I remember your father as being very smart but apolitical—unlike your uncle." Fernandez paused before continuing on. "Miguel was very idealistic . . . and stubborn. He would constantly argue about the treatment of the indigenous workers with your grandfather, who as you know was a wealthy mestizo. My parents were landowners, too, but they were a little more tolerant of the leftist positions. Your poor grandmother was torn apart by the conflict. She, too, was a proud mestizo, but she loved, even favored, her firstborn son and tried to dissuade him without pushing him away. At the university, a lot of us became radicalized, but Miguel was even more impatient, in addition to being a natural, almost charismatic, leader. He and Pepe's father both dropped out after their first year and started organizing the peasants and, before you know it, became the military leaders of the rebellion. Mind you, there had already been a major peasant rebellion that almost succeeded after World War II, but this one got wrapped up in the civil discontent against Marcos and his repression and strong anticommunist line. Perhaps you didn't realize it, but our military involvement in Vietnam was even more unpopular here than in the States."[90]

Rachel nodded, "Yes, I am somewhat familiar with the history of that era."

"Not really being the military type, I became a political spokesman for the party. I would go around central Luzon talking to various groups of workers and students, and the party was steadily growing in numbers. But Marcos was carefully planning his move, playing on some discontent within the organization. During one of his military sweeps, he managed to turn one of our commanders and corner the main leadership, which is when Miguel and Jaime were killed. Most of the top political leadership, including me, was thrown into prison. But because my parents were influential, I was able to get out after a couple of years."

So that's why no one ever talked of Miguel! Were they ashamed he was a communist . . . or were they ashamed that he was more idealistic than the rest of them?

"And then what did you do?" Rachel asked.

"I just wanted to get away so, like your father, I applied to several universities in America. I ended up at UCLA, finished

---

[90] For a brief summary of the Hukbong (Huk) communist insurgencies of the late twentieth century, see http://www.historyofwar.org/articles/wars_philippines.html. For a more extensive discussion of the largest Huk insurgency between 1949 and 1954, see Benedict J. Kerkvliet, *The Huk Rebellion: A Study of Peasant Revolt in the Philippines* (2nd Ed.), Rowman & Littlefield, 2002. Although the first Huk rebellion officially ended in the 1950s, many remnants of it arose again in the 1970s to fight the continuing inequality of Filipino society and the dictatorial rule of Ferdinand Marcos. A very low-scale insurgency continues to this day.

my undergraduate studies in economics, and returned to Rosales to help out with the family business."

"And you adopted Pepe."

"Not right away. I got married and my wife had already given birth to our firstborn when I received word from Pepe's mom that she was very ill with cancer. She asked if I could take Pepe in for a while, since both her family and Jaime's had disowned them because of his activities. That was also Jaime's wish before he died, in case anything would happen to the both of them. When she died later that year, I formally adopted Pepe and raised him along with my own children."

"So how did you get started with the Family?"

"It's too long a story for tonight, so I'll give you an abbreviated version. After I had received my graduate degree and started teaching economics at the local university here, I received a call from one of my old undergraduate friends. He asked if I knew anything about Golden Lily and the buried treasures around here. Of course, we all knew the legends, but until the Roxas case came to light, none of us realized the truth behind them. He mentioned that he represented some wealthy Asian businessmen who wanted to explore some of the sites."

Rachel turned her head slightly. "And what did you tell him?"

Fernandez smiled slightly. "I didn't tell him anything but rather asked him rhetorically, 'If you find any gold, whose should it be?' He seemed taken aback momentarily, which is when I answered that the 'gold belonged to the people of Asia."

"My friend seemed surprised and said, 'So, you think it should all just be given away to the masses?' Fortunately, I had been thinking about and even writing on the possibility of an Asian Monetary Fund, to rival the International Monetary Fund and World Bank. Those two agencies have been a catastrophe for the developing world. Did you know that, just a few years ago, this nation sent almost *eight times* more in interest payments to international lenders than it received in international relief for Typhoon Haiyan—that's what's known as 'reverse foreign aid.'[91] In any case, I told him that, after the finder's fee had been allotted and the investment costs recouped, the rest of the gold should be used to back a new Asian currency to replace the American dollar."

"And he went along?"

"Not only that, he recruited a lot of his own friends, such as Craig's father, many of whom were quite wealthy. You'd be surprised how easy it was to bring the wealthy Asians together against Western interests—most of them have been cheated one way or another out of their rightful assets over the last century. And despite their recognition of America's leadership and prowess during the last century, most never trusted the Americans and British and other Western financial elites to honor their debts. They want them out of our region, once and for all."

"But I hear America's still fairly popular over here."

"It depends who you talk to—people rarely bite the hand that feeds them. But that's going to change soon, now that China has become our largest trading partner."[92]

Rachel returned to the Golden Lily discussion. "What I'm wondering is how you convinced the others you could open the Lily sites? How were you planning to do it?"

Ben smiled. "Through various means, some of which Craig told you about, no doubt." Brooke nodded in assent.

Fernandez described again how Marcos had obtained several dozen of the white maps and almost succeeded in matching

---

[91]   See http://www.ohchr.org/FR/NewsEvents/Pages/DisplayNews.aspx?NewsID=14482&LangID=F. For a more general discussion of the issue of "reverse foreign aid," see http://www.newleftproject.org/index.php/site/article_comments/aid_in_reverse_how_poor_countries_develop_rich_countries

[92]   As of early 2013, China and the United States were tied as the leading trading partners of the Philippines: http://www.census.gov.ph/content/foreign-trade-statistics-philippines-first-semester-2013

them to the red ones. "He eventually found out about the red maps that Prince Takeda had left with Valmores.[93] He could have opened dozens of more sites but Curtis double-crossed him and ran off with most of the red maps, or at least photocopies of them. The American government knew about Marcos' white maps and was always pressing him to hand over the Golden Lily loot to use in some of its covert operations and to shore up the dollar. Marcos would give them a cut from time to time, but he refused to hand over the white maps, even when they threatened to depose him—which they eventually did in eighty-six.[94] After that, all of his accounts and those of Santa Romana, like White Spiritual Boy—"

"With the impossibly large trillions in them."

"*Improbably* large, but hardly impossible, Rachel, given the massive wealth Asian nations had accumulated before the Japanese rape. In any case, all of those accounts and others were turned over as collateral to the Western financiers, and not one penny was ever returned to the original owners. In fact, almost no compensation has been paid by any Japanese officials to the victims of World War II, and the emperor and his family who designed the conquest were left not only free after the war but extremely wealthy, *thanks to your government*."[95]

For the first time, Rachel noticed the emotion rising in Fernandez' voice. She understood from her time in Asia that enmity toward the Japanese was still strong across the region, even sixty years after the war, so his feelings did not surprise her. But she decided again to redirect the conversation to the maps.

"So the Dragon Family eventually obtained the white maps."

---

[93]   See Seagraves & Seagraves, 2005, *op cit.*, pp. 161-163.

[94]   See footnote #31.

[95]   See Seagraves & Seagraves, 2005, *op cit.*, chap. 8; and, for a more general account, see Herbert Bix's *Hirohito and The Making of Modern Japan* (Harper Perennial, 2001). The estimated total restitution for the alleged tens of trillions of dollars in assets looted by the Japanese in World War II was about one billion dollars (Bix, 2001, p. 693).

"Yes, one of our members was a Marcos confidant who knew where they were being stored. Marcos wanted them to be kept in his family after his death, but our colleague had heard about the Family and decided to do the right thing and give the people of Asia the opportunity to recover the wealth that had once been theirs."

Fernandez paused and stared at Rachel before pulling rolled paper from his jacket pocket. "So Rachel, you have seen the realities of the massive poverty of Asia, despite its modern façade, you have seen the reality of the Dragon Family and our purposes, and you have seen the reality of the Golden Lily fortune. Now, you'll see the reality of the maps."

Rachel unrolled the paper and saw a bunch of little curved lines and Japanese symbols and directional arrows. She mused how similar they looked to the maps she used to see in her childhood treasure hunts. Since she didn't read Japanese, it wasn't clear what any of it meant, although she did recognize the "777" designation at the top. "This is it—this is what's so valuable?"

Fernandez smiled. "No, of course not. It's what's inside those sites that's worth tens of billions each, as you saw. But did you know that, according to our collection, there were at least a half-dozen sites along your route today. How would you have found ours today if you didn't have the map?"

"Obviously, I couldn't have. And it would have required the red maps, too."

Fernandez nodded. "Yes, that's more or less true. With modern imaging and other advanced technologies, the red maps are less essential than before, but they're still important. We've had success with one other site on our own. But the red maps can save a lot of time and, more importantly, they can prevent costly mistakes, such as a site collapse. We've already suffered one cave-in, fortunately not costing us any lives. But we alone have maps of over fifty sites that have yet to be explored, and there may be more. I personally believe that more than half of the original one hundred and seventy-five reputed Golden Lily sites have still not been tapped." [96]

"Why do think that George Perry and his group would be interested in them now?"

Fernandez smiled. "It is true that the 'cabal,' if I may use that term to describe the Anglo-American Bilderberger group controlling the key Western financial and industrial enterprises, has more than enough gold for the time being. But they don't want anyone else to trump them with a competing financial system. As long as the gold is in the ground, it's no problem for them—that's why they haven't bothered to bargain for the white maps in recent decades, leaving so many of the Lily sites untapped. And why a lot of the Sukarno gold is still in the ground in Indonesia. But if the cabal perceives that someone else may gain control of the gold, *that* represents a problem for it. Then, hopefully, they'll be forced to deal."

Rachel had heard the same argument from Brooke in New York, but she was still struggling to grasp the end game of the Dragon's bold plan. Fernandez sensed her doubts and looked her directly in the eye. "Without going into details, Rachel, I want you to know that you have stepped into a high-stakes financial chess match, with powerful players on both sides and brinkmanship and minefields all around. As you—and the Bilderberger cabal—well know, every day Asia gets richer and more powerful and the West gets older and poorer. The result will inevitably be a tilting of the global financial structure in our favor, regardless of whether or not we uncover any gold on our own. But the treasure you could help us find may very well

---

[96] No one knows the exact number of unexplored Lily sites. One lower estimate—that of Powers, 2012, *op cit.*, p. 100—argues that only fifty-five sites remain untouched. But treasure hunting in Luzon remains an active pastime: http://www.southeastasianarchaeology.com/2007/12/28/cave-restriction-to-fend-off-hunters-of-yamashitas-treasure A particular goal is to uncover the famous Tunnel-8 complex near Bambang, described by Ben Valmores to the Seagraves.

represent the tipping point that finally forces the long-overdue repatriation of our wealth to its proper owners—the people of Asia."

Rachel gently nodded to signify her comprehension of his words, but she could scarcely conceal her concerns. Just as she started rolling the map back up, Fernandez grabbed one of the ends and tugged at it.

"Before you leave with the map, Rachel, I want to be blunt. There is a risk in your getting involved. But we will not deliberately put you in jeopardy, and hopefully George Perry won't put his daughter-in-law—"

"*Ex*-daughter-in-law."

"I'm sorry . . . Craig told me about your tragedy last year." Rachel thought to herself, *Yes, you know about it, but do you really care to know what I went through all that time?*

Fernandez then released the map and said in a softer voice, "The only thing I ask is that when you exchange the white map for the red one, you *personally* arrange to bring the red one to us."

Rachel stared directly at Fernandez and replied in a deliberate tone of respect. "I'll make sure the map gets to him, Don Benito, or you'll get it back soon. Hopefully, some good will come out of it."

"It will, Rachel . . . it will." Fernandez smiled and then shook her hand and excused himself. Brooke, who had been silent during most of the exchange, briefly tried to chat with Rachel but could tell her mind was elsewhere. He then reminded her that she would have to be ready by seven the next morning, and they both arose from the table to go to their rooms.

As she was walking up to her room, Rachel thought about her uncle Miguel, Ben Fernandez, Li Shiang, George Perry, and even Jackson. *What is it about men that makes them so intense . . . and even dangerous?*

And then she thought of her grandmother in her wheelchair and what it must have been like to see her oldest son join a force opposed to her husband and then get killed and then see her only other son leave across the ocean, to rarely see him again. *Men may start the conflicts and even get killed in them . . . but in the end it is the women who suffer the most.*

CHAPTER

8

As before, Brooke arrived on time for the departure, this time dressed in a white T-shirt and driving his original rental car. After a quick continental breakfast in the hotel, they rapidly descended into the valley on another cool and misty morning. Rachel was already starting to miss the mountains and pine forests that she had come to relish during her brief stay.

Since her plane left at three o'clock in the afternoon, Brooke planned to arrive at Manila International before noon. Her flight would arrive at Los Angeles that same day and she then planned to stay overnight before leaving for New York early the next day, giving her a couple of days of rest before starting work.

As they headed south, Rachel realized that she had learned very little more of Brooke during the trip than he had revealed to her in New York six weeks earlier. So she decided to probe him about his personal life.

"Craig, I want to thank you for being such a great host to me during the trip. I'm sure there were times when you felt a bit bored by the conversation, but you never once let on."

"Oh, no, Rachel, the pleasure was mine. Even when I was just listening, I learned new things about the Dragon Family . . . and about you and your family."

"But I know practically nothing about you. Tell me a little about yourself."

Brooke chuckled. "Spoken like a true woman—always wanting to get inside a man's head!"

"Speaking of women, do you mind if I ask you if you have a girlfriend or fiancee? I notice that you don't wear a ring on your finger."

"No, at the moment, I don't have a girlfriend . . . or a boyfriend, for that matter."

It was Rachel's turn to laugh. "So, assuming you *do* like women, what type of woman would appeal to you?"

Brooke acted for a few seconds like he was giving it a serious thought. Then he replied, "I like smart and beautiful green-eyed Eurasian women."

"Oh, cut it out!" she said laughingly. "You haven't shown the slightest interest in me the whole trip."

Brooke smiled. "So, you don't think I find you attractive?"

"Nope."

"Well, then, you're wrong. But you have to understand one thing."

"What's that?"

"If I would ever let myself have feelings for you, I wouldn't permit you to go through with this."

"Oh, so you're one of those men who thinks a woman needs a man's permission in life?"

"No, I'm one of those men who believes that, once you're in love, you should always seek permission from your lover before you get involved in anything dangerous."

"So this really is a dangerous mission that the Dragon Family has set me on."

"Didn't you hear what Fernandez was saying last night? Rachel, we're talking about trillions of dollars in assets—that's a lot of money in any corner of the globe. People have been killed for a tiny fraction of that." He paused. "Don't let my courteous behavior entice you into believing this isn't purely business, Rachel."

"I don't believe it."

Brooke turned to look at Rachel. "You don't know what it means to be a member of the Dragon Family . . . even I'm only a junior partner, so to speak."

Rachel switched gears. "But it seems that most of the Family is involved in business or related fields, unlike you."

"I share their ideals, even if not their interests."

"So you're much less materialistic?"

"Let's say I'm much more into intellectual, even spiritual, pursuits. Although I ended up with a degree in comparative religion, I tend to search for more expansive, transcendental experiences—not religious in a traditional sense, but more mystical."

Rachel wanted to probe more. "You know, Craig, I've been thinking how men handle stress. Unlike most of us women, who aren't afraid to let our emotions out, most men either turn their stress inward—as with my late husband, who created a world of his own before taking his own life—or turn it outward and become highly competitive and driven or sometimes even dangerous to others. In your case, though, you tend to turn it—"

"Upward? Yes, I do a lot of mediation and try to relax and quiet my body as my mind drifts higher."

He's very autotelic and idealistic . . . perhaps even monastic. He has Jackson's same underlying intensity, but it seems more under control with him.

"Do you know what I think?"

"What?"

"I think you're the real 'White Spiritual Boy'—without the trillions, of course!"

Brooke smiled but then redirected the conversation back toward Rachel. "So what about you? Why would you take on a potentially risky mission like this?"

"I don't know why, exactly. Perhaps I may regret it, but for now it seems like the right thing to do. For one, I'm interested in Asia and, even though I'm ashamed to say it, this whole venture has shown me how little I really know of this part of the world. I also now realize how much of an impact this could have on the societies of Asia. Do you remember the words you had me say in Tagalog at the first dinner: 'I share your purpose'? I actually believe them . . . if the Family's purpose is truly as it has been portrayed."

"As far as I know, it is. But I guess one should always be a little wary of men who have accumulated so much wealth."

"Another thing you have to realize"—Rachel stopped, after getting a little choked up—"is that this is an escape of sorts from over a year of almost constant hell. Do you have any idea what it's like to see the person you love descend into madness and then die violently by his own hand?"

Brooke waited before responding. "No, I can only imagine what it did to you. I really admire you for your perseverance and strength."

"I wouldn't exactly call it strength. In the first few weeks after Jackson's funeral, I stayed home from work and couldn't leave the bed for almost a month, staying with some friends. I eventually went back to work, but right after I came home I would eat a takeout or frozen dinner and climb into bed again.

"My family wanted me to fly to Texas for the holidays, but I couldn't bear to face anyone, so my mom instead flew up to New York to be with me. We rented a motel room by the beach with a kitchen and read and talked and took walks all bundled up by the shore. My mom, thank God, seemed to know exactly what I needed—she listened for hours, never pressured me on anything, and did all of the cooking. It was very therapeutic for me, although I was still depressed when she left."

Brooke waited before responding. "Did you ever seek help during the whole ordeal?"

"Before he died, yes; but afterward, strangely enough, no. One thing that helped during the bleak New York winter was getting his book published. It provided a little closure and eliminated some of my guilt, and it gave me a bit of purpose. But I still couldn't bring myself to move out of the apartment, feeling there would be nothing left of him for me if I did. Until that night we met for dinner. After you dropped me off and I turned the key, a wave of panic and loneliness hit me and I didn't want to enter the old apartment at all."

"So you're telling me you've picked out a new place, to get away from all of the bad memories?"

"Absolutely. After that night, I immediately started looking and just put a deposit on a new place, in lower Manhattan, near Chinatown."

"That's good."

"But, Craig, there's perhaps a deeper reason I agreed to help out your group. I didn't realize it until I actually visited my relatives and met Ben Fernandez and he started talking about my Uncle Miguel and my *lola* and my father." Rachel paused briefly, then her eyes started to well up. "I now realize that part of me is using this to bring myself closer to my dad; perhaps even my earlier decision to major in Asian studies was unconsciously for the same reason. You know, Daddy was a good father in a certain way—he came to most of my soccer games and school events and watched me graduate and walked me down the aisle. But he never really opened up to me."

"How so?"

"He would come home from work and go watch a little news and sports and go to work in his little workshop in the garage. On weekends, he'd go golfing or to a football game or play cards with some of his friends. He was very masculine in his pursuits—perhaps he would have preferred a boy, as he always told me to be strong and tough. But he never realized how much I wanted to connect with him at a deeper level, to know what his thoughts were, what he was like as a boy, what growing up in the Philippines was like, why he left. To everyone, he was Dan Echon, as American as the next guy, who seemingly could care less about his Filipino past. But I always wanted more."

"He obviously was trying to repress his own painful memories—his family's conflicts, his brother's death—by escaping to a place where everything could be normal and orderly, unburdened by the past."

She looked at Brooke, still focused on the road. *Despite his youth, he seems so wise in his thoughts.*

"And, in retrospect, I realize how much I misjudged my grandmother. I was always respectful, even a little afraid of her. But I didn't know the emotional turmoil she must have felt, first by Miguel's conflicts with the family, and then his death, and then my father's leaving. Because she rarely smiled, I thought she was just stern and even haughty, but now I realize I was wrong. It dawned on me when I stopped by the *hacienda* how truly sad she must have been and is especially now, pleading for my dad to visit her 'one more time.' I now wished I had let down my guard and truly showed my love to her . . . in the twilight of her life."

"It's not too late, Rachel."

"What do you mean?"

"Well, we already passed Rosales, but we're making good time and I left a little time to spare. I'm going to turn around so you'll never have to say 'I should have said or done this or that with my grandmother before she died.' Your magic moment is going to happen."

Rachel tried but couldn't quite hold back the tears. *God, how he understands the important things in life.*

Ten minutes later, they were back at the hacienda, and Rachel crept up on her grandmother. When Rachel turned and faced her, her lola was at first confused but then broke into a joyful smile. Rachel bent down and whispered what a great lady she was and how proud she was to be her granddaughter, and she gave her a gigantic hug, from not only her but also her father. Her grandmother started sobbing and clutching Rachel so tightly with her wrinkled hands that Rachel could hardly breathe. Then, Rachel told her she had to make a flight back to the States, but that she would be back again and write to her in the interim.

Along the road, Brooke and Rachel didn't speak for well over a half an hour, her eyes remaining moist as she struggled with her emotions. As they approached Angeles, Brooke broke the silence. "Well, Rachel, I think we're going to be fine on time. You'll still have about two hours before the flight."

Rachel nodded. She then held his hand briefly and kissed him on the cheek. "Thanks, Craig . . . you have no idea how important that visit was to me."

Brooke smiled. "No worries. But, Rachel, I'm sorry I'm not going to get to buy you that coffee on the Baywalk. I'm taking the EDSA loop around the city instead, to save a little time."

"Next time, Craig. But I'll buy for you if you ever come to New York. Do you come very often?"

"No. I hadn't been there since I stopped by on a return home from Cambridge many summers ago. But I'm sure we'll see each other again . . . somewhere."

Rachel felt the reality set in. *In the end, despite his kindness, maybe it was just what he said it was—business.*

As they arrived at the terminal, Brooke took Rachel's bag out of the trunk and placed it next to the curbside check-in. He then gave her a little box as a "memento of her trip" and bade her goodbye, with a handshake and brief kiss on the cheek. And then he drove off.

In the box was a little note from him—"*May this protect you always.*" Inside the note was a gold necklace with a large gold pendant configured as a dragon hosting a baby tortoise on its back, which Rachel knew was a Chinese symbol for wealth, protection, and success. As she clutched it, she was suddenly gripped by the same wave of loneliness that she had felt when he first dropped her off in Brooklyn.

CHAPTER
9

When Rachel arrived back in New York, she wasted no time in contacting her father, carefully relaying her grandmother's words. Her father listened intently while she described her visit and asked a few questions, primarily about his sister and her family. He said he was glad Rachel had been able to visit his mother, and he promised to call her lola soon but remained noncommittal about a visit in the near future.

She checked her voice messages and listened to one from Karen, who welcomed her back and invited her to a day of sailing and then dinner and fireworks on the Fourth of July at the Northport Yacht Club on Long Island, where she and Jacques kept their boat.

Finally, Rachel mustered up the courage to call her father-in-law, who agreed to meet with her the following week at the elegant Inside Park restaurant on Park Avenue, a few blocks south of the Pacific Group's offices. *I wonder how he's going to react when he hears about all of this.*

George Perry was standing relaxed in his Armani suit as she entered the restaurant, and he smiled as he greeted her at the door with a quick hug. Rachel mused how Perry seemed to be perpetually tanned and fit, owing to his weekly regimen of racquetball and ultraviolet light treatments during the winter and tennis and golf and occasional yachting during the rest of the year. After he had helped her to her seat, Perry said in his patrician voice, "How are you managing after all these months, Rachel? Patricia and I have been totally remiss in not reaching out to you since Jackson's death. Actually, Patricia's said she's talked to you a couple of times—I guess I'm the one to blame."

"I'm okay. It just feels weird in the apartment with Jackson not around . . . even if he wasn't right. I've finally decided to move to a new place, in the East Village. I should be moved in before the middle of next month."

"Good, I've been concerned about you living over there in Brooklyn, what with all of the crime."

Rachel stared at her father-in-law's refined visage, framed by his styled silver-gray hair. *Yes, you're right about all the crime, starting with the burglary job your henchmen probably did to find the manuscript.*

"If you need any help with the move, Rachel, please let me know. By the way, Patricia and I are having a big party at the beach house the last weekend of July. We'd like to see you there if you can make it. Be sure to bring a swimsuit . . . I plan to take the boat out."

It's just like him . . . to refer to a mansion as a "beach house" and a forty-meter yacht as a "boat"!

"I might do that. I'm starting to feel a little cloistered in the apartment these days."

"You could drive up with Robert on Friday—he's joining the girls and Ashley, who are spending the week. It'll be just family on Friday night."

Out of Jackson's family, Robert Matthew Perry and his wife Ashley and their two six-year-old twins were the ones to whom

Rachel felt most attached. And Robert was the only one who regularly checked in on her after Jackson's death, taking her to lunch on a few occasions and inviting her over for the twins' birthdays. She would relish a three-hour drive to Newport with her brother-in-law, who was very down to earth and funny and always accepting and caring of his younger brother, even during the latter's dark end days. *He knows I won't refuse to come if Robert offers to take me.*

He stared at her with a faint smile that a bystander might interpret as gentle but which she sensed was a little condescending . . . or worse. By American standards, George Oliver Perry, descended from the famous captain and hero of the War of 1812, came from old money—and lots of it—created by robber baron schemes in railroads and agribusiness and oil in the late 1800s and later cemented by generations of marriages of wealthy families. He, like his father and grandfather and sons, attended Yale University and was reputedly a member of one of its notorious secret societies. Despite his family tragedies—a turbulent marriage, a wife who died of an overdose and now a son who went insane and committed suicide—he seemingly led a charmed life of privilege, from prep schools to Yale, to a cushy naval officer assignment during Vietnam when so many of his generation were cut down, to president of First Manhattan Federal Bank and later the megalithic Manhattan Trust, and then on to a capstone position as secretary of the treasury. His real power, though, came from his longtime tenure as president of the Council on Foreign Relations—the nongovernmental think-tank that was started by J.P. Morgan and a few other industrialists and bankers in the early 1920s. The council was the public arm of the powerful Bilderberger Group and had served as the springboard for almost every major cabinet appointee since World War II.

George Perry generally exhibited a nonchalant politeness toward Rachel and her commoner, mongrel background, with all of its races and ethnicities mixed together. But she knew that he would have been much less tolerant of her had she been the love interest of his elder son, who he was counting on to follow in his footsteps.

The waiter stopped by and they quickly ordered, he a steak au poivre and fries and a Sam Adams, she an Asian chicken salad. Afterward, he asked, "So, Rachel, what did you want to discuss with me?"

She hesitated. "I was approached by someone from the Philippines I once knew at Dartmouth"—she lied—"who wanted me to relay a message from a wealthy group in Asia, known as the Dragons."

"And . . ."

"He said it relates to gold—lots of it—and that he feels you will be appreciative of his offer." She hesitated, feeling her anxiety increase. "He said you and they could work together to find the remaining Marcos gold."

"You mean the Yamashita gold, don't you?"

"Yes."

"Did he mention why he wanted you to approach me specifically, or was I just one of several on his list?"

"No, you were the only one. He said the Dragons have access to a large number of the geographical maps with directions to the Yamashita sites and that you were very well connected and had access to . . . to the other maps, the red ones."

He smiled. "And you would go to bat for any old acquaintance on a matter like that? What's this fellow's name?"

She could feel herself sweating a little more. "It's Craig Brooke—at least that's the name he goes by."

He leaned slightly forward as his light brown eyes bore down on Rachel. "That's interesting. There is a Craig Brooke who works for Imperial Publishing in Cebu . . . but that couldn't be him, could it?"

My God, he knows everything . . . why was I so stupid to use his real name!

"Don't look so shocked, Rachel," he continued. "In my world, a book like that doesn't pass unnoticed. Nor do the people who end up publishing it."

She knew she was cornered so she blurted out the truth. "I did it out of respect for your son, not because I had any role in writing it."

He smiled again. "Of course you did, but I wish you hadn't. Not that a little thing like that really threatens any of us—hell, it must have sold all of ten copies by now—but because it's just so wrong in all of its facts and innuendo. You know that, right?"

"I don't know what to believe. All I know he was passionate about it, even if it destroyed him in the end."

Perry realized he was too intimidating and began to soften his approach. "Look, Rachel, you realize the whole notion that a small number of us New York bankers can even begin to control the world's financial system is preposterous, right? Do you really think that the current world is ideal for anyone, whether it be you, me, we Americans in general, or the Europeans? So what if a group of us tried to keep a bunch of countries from going communist or want to curb overpopulation or take the risk of lending to marginal nations that are in need of credit? Is that so wrong?"

"Fair enough, but you're not denying that American intelligence agencies and our financial networks are throwing their weight around everywhere, are you? Look at what's happening in the Middle East—our fingerprints are all over the strife there." Rachel was surprised she had the courage to mount even that much of an argument against her father-in-law, but she could feel the perspiration building.

"Rachel, hold on." Perry touched the tips of his fingers of one hand to the palm of the other, in a time-out signal. "Yes, we financiers have interests around the world . . . and, of course, we have influence in Congress and the White House as well. But you act as if all of us goose-step to the same orders. Do you think I really wanted the mess that's over there in Iraq . . .

and now the whole region? Saddam was a son-of-a-bitch, but we could always do business with him. Same with Gaddafi. People think we need to control all of that oil over there, but whoever owns it has to sell it and deposit their petrodollars somewhere."

"Unless they demanded something other than petrodollars for it." She saw him recoil slightly. "So, how is it that we ended up intervening in all of these countries?"

Perry's eyes widened and his voice became more animated. "It was all because of those damn Zionist neocons"—but then he caught himself almost immediately. "Sorry, I didn't mean to be insensitive, Rachel."

Rachel tacitly nodded. Even though she was slightly taken aback by Perry's lapse, it didn't surprise her that Perry might harbor anti-Zionist, perhaps even anti-Semitic, beliefs, although Rachel didn't equate the two. Despite the relish of so many conspiracy theorists to blame all of the Anglo-American secret machinations since World War I on Jews, Rachel knew that most of the most powerful men in America were not only *not* Jewish but often hostile to Jews; indeed, she supposed George Perry and many of his ilk learned to swim and play golf and tennis in country clubs that didn't even admit Jews back then. What slightly bemused her, though, was that Perry didn't realize that she rarely even identified as Jewish anymore. Her mother had chafed under the domination of her grandmother and had never pushed religion on her—only the need to excel academically, which she did by becoming salutatorian at Westlake High. She had attended a Jewish day school in Austin through the fifth grade with her grandmother's blessing and money but had insisted on going to public middle school. She also had briefly considered passing on her bat mitzvah, but again her grandmother won out. Rachel did admire the accomplishments of the Jews in science and the arts, but she also couldn't overlook the disproportionate Jewish representation among the great financial swindlers of the late twentieth century. And she had an increasingly negative view of Israel, even defending the Palestinian cause in arguments with some of her Jewish coworkers.

The awkward moment placed Rachel at a temporary loss of words. She knew she had scored a few points in the argument but that George Oliver Perry was too experienced and agile at rationalizing for her to be able to expose his true role in the Bilderbergers, which she knew was much more extensive than he would ever let on.

Fortunately, the food arrived to break the silence. Perry then resumed on a different tack that surprised her. Staring directly at her, he said, "Rachel, you know how it is when kids hit their teenage years and a lot of them start rebelling against their parents? It probably never happened with you, but that's the way it was with Jackson. Our relationship began to suffer and he started to reject everything I was involved in. I blame myself to some extent—I wasn't really there for him after his mother died. I don't know what happened, but he seemed to get more and more erratic as he went through college. I know he was into drugs for a time, and that probably contributed to his paranoia. We really hoped that you might be able to pull him back from the abyss—especially since you seemed so right for him. It's been very difficult for all of us to deal with. For you, I can't even begin to imagine the pain you've felt."

Rachel could feel herself welling up. Despite her attempts at blocking off the memory of Jackson's illness and suicide, his father's words churned everything up inside of her. Just when she could barely hold back her tears, Perry put his hand on hers in a comforting gesture. *He seems genuinely concerned about me . . . is he really the monster Jackson made him out to be?*

After a half-minute of silence, Perry sensed a return of her composure and returned to the topic that had brought them there. "So, yes, Rachel, I do have access to the red maps. You don't need to know the details, but let me simply state that there were some financial arrangements that involved Manhattan

Federal a long time ago. But I'm not sure I'll be able to pry any loose."

Rachel then pulled a photo out of her purse showing the gold inside the Luzon site she had visited, with no other identifying information. "Brooke said the Dragons had opened this site recently and were prepared to go it alone—but for various reasons were prepared to deal."

Perry knew he needed to come up with more. "Okay, Rachel, here is what I would suggest. As a test case, arrange to have him send you a white map of a '777' site, one of the richest supposedly. I'll then provide him with a corresponding '777' red one from our own set. Where does he want the maps sent?"

"He wants me to handle them—to ensure chain of custody from you. And he wants an original."

Perry stared at her. "Rachel, there are no original red maps as far as I am aware—they were destroyed a long time ago. And I don't think it's good idea for you to be so involved."

She remained impassive, and he turned away briefly before looking directly at her again. "I don't know what Brooke told you, but we're talking about potentially vast sums here. If any missteps take place, there could be serious repercussions . . . and I don't just mean financial. The people I deal with are not as monstrous as Jackson led you to believe, but they're far from saints—especially when crossed." He paused. "You did nothing wrong by bringing this to my attention; in fact, I'm glad you called me about it. And if you bring me a map, I'll pass it on and provide you with one of ours—a valid photocopy. And if something goes wrong, I'll have to take the fall. But let me be frank with you—if you continue to stay involved after this one, you could be in very serious danger. And I'm much too fond of you to let that happen."

Rachel looked down at her plate. She knew she was in too far for her own good, but was the same man Jackson claimed was starting coups, pushing wars, and stealing resources around the world being honest with her? *Will he really protect me if I get out after the first round and something goes down?*

Perry stared at her and seemingly read her thoughts. "It'll be okay, Rachel." Then after quickly consuming the rest of his meal, he rose from the table and helped her from her chair. "I'm sorry but I have to leave now. I'll call my driver and he'll take you back to your office." Then, he added, after another brief hug, "Please do try to make it in July . . . you'll enjoy the company."

CHAPTER
10

Although Jacques Delacroix had a penchant for Mercedes sports cars, he sold his last one when he and Karen moved into their Manhattan condo. So on sailing weekends, Jacques and Karen would typically ride their bikes to Penn Station, place them on the Long Island Railroad to Northport, and then mount them again for the ride to the Yacht Club where their sailboat was moored. Off-peak, the entire cost was about twenty dollars, less than a rental car. But with Rachel and a friend of his joining them for Independence Day, Jacques decided to rent a mid-size SUV that allowed them to drive up right to the club, in less than an hour.

Rachel had figured the other member of the foursome would be one of Jacques' French buddies, but it turned out that he was Juhn Peng, a tall, good-looking Asian man with a Chinese-British accent who introduced himself by the Americanized name "John." Peng was evidently a Canadian citizen and an associate of Jacques' at the international bullion trading house. She was surprised that he seemed to know Jacques so well, given that he wasn't at his birthday party two months earlier.

The Northport Yacht Club was a family-friendly marina, though hardly the most exclusive one on Long Island. It was situated in Northport Harbor, an inlet extending off Northport Bay that led to the Long Island Sound via Huntington Sound and Huntington Bay. Karen and Jacques brought along a large cooler, which contained sandwiches for lunch, their potluck dishes for dinner, and plenty of drinks, mostly alcoholic. Jacques and Peng helped carry the cooler to the boat, while Rachel and Karen carried the beach towels, snorkeling gear, and other accessories.

The plan was to tour around the bay in the morning and view some of the mansions along the Huntington Bay shoreline before enjoying lunch and snorkeling and sunning on the beach at nearby Caumsett State Park, the former estate of department store magnate Marshall Field III. As they left port, the breeze off the water was strong, and Peng showed his skill in trimming the sails, with Jacques mostly watching. Rachel and Karen sat near the stern, catching up on gossip and getting excited about Rachel's impending move to Manhattan, while avoiding any discussion of her recent Philippines trip. They dropped anchor just off the park's rocky beach in about a meter of water. She remembered the time Jackson and she had hung out one afternoon not too far away. She briefly gazed out at the shoreline and mentally tried to bring him back to life, but his face and body were no longer vivid. *With what's been happening recently, Jackson seems so far away now.*

Rachel wore the bright salmon bikini she bought in the Philippines underneath shorts and a polo. As she removed her outer garments and hat, she could tell Peng was eyeing her. She jumped into the water, which felt refreshingly cool after being in the warm July sun. Jacques handed her one of the two snorkeling sets and she began to doggie paddle away from the boat while looking around for some of the sea creatures hanging out on the bottom. The water was surprisingly clear and she managed to find a couple of starfish and sea urchins, which she dove under to see close up. She later stumbled onto a nest of small sand dollars, which she stroked with her foot, enjoying the softness of their velvety spines.

While Rachel and Peng were snorkeling, Karen and Jacques took the cooler and towels to the beach. After a half-hour of swimming and snorkeling, Rachel along with the others opened the sandwiches and drinks and engaged in some chitchat before spreading the towels out and laying down on them, with Peng in between Rachel and Karen. After a few minutes, Peng raised himself slightly and turned and addressed Rachel in Mandarin.

"So, I understand you are fluent in Mandarin and are an expert in Asian affairs?"

"More or less," she replied, also in Mandarin.

"So, do you mind if I ask what you think of recent events in Asia, specifically the burgeoning dispute over the oil in the South China Sea?"

"Wow, that's a pretty heavy question for a holiday outing, isn't it, John?" Rachel replied. "But since you asked, I see China continuing to lead the rest of Southeast Asia in rapid economic growth. And with its upgraded and advanced naval capabilities and massive investments all over the region, I think it will ultimately prevail in any oil disputes in the South China Sea—although not without friction."[97]

Peng continued, "And you don't think America will try to stop it?"

Rachel paused. "Personally, I think American influence is on the wane and that Asian nations no longer see the United States as a fail-safe deterrent to the Chinese claims."

"And the new BRICS fund . . . how is that being viewed?"

"I think everyone is in a wait-and-see attitude right now. There's not enough in it now to have a major impact."

---

[97] The South China Sea, a source of many recent maritime skirmishes between China and other nations, is believed to contain proven and estimated oil reserves of over 20 billion barrels of oil and over 300 trillion cubic feet of natural gas: http://www.eia.gov/todayinenergy/detail.cfm?id=10651

"Interesting views, Rachel—thanks. One more thing—have you heard anything about a major currency play? Some of our clients are starting to dump euros and dollars for gold and are buying yuans. There seems to be something about to break on the gold front in the next few months that could really upset the Western currencies."

He's probing me for some inside information . . . or bluffing or even teasing me, what with his bullion-trading background. Either way, he must have gotten wind of my trip from Karen and Jacques!

Before Rachel could answer, Karen, as if on cue, chimed in with feigned anger. "Would you stop talking behind our backs, guys?" Then she burst out laughing. "Rach, you have no idea how weird it is to have your best friend who you've known for almost a decade speaking strange words that I've never heard come out of your mouth."

Rachel kiddingly said, "Get me drunk and you'll hear a lot more words come out of my mouth you've never heard—whether in Mandarin or English!"

Everyone laughed, but Rachel was still mildly peeved, convinced Karen had spilled the beans to Jacques about her Philippines venture.

After about an hour on the beach, Karen and Rachel hiked up the hill on one of the tree-laden paths that led into the estate. There they were able to get better views of the sound, and they encountered deer, rabbits, geese, and even a turtle along the path amidst the background of whippoorwill cadences.

A few minutes into the walk, Rachel confronted Karen about her suspicions. "You didn't mention anything to Jacques about my side trip to the Philippines, did you?"

"No, of course not. Why do you ask?"

"Because his friend seemed to be hinting at some major play on gold that was about to unfold, negatively affecting the Western currencies."

Karen paused. "Rachel, trust me, I didn't say a word about anything to Jacques. Maybe Peng has some insider information of his own. According to Jacques, he's only been working at the firm about six months and is a bit secretive. What can I say—Jacques and John really hit it off and like to hang out together. They talk for hours when John visits our place, on everything from stocks to cars to boating."

"But he wasn't at his birthday party."

"I think it was because he was out of town. Let's change subjects—how'd it go on the trip?"

Rachel took a deep breath. Without naming names and specific locations, she described the trip to Baguio, the meetings, the Golden Lily site, and the maps. She then concluded by telling her about her meeting with Perry the previous week.

Karen listened intently while only rarely interrupting. At the end, she said, "Again, Rach, I give you credit for sticking your neck out there. I just hope the guillotine isn't lurking behind it."

"Krew, think of it this way. I'm pushing thirty, widowed with no kids. Realistically, what other options do I have for my future—attending boring lectures and drinking lattes? If I die, I die. Just be sure to say some nice things about me in your eulogy."

Karen just shook her head. Then she put her arm around Rachel as they headed back to the beach. When they arrived, most of the other sunbathers had gone. Jacques started walking toward them and exclaimed, "*Mon dieu*, I thought you guys got lost and were halfway to Hoboken! Everything's in the boat, so let's hurry up and take a quick dip before we take off. If we're lucky, the wind will hold up until we hit the marina."

They made it back by six o'clock, just as the potluck dinner was being served. Some of the officers of the club cooked burgers and hot dogs and corn, and there were plenty of Long Island oysters on the half shell.

Around eight in the evening, as the western sky broke into a hue of orange and red streaks, a bonfire was lit near the water, and people started singing some patriotic and other traditional American songs. One middle-aged man sang a rousing *a cappella* version of "New York, New York," while another slightly inebriated fellow tried to lead a verse of "Take Me Out to the Ballgame" game in honor of the Yankees' victory over the Sox earlier in the day. Jacques even attempted to join in the act with his own off-key rendition of the "Marseillaise," reminding everyone of France's critical role in helping "you *Americaines*" in defeating the British, but he was booted off after the first verse.

Peng seemed highly amused at the spontaneous choir of boaters and their kids. He moved closer to Rachel and asked what she thought about all of the singing.

"Oh, it's great fun, don't you think? Or do you think it's all sort of hokey?"

"No, I like it all, actually. But why are you Americans always invoking phrases like 'God shed His Grace on thee' and 'God bless America'?"

"Oh, I don't know . . . that's just the way we are. Do you think it's pretty arrogant to be asking God to do anything for us? You know, our President Lincoln once said, 'It's more important to be on God's side than to have God on our side'— or something to that effect."[98]

Peng smiled. "It's an interesting quote, but one most people in Asia and Europe wouldn't even dream of. After all of the human-made catastrophes of the last century, most people start to doubt that God really cares about what happens. You still

---

[98]   http://www.brainyquote.com/quotes/quotes/a/abrahamlin388944.html

have the luxury in this country of believing that way because you've never been humiliated or crushed militarily as a nation."

Rachel shrugged. "John, you're way over my pay grade with your thoughts . . . you need to lighten up a bit, just for today!" Then, looking out at the children who were starting to light their sparklers and tanks and black snakes amidst the fireflies popping up everywhere, she said, "I just want to watch the kids have fun, like I used to as a little girl, and then see the fireworks." Switching to Mandarin, she added, "You know where fireworks came from, don't you, John?"

Peng let out a laugh and high-fived Rachel. Then he went and grabbed the last Heineken out of the cooler and sat back down next to Rachel and exclaimed, "Let the fireworks begin!" Right on schedule, the first missile pierced the darkened sky over the harbor, accompanied by a stereo blaring the "The Stars and Stripes Forever."

The ride back was quiet, with Jacques focusing on the road and Karen and Peng napping. Periodically, Rachel would gaze at Peng with his head against the window on the other side of the backseat, as if to get inside his mind.

As much as I want to believe Karen that he's just another young bullion trader, something tells me he's not all he seems.

CHAPTER
11

A week after the Fourth of July outing, Rachel rented a pickup and had Karen and Jacques help her move into her new one-bedroom apartment in lower Manhattan. She kept a few things of Jackson's, boxed up a few other things to give away to his family, and donated everything else she didn't move to the Salvation Army. Only two trips were required, aside from the movers' truck for the large items.

To celebrate, Karen and Jacques took her out to Da Nico's in Little Italy, where they ended up downing two liters of Chianti before the night was through. After the meeting with Brooke, the trip to the Philippines, and the invites from Karen and Jacques, Rachel was finally starting to come alive again after her months of hell. But she viewed the upcoming weekend at Newport with some trepidation and was already half-wishing it were over.

Robert Perry called her on Tuesday night. He aimed to get out of the city by three that Friday afternoon and arrive in Newport for dinner. The plan was for him to swing by and pick

Rachel up at the Pacific Group before heading up FDR Drive to Interstate 278 and then onto Interstate 95 through Connecticut. Rachel almost missed him pulling up in the new Jaguar he had just purchased, as he was wearing dark shades and had grown a well-trimmed beard. But it wasn't long before he brightened her mood with his wisecracks and jokes. If Jackson had come to display the intensity of his father and the moroseness of his mother, Robert was of the opposite persuasion. It wasn't that he was lacking in smarts or leadership—he graduated magna cum laude from Yale in government and had received several commendations as a lieutenant commander in the navy, but unlike his father and brother, Robert would fit in as easily at a working-class bar downing beers while watching a football game as at a black-tie affair.

Perry told her he was glad she was coming along for the weekend, as the twins were really looking forward to seeing their Aunt Rachel. He also congratulated her on her new apartment and how she "had begun to move on". He himself seemed different emotionally from when she had last seen him a few months earlier. Then, and in the months immediately after Jackson's death, he was more somber, sharing in her grief. But, one thing you could always count on living in the North— as the seasons changed, so did one's mood. Perhaps everyone would again get depressed as the days grew shorter, but now Rachel could feel she was starting to blossom again—and feeling nowhere as guilty at enjoying life as she would have thought even a few months earlier.

They made good time getting out of the city. As they crossed into Connecticut and the traffic began to thin, Rachel complimented her brother-in-law on his new car.

"I can't believe how smooth your new Jag is, Robert. If I ever drive again, I'll have to get one of these."

"If you want to drive one of these, Rachel, you have to get the hell out of Manhattan. From what I've been told, the parking space for a year there costs a lot more than the car itself."

"No kidding."

"So, Rachel, I understand you just returned from a trip to Asia . . . how was it?"

"Oh, it was very interesting. I attended a conference in Singapore and found out about some new trends, especially involving female entrepreneurship."

"So, I guess that's the next region to end up with emasculated men!"

"Oh, stop it," Rachel blurted out as she punched him kiddingly. Then she added, "And the trip to the Philippines was pretty interesting . . . and emotional. I spent some time with my aunt's family on the west coast of Luzon and then visited my grandmother at the old hacienda in Rosales nearby. She's in a wheelchair and not doing well and really wants to see my dad. And then we spent a couple of days in the mountains, with its pine forests and all. Have you ever been to the Philippines?"

"Actually, I did spend a couple of days there when I was in the navy, on one of my two deployments. I was on the USS *Essex* out of San Diego. We had just finished participating in a joint exercise with the Philippines and we were given shore leave at Subic Bay. I was surprised to find that most Filipinos still seem to like the United States . . . especially the women."

"You don't have to tell me the rest of the story. Just remember most Filipinas are not like the ones that hang out at naval bases."

If I didn't know better, I wouldn't for a million years guess that he's heir—now, sole heir—to one of the greatest fortunes in America.

Rachel continued, "Robert, can you answer a personal question that's been bothering me for a long time?"

"No, I 'm not going to have an affair with you."

"Would you cut it out, already!" Rachel laughed, but then grew serious again. "You know, your father has always been very polite to me . . . and you seem to have a good relationship with him and have been following in his footsteps. Why didn't Jackson?"

"Well, I guess he was just a little more rebellious."

"But, you know, you even look a lot more like your dad, with your dark wavy hair. And your mannerisms are pretty similar, although you're a bit more laid back."

"Perhaps."

"Would you say Jackson took more after your mother, and that's why he was perhaps a little more affected by her death?"

"I don't know. I was six years older than Jackson when she died—almost in middle school. But that doesn't mean I didn't take it hard. Did you know I still wear a gold chain with a picture of her in a locket?"

"No, I didn't." Rachel paused again. "I know Jackson's gone, but I just wished I knew a little more about him . . . why he ended up the way he did."

Robert remained silent as he stared at the road, so Rachel continued to probe. "So, do you think you'll follow in your father's footsteps someday, like joining the Council on Foreign Relations and even going into governmental service?"

"I actually don't like to think about those things, Rachel. I'm enjoying coming home at regular hours to be with Ashley and the girls. But I expect that someday I'll be taking over for my father in some of those functions. Not that I would do things exactly the same."

"How so?"

"A lot of us 'Gen-Xers' don't see the world the way our parents did. None of us is so arrogant as to claim 'American exceptionalism' anymore; we all know American influence is declining, what with China and Russia and even India and Brazil on the rise. And there's going to be some serious reckoning as the energy and debt loads keep mushrooming. But I'm sure my father wasn't thinking about all of the power he's now wielding when he was my age, either. I know he comes across a certain way now, but I still remember him when he was younger and more carefree . . . and probably a lot happier. As he's grown in influence and power, the weight of it all has grown on him, too."

"I can only imagine. Did he ever mention to you about giving it all up and enjoying other aspects of life?"

"Dad? Are you kidding?" Robert let out a chuckle, then grew more serious. "No, Rachel, he's never mentioned anything like that to me and I've never proposed it. I hope I can do it someday, but I can only surmise what an intoxicant power like my dad's can be."

"Do you ever argue with your dad, Robert? When we had lunch a few weeks ago, we started talking a little politics and I put up a little stand against him, but I got a taste of how tough it would be to take him on in a debate."

"Oh, we get into friendly discussions now and then. When I was younger, he would generally compliment me on my arguments but end up cautioning me that 'things will look a lot different when you reach my age and vantage point.' I can assure you, though, that my discussions with him were nothing like the heated ones Jackson had with him."

"I can only imagine."

Then, carefully contemplating his next words, Robert opened up even more to Rachel. "I don't know what you were getting at, Rachel, but I'm going to tell you something I shouldn't. I'm doing this because I know you're looking for answers . . . and with the hell you've been though, God only knows you deserve them. But I want you to promise *never* to let loose to anyone what I'm about to tell you."

"I promise, Robert."

"Jackson didn't look and act like my father because my dad wasn't his real father . . . and that lay at the heart of their stormy relationship." Realizing that Rachel was too stunned to say anything, he continued. "I don't know what happened, but my mother was unhappy in their marriage and getting depressed. She was probably desperate for an emotional lift, and she started having an affair with an old friend from college."

Robert's words cut like a knife, but Rachel sensed deep down it was the truth, even as she struggled to comprehend it. "Did Jackson ever get wind of any of this?"

"No, I don't think so. At least I never told him. The affair ended when my mom got pregnant with Jackson. But one night about a year after he was born, when I was supposed to be asleep, I overheard my dad arguing loudly with my mother, claiming she had humiliated him and was nothing but a slut and that she could keep her 'bastard child'. Even though the marriage was headed for a divorce, my mother was crying and begging my father not to leave. She promised him anything, and I believe she tried to make the marriage work, but my father started having affairs of his own by then and basically checked out. I'm sure he eventually told her he wanted a divorce, which is probably what set her off on her final downward spiral of booze and pills."

"And that's why your father never warmed up to Jackson, right?"

"Yeah, he neglected Jackson except when he would criticize him. My mom tried to protect him, knowing my dad's feeling toward him, but her death left him extremely vulnerable. I felt sorry for Jackson and tried to cheer him up as much as I could. But a few years later, I was off to boarding school."

Rachel couldn't bring herself to say anything, but Robert saw the tears flowing down her cheeks. He put his hand over hers and glanced at her. "Rachel, I loved my brother . . . and I was so glad for him when he married you. But no one is going to hold it against you if you start enjoying life again. You're way too young to give it all up."

They arrived around six, with the evening still warm. Everyone except George Perry was there to greet them, with Robert's two little girls gravitating to their Aunt Rachel, who fortunately had remembered to bring a couple of little jewelry bead kits and candies for them. The Perry house was a white, wooden-frame gabled mansion at the Southeastern point of Newport, with its expansive grounds projecting out to the Cliff Walk and the Atlantic breakers that lay below. True to the naval tradition of the Perrys, in the middle of the circular driveway was a flagpole, surrounded by two anchors and a planter full of roses and hydrangeas.

Just before dinner, George Perry ambled down the stairwell and joined the family. Their chef had prepared a Mexican meal, with enchiladas, fajitas, poblano peppers, rice, beans, and, of course, plenty of margaritas for the adults. Perry kiddingly remarked that the Southwestern theme was in honor of Rachel and her Texas roots. Afterward, Rachel played with the girls until it was time for them to get ready for bed. Then she went out to the back patio, where George and Robert were smoking cigars and sipping on whiskey sours as the last faint tinge of twilight lingered in the western sky and Venus and a few stars began to appear in the darkened eastern sky. As Rachel went out to join them, George Perry got up and moved over to let her sit in between them. He even jokingly offered her a cigar, which Rachel declined, to a little ribbing from her brother-in-law.

"Robert and I were just talking about some of our days at sea, in the navy. In these parts, the navy is a big tradition. We grow up with the water, a lot of us learn to sail, and a lot of naval shipyards and installations are still in these parts. Even now, a large contingent of our naval officers come from Southern New England. It's a little different living in Texas."

Rachel didn't know how to respond at first, but then she mentioned how she and her family would spend hours on Lake Travis in the summer and early fall waterskiing and wakeboarding behind her dad's motorboat. She then remembered her visit to the Nimitz and Pacific War Museums in Fredericksburg, Texas, on one of her middle-school field trips.

"But you do know our greatest admiral grew up not too far from Austin, hundreds of miles from the coast," she said.

Robert was a bit perplexed, but George Perry knew exactly who she was referring to. "I agree with you that Chester Nimitz was the greatest admiral of the *twentieth century*. But you're being a little sacrilegious in these parts if you say he was the greatest admiral in *all* of American history."

Robert added in a mock stern voice, "Don't you dare forget the hero of the Battle of Lake Erie and the admiral who opened up Japan—our illustrious ancestors Oliver Hazard and Matthew Perry."

Rachel conceded her faux pas with a smile and a simple "My bad."

But her father-in-law came to her rescue. "But Robert, you do recall that Oliver wasn't really an admiral—his official title was 'commodore'—so it only boils down to Matthew. Although I might add that Oliver Perry was the more famous of the two Perrys to this day."

Robert then chimed in, smiling. "Only because Oliver's your middle name."

George smiled and then took out a quarter he regularly kept in his pocket and showed it to Rachel. "But whose face is on the United States quarter?"

Rachel stared at the coin and saw it was a 2013 commemorative, in honor of the two hundredth anniversary of Oliver Hazard Perry's victory over the British on Lake Erie.

"I know you've probably never studied American naval history, Rachel, but next to the battle of Midway—in which your Admiral Nimitz brilliantly planned the victory—the Battle of Lake Erie was the greatest American naval victory in history.[99] Though a relatively small affair, it allowed us to

---

[99] In the Battle of Lake Erie in 1813 at Put-in-Bay, Ohio, Oliver Perry maneuvered against the Royal Navy task force and at one point had to row in heavy gunfire from his damaged flagship, the USS *Lawrence*, to the USS *Niagara*, whose command he assumed. After every British

control Lake Erie and defeat the British-Indian alliance led by Tecumseh. Oliver Perry, though a lot younger than Robert here, showed great daring and courage in the face of the British assault. There're all sorts of things named after him in the navy, including an entire class of frigates."

"You're right, that's some history I wasn't aware of. But why did you mention earlier the words 'sacrilegious *in these parts*'?"

"Oh, that's because we Perrys and Newport go back a long way. Oliver and Matthew were both born in nearby Kinston, but they grew up in the Perry homestead a few miles from here on Walnut Street and were interred at the Island Cemetery, just up the road. Robert, you need to show Rachel those sometime."

Robert turned to Rachel, "Sure thing, maybe even before you leave on Sunday." Then he added, with a wink in his eye, "Unless, of course, you are turned off by looking at old homes and graves, Rachel."

"Now, that's what I call *really sacrilegious*, son!"

All three of them broke into a good-hearted laugh. *I've never seen George so relaxed. Maybe this place helps to take him away from all of his . . . messy business.*

Perry stared out at the sea and the rising moon and the stars beyond that dotted the clear sky, as the three of them enjoyed a few moments of silence, broken only by the regular sound of the waves crashing against the cliffs. Then Perry opened up about a new twist in the family legacy.

"Did you know that Oliver and Matthew—and we, of course—can trace our ancestry all the way back to William Wallace of Scotland?"

---

ship and sailor was captured, he wrote to President William Henry Harrison the famous words, "We have met the enemy and they are ours." Perry's decisive victory effectively ended the War of 1812 in the Great Lakes Region and was commemorated not only by the two hundredth anniversary coin but also by a stamp with the famous "Battle of Lake Erie" painting by William Henry Powell on it.

"Really? Do you mean the guy Mel Gibson played in *Braveheart?*"

"The same. Although you couldn't have mentioned a more historically inaccurate movie than that one."

"Sorry about that."

"No problem. It wouldn't be the first time history was portrayed incorrectly."

I guess the veiled reference to Jackson's book means that he wants to start talking business now.

After a subtle signal to Robert, the younger Perry excused himself and Rachel was left alone with her father-in-law.

"So, Rachel, did you manage to bring the map?"

"I did . . . it's in my room."

"Good." He then pulled out a folded paper from his shirt pocket and offered it to her. "Here's the red one you requested. I ask that you leave the white map outside your bedroom door, precisely at ten o'clock."

After Rachel nodded in agreement, Perry handed her a slip of paper, "One more thing, Rachel. Please give Mr. Brooke this special number if he wants to contact me in the future. And no matter how hard they try to convince you, you have to stay out of it from here on out. *It will get pretty dangerous if things go bad.*"

Rachel nodded but stared straight ahead at the ocean. Neither spoke for another long stretch, but then George Perry patted her hand and got up out of his chair.

"C'mon, Rachel, let's go in now. It's getting a bit chilly, don't you think?"

Rachel slept fitfully and was awakened early by an unusually bright sunrise, which presaged a beautiful day for the Perry's annual summer party. They were expecting over one hundred and fifty guests, a few who would stay in the house and several more in the guest houses, with the remaining either leaving late or staying in one of the many Newport hotels. Aside from a few family members and friends, most would be employees or clients of Manhattan Trust and its partners.

Patricia made scrambled eggs and bacon for everyone. After breakfast, Rachel agreed to take the girls around the Cliff Walk. Rachel had fun throwing pebbles at the ocean with the girls and watching the seagulls devour some bread they threw out. Periodically, they would go down to the rocks and she would make up pirate stories about lost treasure, enhancing the tales of gold and gems with her newfound experiences in the Golden Lily cave.

When she got back, she helped around the house setting up for the lunch. It was to be an informal meal, with catered sandwiches and snacks and drinks. The guests started to arrive by late morning, most of them from the New York area. Just after one, Rachel could see from her bedroom window a large contingent of younger adults, mostly attractive females, arriving in a couple of late-model sedans. To her surprise, her old college roommate Frankie exited one of the cars in a bright red sundress. And shortly thereafter, she got an even bigger surprise—John Peng and a male friend drove up in a black Lexus convertible with the top down that struck Rachel as vaguely familiar. *This is way too much for a coincidence!*

Rachel rushed down the stairs and greeted Frankie, who she had only seen twice since Jackson's funeral.

"Frankie, what are *you* doing here at George Perry's bash?"

Frankie smiled, then gave Rachel a hug. "Oh, I'm just here with a few friends who work for Manhattan. It's great to see you again after all these months, Rachel."

"Come up to my room, Frankie. We'll talk a bit before everyone arrives."

"I've got a better idea. Let me head to the pool cabana and change into my swimsuit. You do the same in your room and meet me by the pool. We'll catch on things while we have a few drinks and lie in the sun. As you can tell, I could use a little."

"Sounds good." *But I wonder why Frankie doesn't want to be seen with me in the house.*

A little while later, Rachel headed to the pool, wearing a t-shirt over her salmon bikini. Frankie was already lying on a pool lounger in her revealing turquoise Brazilian string bikini.

As Rachel took off her t-shirt, Frankie lifted her sunglasses and turned toward her. "God, you look great, Rachel. I'm so glad you're coming back to life. I've felt guilty in recent months for not getting together with you. You seemed like you were halfway to zombie land when I saw you last March."

"Yeah, things have picked up recently, Frankie. I've been to a couple of outings with Karen and Jacques, including his birthday. I took a trip to Asia in June, and just last week I moved into a new place in the East Village."

"No way! Hey, we're practically neighbors now, so let's get together soon. But why the fuck didn't Karen invite me to Jacques' birthday party?"

"She said she did but you were out of town. Don't you remember?"

"Oh, yeah, that's when I was in Vegas with Ron. Damn, Rachel, I need to slow down a bit—you know I've been more than a little ADHD when it comes to men."

"Oh, really?"

Frankie laughed. "And how about you? Are you dating anyone yet . . . male or female?"

Rachel laughed but was not inwardly amused. *She had to bring that up again!*

"No, but I've met a very interesting man recently. The problem is that he lives in the Philippines."

Before Frankie could retort, Rachel saw Peng and a couple of young women come into the pool area with their drinks and sit down. Rachel put on her sunglasses and tried to look away, but she realized he would recognize her bikini. *Damn, I should have worn the old one . . . but who would have expected to see him here?*

Rachel was surprised, even alarmed, when Frankie smiled and waved to Peng. She now realized that what she was seeing was no coincidence, but what was it? She tried to stay calm and keep things in perspective. *Let's not get paranoid, Rachel baby, like your late husband.*

"I've seen this fellow before, Frankie." Then, to test her, she asked, "What's his name?"

"I believe his name is John."

"Where do you know him from?"

Frankie paused for a second. "Oh, I see him now and then hanging around our building. I think he represents some big account in Manhattan Trust."

Just as Rachel was about to probe a little more, a young man dressed in whites came by and announced to the younger guests that there was going to be trip up Vineyard Sound to Woods Hole and back on Perry's yacht, the *Commodore II*. It would be limited to thirty on a first-come basis, leaving at three from the boat ramp and arriving back at five-thirty, well in time for dinner.

Frankie said to Rachel, "How about joining me for the trip, Rachel? I'm sure it'll be a lot of fun."

"I don't know, Frankie. I just want to relax by the pool here. I'll think about it."

But when the time came, the pool was emptying and Rachel didn't see Peng around, so she decided to accompany Frankie to the boat. The trip to the boat ramp was about a quarter-mile, where a small speedboat was ferrying passengers to the nearby yacht, which had a retractable keel and could sit in as little as three meters of water. After she got on the yacht, she saw Peng and his friend approaching it on a pair of jet skis, which they deposited on the ramp before climbing aboard. *Damn, I thought I could avoid him by coming on the trip.*

The yacht left with a full load of passengers, all appearing to be in their twenties and thirties, plus a complement of snacks and drinks, mostly alcoholic. It quickly reached its cruising speed of twenty-five knots as it hit the open water and some of the nubile young women started dancing provocatively to the hip-hop music coming from the deck. Rachel could see a few of the passengers inside were snorting some coke, and she noticed that a few of the girls had begun to take off their tops and rub their breasts against some of the men on board. But by the time they had reached Woods Hole and made the turn into Hadley Harbor, Rachel had already downed a couple of Smirnoff Ices and could have cared less what cavorting was going on in the cabin by Frankie and some of the others. She was leaning against the stern's low railing when an inebriated young German man started to snuggle up to her from behind and sway with her to the music, putting his arms around her waist and gradually moving his hands up until he pushed against the underside of her bikini top and then eventually poked his fingers behind it to touch her breasts. Not wanting to be fondled in public, Rachel pushed his hands down and away from her, but he responded by grabbing her arm and turning her toward him.

"What's your problem . . . can't stand a little fun?"

"You're my problem!" as she tried to shake her arm lose.

As she swung around to release his grip, the tipsy young man lost his balance momentarily and fell backward over the stern.

To cries of "man overboard," a couple of lifesavers were thrown into the water and the yacht, which was below cruising speed as it passed through the harbor, quickly circled around and rescued him, to the cheers and laughter of the passengers. But when he got on the boat, the young man was seething.

"You little bitch," he yelled at Rachel. "I thought you were all supposed to be 'party girls.'"

"Party girls? What the hell are you talking about? I'm George Perry's daughter-in-law!"

By now, most of the passengers were watching the confrontation and cried out in unison, "Ooooooo."

The young German's demeanor changed suddenly and he was now full of contrition. He added sheepishly, almost in a whisper, "I'm sorry, okay? Please don't say anything to Mr. Perry about all of this."

Rachel looked directly at him with a stern face for a couple of seconds and then burst out laughing. She put her arm around the embarrassed young man and whispered in a voice loud enough for the other passengers to hear, "Don't worry, honey, what happens on the *Commodore II* stays on the *Commodore II*!" Everyone then joined in the laughter and resumed their debauchery.

Halfway through the return trip on Buzzards Bay, Rachel saw John Peng approach her. "Good work, Rachel," he said to her. "Your little 'incident,' shall I say, was the highlight of the trip."

Rachel nodded and smiled. "Oh, hi, John, didn't expect to see you here."

Peng replied. "Actually, I can't say the same. I knew you were once married to Perry's son."

"Who told you—Jacques?"

"Yes."

Rachel looked out at the ocean, then turned back to Peng. "My friend Frankie, who I also didn't expect to see here, said you're doing some business with Manhattan Trust."

"No, not me . . . I'm just a lowly gold trader. But my family, on the other hand, does have substantial holdings in Manhattan."

"And how do you know my friend Frankie?"

"Ah, you're talking about the girl who was lying next to you at the pool." *The one I know as Angel.* Peng stared at Rachel and said, "She may be your friend, but I can assure you she's nothing like you."

"Frankie and I go back a long way, so you're not telling me anything I don't already know. But I still don't understand why she's here today."

"So, you really haven't figured things out, have you? You see all of these young men here? Most of them, whether they're European, Arab, Asian, or whatever, represent families who park large amounts of wealth in America—mostly, Manhattan."

"And the women?"

"Rachel, don't push me over when I tell you this. They're like the coke and booze—perks for coming. Perry evidently doesn't want any serious shit going on at his house, so he makes sure it all takes place on his yacht . . . or afterward in the guest houses and hotels. To be honest, I don't think you were even supposed to be on the trip."

"So, that German fellow wasn't shitting me—he actually believed I was part of the takings, his very own 'party girl'!"

Peng smiled. "I think the proper term these days is 'escort'—high class."

Rachel was stunned. She didn't put it past Perry to arrange something like this—but Frankie? As she was leaving the boat, Rachel was feeling light-headed and sick to her stomach and trying to avoid Frankie and hoping that someone might be heading back to New York that night, with whom she could catch a ride. If not, she would spend the rest of the night in her room. She could smell the spare ribs and brisket on the outdoor pit, but her appetite was shot.

When she arrived back at the house, Patricia Perry saw her.

"God, Rachel, you look as though you've seen a ghost!" After realizing her insensitivity, she then added, "Was it the waves? Are you okay?"

"Not really." *No, it's not the waves or any weird apparitions of Jackson at our wedding here, or anything else; it's that your husband hired a pack of expensive whores . . . including my old college roommate!*

"Why don't you get some rest, poor thing? If you don't feel like staying, I'll check around to see if anyone is heading back. And, there's some Alka-Seltzers in the hall bathroom, if you need to settle down."

"Thank you, Trish."

It turned out that one of the older couples had to get back that night. They lived in Englewood Cliffs but had agreed to swing by Lower Manhattan to drop Rachel off. Rachel went into the twins' room and told them she was sorry she was sick and had to leave early but that she would host them some weekend in the city and take them to Central Park and the zoo. She then said her quick goodbyes to Robert and Ashley and took her belongings as well as a plate of food prepared by Patricia, for when she "felt better." The red map was securely rolled up in her purse.

The couple sat in front and were mostly quiet on the way back, while Rachel dozed in and out of sleep. At one point, she heard the woman remarking on how many "nice, good-looking young people were at the party, most probably friends of Robert and Ashley". Then the man added that he was sorry they had to leave early and that they couldn't "get the younger generation's take on the world."

Rachel mused, *If they only knew.*

CHAPTER
12

Rachel woke up the next morning feeling much better. She planned to take the bus into Chinatown from her new one-bedroom overlooking Tompkins Square Park, where she could engage in a couple of hours of Mandarin and take in the atmosphere of the district. She already was in love with her new apartment, from its wood floors and bright windows to the leafiness of the park next door, and her proximity to the sensory mélange of Chinatown made her feel as if she was back in Taipei again.

She checked her text messages and saw she had a semi-contrite one from Frankie. It read "Sorry bout yda. Plz let me explain. Can u do lunch this week—on me?" Rachel was still miffed at Frankie but curious to hear her explanations, so she quickly texted back and they agreed on a Wednesday luncheon at Dos Caminos at Third and Fiftieth. She hoped she wasn't making a mistake, as a lunch with Frankie would almost certainly turn into a "three-margarita" affair and cut well into her busy afternoon work schedule.

She started thinking about Frankie and the memories began to flow. She remembered from a course she had in cognitive psychology that our most prolific autobiographical memories are from our late teens and early twenties—the "coming of age" ones. And she realized just how many Frankie was involved in, from the time she first met her on the freshman trip to Mount Moosilauke and confirmed that she would be her first roommate at Dartmouth. Rachel often mused how the housing person who paired an intense, overachieving, and slightly uptight Asian-Jewish girl from Austin with a free-spirited upper-crust preppie from New England must have been yucking it up half-drunk at the time.

Frances Hinman Stewart came from a long of Dartmouth alums, the only one Rachel knew of in her class whose family name was attached to one of its dorms. Frankie grew up in Wellesley and went to Milton Academy near Boston in middle school before transferring to Deerfield Academy in Western Massachusetts for high school and eventually receiving early admission to Dartmouth. To the admissions office, Frankie was a brilliant student whose essays were among the best ever submitted, as well as a talented thespian and equestrian— and, of course, a legacy student whose father had contributed millions to the college. What the admissions office wasn't aware of was that she had given her first blow job and smoked her first weed at fifteen, lost her virginity and contracted her first sexually transmitted disease at sixteen, took her first coke hit and underwent an abortion at seventeen, and had her first breast enhancement—a "back to school special"—before she even matriculated.

To Frankie, college was one big party sandwiched around her sporadically attended courses. She quickly demolished Rachel's previously sheltered existence, before she even took in her first college class. The night of the freshman mixer, Frankie brought home a male student and paid Rachel a month's spending money if she would move to the commons area for a few hours. Rachel went along then but refused after that, so Frankie started paying some other girls down the hall to use their bedrooms but eventually started having sex when she knew Rachel wasn't around. She also paid Rachel and some other girls in the dorm to wash and iron her clothes, which Rachel appreciated given that Frankie would otherwise have just left all of her clothes lying on the floor. Though she could be smartly dressed when she went out, Frankie was a slob when it came to her private wardrobe organization. One thing Rachel realized from the outset, though, was that Frankie had a brilliant mind—a true procrastinator-scholar. Frankie would basically spend most of the semester skipping classes and getting high on pot and coke before pulling off a bunch of all-nighters toward the end of the semester, whipping up incredible papers in a fraction of the time it would take Rachel. She remembered how at the end of her sophomore spring semester Frankie didn't bathe for three straight days—and even sacrificed getting high and having sex—while desperately finishing up some papers. She ended up majoring in psychology, but long before she graduated she knew more about gauging people's inner thoughts and motivations than most of her socially inept professors.

Although Frankie was the alpha female in the dorm—even getting some of the other girls to synchronize their periods to hers—she ended up following the lead of Karen and Rachel in joining Delta Gamma, with the three of them pledging together in the spring of their freshmen year. Delta Gams were generally more sexually active than some of the other sororities on campus, but Frankie had spread the truth about Rachel that she was still a virgin, which made Rachel feel more than a little uncomfortable among her sisters. So to make up for it, Frankie secretly provided a one-time stipend to a male student who Rachel had intimated she wanted to get to know, but the sexual escapade turned into a huge fiasco, with Rachel so upset she vowed never to have sex again while in college. Her pledge didn't last long, though, as Frankie sensed her emotional state and caressed Rachel into having her first lesbian encounter. Rachel didn't really consider herself bisexual, but Frankie proved to be an expert at massaging all of Rachel's erotic spaces, and she became her unofficial tutor on all things sexual. For the next year, before they moved into the sorority and gained their own rooms, the two of them had many more sexual trysts, which were easy to hide given their roommate status. During all of their lovemaking, Rachel felt a lot of raw hedonic energy emanating from Frankie but nary a speck of true emotion.

―――――※―――――

When Rachel arrived at the restaurant, Frankie was already waiting out front in a black summer mini, her twisted blonde locks extending past her shoulders. Knowing that the taller Frankie would probably be stylishly dressed, Rachel decided to forego her usual workday pants outfit and wore a pleated white pencil skirt along with a lavender silk blouse and heels. After a brief kiss, the two of them walked to a table in the back corner of the room, turning more than a few heads in the process.

After ordering their quesadillas and ceviches and a couple of tequila punches, Rachel stared at Frankie, who was still a looker despite a few small creases starting to form around the mouth. Frankie opened the conversation. "Rachel, first of all, I'm sorry I haven't been in touch with you much since March. I know you've been going through hell and I should have been there more for you."

Rachel was nonplussed. "I appreciate it, Frankie, but I'm actually doing a little better these days."

"I could tell when I saw you." Since Frankie knew exactly what Rachel was wanting, she quickly got to the point. "Okay, before you start asking any questions, please let me explain about last weekend. Yes, I was working for your father-in-law, as were a few other girls from the agency."

"So, you're an escort nowadays."

Frankie waited a few seconds before replying. "Rachel, I've *been* an escort, for over two years now . . . ever since I got laid off from the Wall Street firm. I went from six figures to nothing, and I had a three-grand apartment and a thousand-dollar-a-month coke habit to support. When a bunch of us were pink-slipped, a girl who had been doing occasional escort work even while day-timing with the firm told me I could make a lot of money quickly—even more than I was making with the firm. All the while you and Karen were thinking I was playing the field and traveling here and there with different men . . . those were my clients."

"But, how could you . . . *do it for money*? Damn, Frankie, you're an Ivy League graduate!"

"Well, as you know, I've done a lot fucking for free as well. What I'm mostly selling is unencumbered sexual fantasy, so it's mostly about acting anyway—which you know I've always been good at. You may not agree, but I actually see this line of work as a whole lot less destructive than all the screwing of investors and the general public I did when I was on Wall Street."

"Didn't you ever think you might run into a close family member or friend along the way? What if a client turned out to be your father—what would you say?"

"Well, first of all my dad doesn't venture down to New York very often, least of all to see me. But, I'd probably say something to him like 'Isn't it great that we finally have something in common, Dad—now that we're both whores'."

Rachel just shook her head. "Tell me one thing—what does it mean you were *working for George*? Are you just contracting out your services or are you—"

"Fucking him?" Frankie paused. "It's actually a little of both."

"How could you? *My own father-in-law!* Does he know you're my friend from college?"

"I don't think so . . . although George knows a lot of things about people he shouldn't. He may have seen me briefly at the wedding, but my hair was darker and shorter then and I was there under my real name."

"As opposed to 'Angel'."

"Or Alexis or Monique or Sonya . . ."

"Okay, I get it. But you don't go to the house, do you? Has Patricia gotten wind of any of this?"

Frankie stared directly at Rachel for a few seconds. Then she said quietly, "Patricia's been involved a few times herself."

"Jesus!"

Frankie put a finger to her mouth. "Sshhh, not so loud, Rachel."

Rachel was steaming and becoming nauseated. "Please tell me one thing. Jackson always fretted that George might be into some weird pedophilia stuff he once read about that reached the highest levels of our government. Tell me he was wrong." [100]

Frankie sighed. "I don't think that's the case with George—he despises that sort of stuff. I shouldn't be saying this, but he's actually a pretty conservative guy sexually."

"Please don't say anymore."

"Okay, but if you want to know the truth, your father-in-law isn't the moral monster you might think he is."

"What would you know about morality, anyways?"

Frankie then grabbed Rachel's arm and pressed her taut face closer to hers and replied in an angry, low voice. "Don't do you ever talk to me about morality! Do you remember what a sheltered little bitch you were before I started showing you about life? Tell me, how many lepers have you been treating in India these days? And how many starving orphans in Haiti have you been feeding, huh?"

Rachel knew that Frankie was spot on. Outside of a little work for the Nature Conservancy, she hadn't regularly volunteered for anything since college. And she did owe Frankie immensely for bringing her out of her shell and showing her the ropes. *She's always been generous to me . . . who am I judge what she does in the bedroom?*

---

[100]   See footnote #3.

Frankie continued with her edgy tone. "You know, I didn't grow up like you, Rachel. I didn't have a lot of barriers to rein me in, like parents and grandparents who gave a shit about me and neighborhood schools and religious teachings. My father was only in the house until I was three, and he didn't always come home even then. After that, whenever I'd see him he'd always have some new girlfriend under his arm. So is it surprising I ended up with a craving for men? And then my mom started fucking around, when I was barely five. I'd spend a lot of lonely nights, creating a fantasy world of dashing princes and princesses, watching my little brother play with dolls—little did I know the little shit would go transgender on me in his teens! By thirteen, I was already on my own in boarding school, trying to gain some human attention any way I could. Through it all, one thing I learned is that when you have money it's about taking— from the opposite sex, from business clients, from whomever. Even when the rich are giving to charity, there's an angle to it, whether it be adulation or a tax break or having your name plastered over some building."

Rachel listened intently, then replied in a soft voice. "You're right, Frankie, I'm hardly one to judge or throw stones. Especially now that I've got a big window in my apartment looking out onto Tompkins Square."

Frankie finally cracked a smile. "Now you're finally talking sense . . . Freckles!"

Rachel recoiled at the mention of her old sorority nickname. But after the initial peeved look, she burst out laughing, followed by Frankie, just as their dishes were being served.

After a bite of her quesadilla, Frankie smiled at her. "So, when do I get to see your new digs?"

"C'mon, I just moved in. Half of my stuff isn't even put up yet."

"I'll help you with your stuff . . . and more."

"No, Frankie, we're done with that."

"I promise I won't even charge you anything."

Rachel just smiled and rolled her eyes in exasperation. "I'll tell you what—I've got a trip to Los Angeles coming up in a couple of weeks. After that, I'll invite you over."

Rachel looked down and brought another forkful of her snapper ceviche to her mouth. When she raised her head, she saw Frankie was staring at her intently.

"There's something else worrying you, isn't there?"

"Yeah, there is, Frankie. But there's actually two things. One of them is that guy, John Peng, who was at the party and said he knows you. He was with Karen and Jacques and me on the Fourth, when we went sailing out of Northport and then stayed for the evening fireworks. For some reason, he really bothers me. I just don't think it was a coincidence that he shows up at both places. What do you make of him?"

"First of all, I don't want to talk about my clients. But as far as I know, John is on the level, so I wouldn't worry about him. I don't know how he knows Jacques and Karen, but I can tell why he was at Newport—his family has a shitload of money invested in Manhattan Trust. Perhaps you've heard of his uncle—Li Shiang?"

"Li Shang, the Chinese-Taiwanese industrialist? I not only know who he is, but I've actually met him. But I didn't know he was related to Peng."

This is getting even more suspicious. Are Shiang and Perry teaming up . . . or are they playing one another? And what's Frankie doing in the middle of all of this?

"And the other thing?"

"This trip to Los Angeles."

"I take it you're going to see someone there. I hope he's tall and good-looking."

"Actually, he is."

"Oh, that's the Filipino guy you mentioned at the party."

"Yeah, but it's not what you think. It involves some serious business."

"How serious?"

"Frankie, without going into the details, I've managed to get caught in some high-stakes financial game. We're talking potentially tens of billions up front . . . and a lot more down the road."

Frankie's jaw dropped. "How the fuck did you get involved in all of this—this is something I should be in the thick of. Especially if he's tall and handsome!"

Rachel passed on Frankie's attempt at humor. "I wish you were, Frankie, believe me—for my sake, not yours. But I committed to him personally. All I've got to do is this one last thing, and then I'm out. So think good thoughts for me if you ever want to see my apartment."

"So, you're not planning to tell me any of what's going on, are you?"

"Someday, but not now; plus, it's a long story. But I do have a question for you."

"Shoot."

"If you needed to carry something very valuable, where would you hide it?"

"Didn't I already tell you about that once, Freckles?" She looked up briefly, and then smiled deviously and said, "You know, if it was *really* valuable, and I had to carry it on me, I'd definitely put it in my bra. A little extra padding never hurt a girl's looks."

"And if it could be worth billions?"

Frankie started tapping her fingers lightly on the table while staring concernedly at Rachel. "You need to hide it in a little place called 'luck,' Rach—lots of it."

CHAPTER
13

On the eve of her departure for Los Angeles, Rachel checked over her list. She had made two copies plus the original of the red map provided to her by Perry, with one copy left with Karen and the other ensconced in her new apartment. The instructions for the arrangements in Los Angeles had been transmitted through a secret email account that Rachel had set up under a pseudonym, checking its encrypted messages from Brooke only at Karen's condo. The plan was for Rachel to meet Brooke at the main food court in the United terminal, which was chosen because both domestic and international United gates were nearby. Rachel would fly out on a Friday night after work, stay overnight near the airport, and then return to the airport on Saturday night for a red-eye back to New York. It was then that the rendezvous with Brooke was supposed to occur. *I need to get a good night's sleep . . . and make sure I don't forget to wear that pendant he gave me.*

Fifty kilometers north at his estate in Chappaqua, George Perry was also finalizing plans for Rachel's trip. Despite her precautions, he had domestic surveillance keep him abreast of all of her flight plans. Perry arranged to have agents at the gate in La Guardia, on the flight to Los Angeles near her seat, and all over Los Angeles International. He also had agents monitoring Brooke's return flight to Manila and stationed at customs at Aquino International Airport. The goal was to thwart the map transfer and to further penetrate the Dragon Family network. Although the Bilderbergers knew of some of the members of the heretofore opaque Dragon Family, Perry mused how this little deal Rachel had arranged was going to make the Dragons as transparent as the bay window he was staring through. *How stupid they are to think they can outwit the group that has controlled the world's financial system for over a century!*

Thirteen thousand kilometers west in Manila, Benito Fernandez was reviewing the plans he would give Craig Brooke the next night to retrieve the maps in Los Angeles. Brooke, who had done such good work for the Family and was slated to become one of its future leaders, would fly round-trip from Manila to Los Angeles, but this time he would be the decoy. Another young member of the Dragons would be at LAX International to actually retrieve the map and carry it back to Manila via Singapore, while Brooke would arrive separately on a later flight. Once the red map was in their hands, the Dragons would link it to one of their site maps and the effort to recover the gold would begin in earnest. Fernandez had already planned for deception on the part of the cabal with a series of moves of his own. *The Bilderberger cabal has no idea what will hit them if they try to cross the Dragon Family—but we do, because now we've penetrated their operation.*

Rachel had trouble focusing on her work the next day, despite her deadline to finish her part of a preliminary analysis for an American consortium on the potential competition of the burgeoning Chinese electric-vehicle industry. She skipped lunch and had only a sandwich from the vending machine and a piece of fruit she had brought from home and was able to finish just after five in the evening. She quickly made her way to the street with her small carry-on bag and hailed a cab to La Guardia. The flight wasn't scheduled for departure until eight-thirty, so she figured she had plenty of time to catch a meal and relax before the flight. She had brought along two of the books in the Rosales saga, written by the great Filipino author F. Sionil Jose. They were highly recommended by Brooke as a way to understand better the history of her father's ancestral region and the way in which the unrest of the times pulled families apart, much like her father's. She had already started to get engrossed in the first of the novels, figuring they would occupy her attention on the flights and on the Saturday in between.

She studied the faces of the people waiting to board. Relative to other flights, the ones to Los Angeles always seemed to include a higher percentage of attractive and outgoing passengers. She imagined that some might be in the entertainment industry, and she was embarrassed that she was secretly hoping to see some "stars" on her flight, perhaps even one in the seat next to her since the Dragons had placed her in first class. There were also a bunch of businessman returning home for the weekend as well the usual array of mothers with young children and older people visiting relatives.

When she got into her window seat, she saw another young woman had taken the seat next to her. Just before the doors closed, a middle-aged man sat down in the aisle seat opposite to them and glanced at Rachel. Despite Rachel's nose in her book signaling she didn't want to be bothered, the young woman next to her was excited to be flying, and Rachel figured she probably had been bumped up into first class because of the full plane. The young woman no doubt thought Rachel was in the entertainment business because she started asking all sorts of questions with her thick Brooklyn accent about the studios and Rodeo Drive and the like. Rachel made up a story that she was going to see her boyfriend and that they were going to spend a day or two at the beach before driving to Vegas for a couple of overnights. The young woman made Rachel laugh and even feel a little flattered when she told her that she resembled some movie star she had recently seen but couldn't remember the name of. She even asked about the gold dragon pendant around her neck that Brooke had given her and listened intently as Rachel explained its significance.

Eventually the girl quieted down and started listening to her headphones. Rachel returned to the first of the two novels, which followed a Rosales mestizo ranching family like her father's through the prewar childhood of its main protagonist, culminating in the kidnapping and brutal death of the landlord father by some local peasants. It suddenly dawned on her that the same fate could have befallen her grandfather in that era—*in which case I wouldn't even be around to read all of this.*

After deplaning, Rachel went straight for the shuttle to her hotel, noticing that the man who had been in the opposite aisle seat was following her. When she got to the hotel, she looked around but didn't see anyone from the plane. Nevertheless, she was wary and never left the hotel until she returned to the airport, ordering room service for breakfast and lunch. She did lounge by the pool briefly to capture the midday sun, retaining the red map in two pieces, one in each cup of her bikini top.

When she returned to her room, she quickly finished the first novel and started on the second one, which told the tale of two brothers during the first Huk rebellion after World War II, one a pseudo-leftist who loved the good life and who in the end tried to preserve the Rosales family holdings, and the other a committed revolutionary—like her Uncle Miguel.

Around seven-thirty, Rachel gathered her things and headed back to the airport. The plan was for her to sit and wait until she saw Brooke and then the both of them would "coincidentally" enter the McDonald's ordering line together, at which time she would unobtrusively hand over an envelope to him, which ostensibly contained the map. In reality, the two halves of the actual map were contained in napkins she adroitly placed on her tray, which she then planned to deposit in the trash receptacle. A second member of the Dragon Family would then pose as a janitor and empty the bin, quickly retrieve the map-napkin combination, and change out of his janitor's clothes. He would then board a plane bound for Singapore while Brooke returned on the next flight to Manila, throwing away the envelope Rachel had given him along with the rest of the emptied dinner tray when the flight attendant came around. Upon arrival, he planned to quickly catch the next flight to Cebu without meeting anyone from the Family. So even if the cabal managed to bribe customs to search him, they would find nothing.

Rachel pretended she was reading her book while her eyes were actually darting around the court searching for Brooke. Her heart rate began to increase in anticipation of laying eyes on him, although she was under no illusions that their encounter would be anything but brief. Then she recognized him, almost comically disguised in a white hoodie and thick glasses with blonde streaks. She quickly moved to the ordering line, with him right behind. After she ordered, she went to the soda fountain and started pouring her drink. He ordered only a drink, quickly took his cup, and started pouring his drink next to her. In the brief time her food tray was being prepared, he managed a quick glance at her and relayed in a low voice the code words, "Your necklace looks beautiful on you, miss." Then, as her heart fluttered slightly, she discreetly placed the envelope in his hands as he started walking toward the gate—never once raising her gaze at him.

She had hoped for an acknowledgement from him, any type of sign, that the personal connection they had established on her Asian trip wasn't merely a mirage. But by the time Rachel sat down, he had already melded into the crowd, and she started feeling the suffocating emptiness again. *I guess that's it, then. All we were in the end were two ships passing in the night . . . on business. But at least I'm free of all this damn "business" once and for all.*

She slept fitfully on the flight back to New York, arriving early on Sunday morning. When she arrived at her apartment, she immediately opened a bottle of wine, drank a little of it, and then went to sleep for a few hours. When she woke up, she called Frankie and invited her over for the next weekend. Frankie reminded her, though, that her weekend schedule was moment-to-moment and that it might be best to get together that evening. Rachel said she would order a pizza and make a salad if Frankie would bring over the tequila and lime, and they reminisced and gossiped for a couple of hours. Frankie's eyes then showed her faux-amorous look, and Rachel didn't resist. Frankie's touch and tongue, starting with Rachel's breasts, had gotten even better than when they were in college, but she felt something else—Frankie actually seemed to be reaching out emotionally, not just hedonically, wanting Rachel to caress her more. *Something's changed in her—perhaps after all these years the sex alone isn't enough.*

Unfortunately, Rachel was not in a position to reciprocate emotionally. As she was being caressed, in her fantasies Frankie had taken on the form of her White Spiritual Boy—Craig Brooke.

As Frankie and Rachel made love, George Perry received a phone call. The caller said, in a calm but muffled voice, "We lost sight of the map, George. We managed to shake him down at customs, but he had nothing on him."

Perry responded "Yes. But the 'correction' to the red map was flawless. When the posers fall for it, they'll be in for a nasty surprise when they punch through the site we gave them."

"Let's hope so . . . for your daughter-in-law's sake."

Halfway around the world, after arriving back at his high-rise apartment in the upscale Nivel Hills section of Cebu, Craig Brooke had an encrypted email waiting for him from Ben Fernandez. It read "Map picked up in Singapore and now in Manila. You handled Echon well."

Brooke responded with a perfunctory, "Thanks . . . glad it all worked out." *But, the truth is that I didn't handle her well . . . because I put the woman I've come to love in total danger. And I can't even allow myself to tell her.*

CHAPTER

14

The two Lily sites were located on opposite sides of the Cordillera Range. The white map provided by the Dragon Family pointed to a site west of Baguio, down the mountainside toward the little village of Pugo at the border of La Union and Benguet provinces, a half-hour or so drive from Baguio. The map provided by the cabal, on the other hand, was for a site not far from the one the Dragons were already working. As per the agreement, both had been marked "777" by the Japanese.

The American site was the most interesting, in that it was found in the area known as Marcos Park. Marco Park was located just off the Jose Aspiras Highway, formerly the Marcos Highway, that led from Baguio to the coast. The entrance to it was located just past the intersection with the highway that led south through Pugo to Rosario. Marcos Park contained what was once a large thirty-meter bust of Ferdinand Marcos carved partly into the foothills of the Cordilleras, facing the Lingayen Gulf. In 2002, long after Marcos was deposed, an explosion from the inside ripped the façade apart.[101] No one claimed

---

[101] See http://english.peopledaily.com.cn/200212/30/eng20021230_109309.shtml

responsibility, although various theories posited the responsible party to be either leftist elements enraged at the Marcos legacy or treasure hunters enticed by the legend that Marcos buried some of his Yamashita treasure there. After the explosion, no Golden Lily treasure or secret passageways were found inside, which led to several more theories. The first and most obvious, of course, was that the site wasn't linked in any way to the Yamashita gold. But this theory was contradicted by the suspicious location of the massive statue, far away from the Marcos family holdings and political stronghold in Ilocos North. The second theory was that Marcos established the park in the general whereabouts of a Golden Lily site based on his white maps but that he didn't have all of the specific engineering information for the site, which would have required the red maps that Curtis burned in 1975. The third theory was that Marcos Park was indeed a Yamashita gold site but that Marcos chose not to develop it immediately and instead erected his bust away from the actual entrance to the buried treasure for safekeeping. This theory held credence because, along with his ruthlessness, Marcos had a very clever mind, as exemplified by the high honors he scored on his bar exam while studying from prison during his conviction and incarceration—later overturned on appeal—for murdering the political rival of his father in the 1930s.[102] It was this last theory that proved correct when the American cabal was finally able to match the Dragons' white map with one of their own red ones.[103]

The Dragon Family decided to release the white map of the Marcos Park site to the Bilderberger cabal because it was close to its home base and also because of the irony that it was the Americans who staunchly supported Marcos for two decades before pushing him out the door when he refused to hand over his gold in 1986. But the Americans were also pleased when

---

[102] See http://en.wikipedia.org/wiki/Ferdinand_Marcos

[103] It is interesting that a similar planned bust of Marcos at Mount Apo was also the alleged site of a secret gold horde (Seagraves & Seagraves, 2005, *op cit.*, p. 219).

they realized how readily accessible the site was and how easy it would be to transport the treasure down the Aspiras Highway to the coast and smuggle it out to sea. Their plan was get a few members of the cabal and a few trusted locals to pose as investors interested in developing the park. It might take a few months to get a permit, but in the end it would arouse much less suspicion if they carried out the exploration under the guise of normal commercial site development.

The Dragon Family was also very pleased with the red map they had been given. It was linked to a site less than twenty kilometers from the one Pepe Santos was currently exploring, but adjacent to the National Highway just south of its junction with the Benguet-Nueva Vizcaya Road. This was the legendary "Many Monkeys" site that reputedly contained not only a large Golden Buddha but also over ten billion in gold and gems.[104] The Dragons could begin exploring it when Pepe and his men had emptied the current site of its treasure and the rains began to let up, probably by early-October.

Benito Fernandez mused when he looked at the "Many Monkeys" map and then at the hillside. *How could we have missed the obvious?* Although the hillside looked totally enshrouded in forest, there were at one time large boulders covering it, among which a large troop of macaques would lunge about. The Japanese expanded the underground spaces by digging a series of tunnels underneath the hillside connecting the original cave chambers and by joining together many of the boulders with reinforced concrete, thereby creating sealed vaults between them. The antechamber and a few small passageways were known to Santa Romana and the Americans and even Marcos, but because there was only a small amount of gold supposedly found there, everyone seemed to lose interest in further exploration of the site. Fernandez, however, knew

---

[104] The "Many Monkeys" site was actually visited by the Seagraves (Seagraves & Seagraves, 2005, *op cit.*, pp. 80-81), and its description is partly based on their account.

better—because the Japanese labeled this a "777," he had always suspected most of the gold had to be still inside. Studying the red map, Fernandez now knew why everyone had missed the bulk of the gold cache. What appeared to be a solid rock wall in the back of the antechamber was, according to the map, only a meter-thick facade. And not only was there a huge chamber beyond, but there were at least a half-dozen tunnels leading from it to the back of the hillside that were large enough for army trucks to enter. The map showed various traps and dangers, but nothing surrounding the back wall of the antechamber itself.

Being close to the National Highway, the "Many Monkey" site would be harder to conceal than the one Pepe Santos was finishing up. So the Dragons knew that once they began, they would have to work fast and bring a lot more security on board. Fernandez, working with Pepe, came up with an ingenious plan. Rather than approach the site from the front, facing the highway, the Family would work from the back side with a minimal team, which would leave the small two-lane road running behind the site a kilometer and a half up from its intersection with the National Highway. It would traverse a mostly dry creek bed for a hundred meters or so and then cut through another two hundred meters of bush to a new back entrance to the cave that would be carefully opened up using a small amount of explosives. This new entrance would eventually link up with an existing passageway leading to the main chamber.

With only battery-powered lights, the Family worked round the clock inside the cave, systematically moving the gold bars toward the entranceway. Under cover of clouds and darkness and posing as loggers, they simultaneously began to remove a narrow swath of trees from the creek bed to within twenty-five meters of the back of the cave, leaving the remaining bush to disguise the entrance. The final push took place over two nights, which weather forecasts predicted would be dry, enabling the ground to harden. On the first night, Pepe and his assistants and about seventy-five other Family members, both male and female, surreptitiously carried a total of fifteen thousand gold ingots from the back entrance to small clearings spaced ten meters apart alongside the newly created bush road and concealed by the roadside canopy. They piled the twelve-and-a-half-kilo bars into stacks of fifteen hundred each, which could be handcarried by a team of fifteen in a total of fifty individual trips. Just after sunset on the second night, the first wave of ten heavy-duty off-road pickup trucks backed into the bush road one by one, pulled up to each clearing, and were loaded by hand with one hundred and fifty hundred bars each in less than fifteen minutes. After that group drove off, a new set of ten trucks was quickly backed in and their beds filled. In all, one hundred trucks in ten waves, carrying over ten billion dollars in gold, were loaded within a four-hour time span between ten at night and two in the morning. Only the large Golden Buddha, too massive to be quickly removed, remained in the underground chamber—to watch over the skeletons of those buried alive by the Japanese.

Within a few minutes, each ten-truck convoy was on the National Highway, heading south under local police protection to San Jose City before breaking into smaller groups of five, one swinging northwest and passing through Rosales, the other moving southward to Santa Rosa before turning west. The trucks maintained spacing once they hit the North Luzon Expressway and turned south to Angeles and the Clark Freeport Zone, where all one hundred arrived before dawn and were secretly let in through the gate by a team of Family members. By the next morning, another large contingent of Dragons ensconced in a secure warehouse near the tarmac unloaded all of the trucks, and over the next three days every single one of the gold bars had exited the country by plane, crated up and listed as machinery cargo. The entire operation was a testament to the Dragon Family's organization and commitment of several hundred members—Pinoy "people power" in its truest sense.

Despite the cabal's hopes, the missing reference to the thousand-pound ordnance on the "Many Monkeys" red map proved inconsequential. Without even glancing at the map, Fernandez knew long beforehand of the danger on the other side of the back wall of the antechamber. By coming in from the rear, Pepe and his men easily spotted the bomb, which was designed to go off when the hidden wall was punctured. They safely disarmed it and the operation went smoothly after that. But as they were leaving, Pepe's men re-armed the ordnance and set a timer to go off early the next morning. They knew that the collapse of the hillside from the tremendous explosion would be so large that no serious rescue mission would be attempted. They also made sure that Pepe's truck with his insurance and registration were left nearby.

The bomb went off with a massive explosion at dawn the next day and was heard loudly in Aritao and Bambang and well beyond, while the collapse of the hillside was observed by travelers along the National Highway. The papers in Benguet, Nueva Vizcaya, and Pangasinan provinces all ran stories about the presumed death of Pepe Santos, a mining engineer and amateur treasure hunter. A short blurb even ended up in the *Manila Times*, with a caveat to wannabe Yamashita treasure hunters warning them yet again of the tragedies that might befall them while searching for the phantom gold.

George Perry was very pleased after hearing the news. Just as he had planned, the Dragon Family had fallen for the ruse and had blown up the cave when they tried to break into the wall without realizing the destruction awaiting them on the other side. Moreover, he delighted in the word that everything was now in place to make a quick recovery of the treasure at Marcos Park. *The Dragons' gold may have been lost, but not ours!*

The red map Perry and associates were able to link to Marcos Park clearly showed what the treasure hunters who created the

2002 explosions failed to realize: the treasure wasn't in or even directly underneath the Marcos bust. It was in a set of tunnels fifty meters down the hillside, with the only entrance buried underground near the road. It would be no problem to open the entranceway, expand the passageway, open up the floor, move the gold from the tunnels to the main chamber, and then get a forklift to drop the pallets of gold bars from the large main chamber above to the passageway level below. All of this would be done under the guise of redeveloping what had become a sore point, the bust and site being a self-glorification of the most corrupt and ruthless man in modern Filipino history. Adding poetic justice, the federal permit for the work was signed personally by the president of the Philippines, the son of Marcos' great rival and the man he allegedly had assassinated in 1982— not to mention one of the closest allies of the Western financial cabal.[105]

Because of the use of heavy machinery, the entire operation wouldn't take long. The expansion of the underground passageways had just been completed and the loading of all of the gold onto pallets was expected to take less than a week. The rest of the operation would be over in one night, beginning when forklifts would load all of the estimated fifteen billion in bullion into several dozen large pickup trucks. It would take less than two hours to load the gold, a half-hour for each convoy to reach the coast, and an additional hour or so to load all of the treasure onto a fleet of speedboats on a make-shift dock near Agoo. The boats would quickly transport the gold out into the Lingayen Gulf beyond Filipino territorial waters under cover of fog and darkness to some cargo ships hired by the cabal. There would

---

[105]   Benigno Aquino III, the son of the slain senator and his widow, former president Corazon Aquino, was elected president in 2011. His staunch support of the United States was evidenced by his government's agreement in 2014 to allow the return of American military forces to bases in the Philippines: http://www.theguardian.com/world/2015/jul/16/philippines-reopens-subic-bay-as-military-base-to-cover-south-china-sea

be no Philippine Coast Guard cutters cruising the area, since they had all been conveniently scheduled for an exercise off the coast of Central Luzon that night. Perry figured that, at worst, the whole operation would be complete before Thanksgiving. He would thus duly note its success under his breath while giving the Thanksgiving dinner blessing.

But just as the final evening approached and the first trucks were leaving Rosales and heading north to the site, a nasty surprise was in store for the cabal's remaining members at the site. The head of the Benguet provincial police drove down in a couple of squad cars and asked if the "contractors"—mostly intelligence officers and engineers working for the cabal—had a provincial construction permit. The cabal's team protested they didn't need one and became testy when shown the phony provincial permit form they were allegedly missing. This led the police chief to ask if he could look around, but he was blocked. A call went out to Perry from the site team, but the cell-phone reception was too poor and the call was dropped. At that point, the Benguet chief phoned for backup, not only from his own force but also from the Baguio police chief, who was also working for the Dragon Family. Rather than the half-hour normally required for the trip from Baguio, a total of a dozen squad cars, already in waiting, arrived within minutes. The site team, realizing they were outnumbered and outgunned, agreed to be taken into custody in Baguio.

At that point, the same trucks used in the "Many Monkeys" extraction quickly descended on Marcos Park from the direction of Baguio. They perfectly replaced the cabal's trucks en route from Rosales, now blocked by road construction arranged by a public works team also working for the Dragons. The forklifting went on as planned, but its lead operator was now Pepe Santos, who miraculously had been revived from the dead. With all of the gold already loaded in pallets, and forklifts replacing the people power used at Many Monkeys, all of the trucks had within an hour and a half left for the coast—not to the Americans' destination just south of Agoo but to a point fifteen kilometers up the road at Caba, where an entirely new fleet of darkened speedboats was waiting to be loaded with the massive gold stash, to be taken just past Filipino waters to where a Chinese cargo ship and its naval escort lay in wait.

All in all, it was a remarkable night, filled with logistical skill, audacity, cunning, and deception. Most of all, the locals agreed, *the speedboat rental business in the Lingayen Gulf had never been better.*

George Perry was rudely awakened from the beginnings of a vivid dream by a call on his cell phone just before midnight. On the other end was the head of the Federal Reserve.

"Things did not go well last night, George."

"What do you mean?"

"The Marcos Park team was just arrested and placed into custody by the local police and the gold was absconded by the Dragons. And all of the gold at what turned out to be their site—the 'Many Monkeys' one—was stolen right in front of our very eyes! It turns out that they didn't fall for the ruse at 'Many Monkeys' after all. What we took for an explosion and cave-in was all a massive deception, probably to lure us into overconfidence. And, to top it off, we just learned that a site just up the road from Aritao had all its gold removed earlier in the summer. A total of *fifty billion* in gold is now in the hands of the Dragon Family! Already the dollar's starting to slide hard against gold and the BRIC currencies. And that's not good."

Perry was shocked. "I don't believe it! How could this have all happened?"

"For one, you forgot about the local police. Did you manage to pay them off?"

"It was all arranged—we've been double-crossed. Hell, we even had the president involved!"

The caller on the other end remained silent as Perry feverishly replayed in his mind all of his actions during the past months. "But I did everything as planned."

"Yes, you did . . . but he says you *didn't do it well enough.*"

"What else did he say?"

She paused. "He said it's time to play your daughter-in-law card."

"Please don't make me do this. She did what I told her to do and then got out of the way. She's completely innocent of all this."

"Since when did innocence ever get in the way of business, George?"

CHAPTER
15

Less than forty-eight hours after the Dragons moved the gold out of Marcos Park and half a world removed, Rachel relished the feel of the crisp air as she left the apartment building for her Saturday morning run. It was the first weekend in November, and Thanksgiving was less than three weeks away. Rachel was feeling better than she had in over a year and was delighted to be going home for the holiday, for the first time since she and Jackson married. She had decided on Thanksgiving rather than Christmas because Karen and Jacques had invited her on a ski trip to Vermont over the winter holidays. Since her trip to Los Angeles, life had been returning to the normal rhythm of a twenty-eight-year-old single woman in New York. She found living in Manhattan more invigorating than Brooklyn and especially relished the shorter commute, her early-morning jogs in the park, and her Sunday afternoons speaking Mandarin at her favorite Szechuan restaurant in Chinatown. Frankie had been over a few times, a coworker had twice treated her to the Met, and Karen and Jacques had invited her out sailing on Labor Day. And, as promised, Rachel hosted Robert's twins the last weekend in August, just after she returned from Los Angeles. As she promised, she and the twins went to Central Park and visited its zoo and had some hot pretzels and hot dogs while the next day they ate in Chinatown and then rode the ferry to Liberty Island and toured around the Statue of Liberty.

She often thought about getting in touch with Brooke, just to say hello and test his reaction. One day in late September she finally mustered the courage to do so and sent him a text, again thanking him for his kindness on the Luzon trip and hoping he was doing well. His response to her was polite and even a little playful, but no follow-up text or email or phone call ever came. *Maybe I misjudged him and he's lost interest in me—if he ever had any. Or perhaps he thinks this whole deal isn't over and I'm not out of the woods yet.* Since neither one of those thoughts appealed to Rachel, she kept trying to repress them as she went about her business.

She considered discussing her relationship with Brooke with Karen and maybe even Frankie. But she pretty much knew what they were going to tell her—she was too young and attractive and intelligent to be withering away waiting for some white rajah mystic halfway around the world who didn't seem interested in her. And Rachel also knew she'd reject their advice straight off, so why even bother to bring them in? Perhaps it was only an exasperating delusion that someday she and Brooke would end up together, but it nonetheless helped to prop up her still-scarred psyche.

The autumn highlight had been a road trip by all three Delta Gam sisters to the Dartmouth-Princeton homecoming weekend in mid-October. Karen asked Rachel if she could accompany her to Hanover where she had a class officers' meeting scheduled, and the two of them managed to convince Frankie to forego men for the weekend. The three of them left in Frankie's BMW at noon on Friday for the five-hour trip to Hanover. They were chatting the whole way as they passed by the fall foliage, then at the peak of its color. Karen kept probing Frankie about her latest boyfriends and asked if she could send some of her rejects Rachel's way to get her back in the swing of things. Rachel mused to herself, *Is Karen really that clueless about Frankie and her clients?*

They arrived in time for a buffet, mostly consisting of sandwich and veggie platters, put on by the resident Delta Gams. There was a smattering of classes represented by the alums, including a few from their class. Rachel found it amusing that, when Karen introduced herself, the students asked her about the still-infamous Super Bowl party, while Frankie somewhat sheepishly acknowledged her role as the only Delta Gam ever included in *Playboy's* "Women of the Ivy League" spread. After the buffet, everyone headed for the homecoming parade and bonfire. As they entered the college green in front of Baker library and the setting sun created a montage of fiery reflections in the windows of Dartmouth Hall and nearby Bartlett Hall, where the Asian Studies Program was located, Rachel reflected back on her undergraduate studies. *What would Professor Mirsky and some of her other Asian history professors make of all the stuff Fernandez and Brooke and the others relayed to me? Would they believe it—or did they already know about all of it?*

After the parade, full of Dartmouth teams and alums from over fifty graduating classes throwing candy to children lining Main Street, Rachel and Frankie and Karen mingled for a bit afterward on the green during the speeches and bonfire before joining a bunch of other twenty-somethings for a couple of drinks on the crowded porch of the Hanover Inn. Just after midnight, all of them headed up to their suite at the inn, which Karen obtained courtesy of the alumni association.

The next morning, Karen got up early to attend the morning breakfast for class officers, while Rachel jogged around campus in the crisp fall air and Frankie slept in. They all attended a barbecue lunch for young alums on the lawn in front of the gym, where Frankie started flirting with one of her old Theta Delt coke buddies, a former Dartmouth linebacker turned up-and-coming (and recently engaged) Wall Street lawyer. Frankie asked him and a couple of his friends to join them at the game, another disappointing loss for the Big Green. Even though Frankie, Karen, and Rachel had already made dinner plans at the sorority, Frankie asked to beg off, explaining she'd catch up with them later. Rachel just shrugged, barely concealing her reproach. *Is Frankie going to volunteer a solo bachelor's party for her friend—or merely exchange some sex for coke?* Rachel and Karen then headed to the sorority, where they and some other sorority alums had offered to prepare chili for the students. Delta Gamma wasn't hosting a homecoming party, so almost all of the students were planning to head off to other parties, leaving Rachel and Karen to commiserate with the other alums in the house. What Rachel found interesting was that, although some of the under-thirty alums were married, none had any children, including her, Karen and Frankie. *If this is what's going on around the country, so much for the next generation.*

Neither knew when Frankie came into the room that night, but she was sound asleep when they roused her the next morning to head northeast of town to Moose Mountain, which provided a panoramic view of Hanover and the Connecticut Valley seven hundred meters below. The morning air was brisk and the trail was enflamed with the yellow, orange, and red autumn hues of the maples, oaks, and birches. Rachel and Karen easily made the hour and half trip to the summit, but Frankie was puffing after just a few minutes. Rachel mused, *Maybe it's going to finally dawn on Frankie that fucking isn't the same as exercising.*

On the way home, Frankie and Karen chatted in the front seat while Rachel lounged in the back, reading a bit and occasionally glancing at the scenery. When Frankie started asking Karen about investing, Rachel's ears perked up, and her antennae really stood up when Karen told Frankie to pull her money away from any dollar-related investments, as she had gotten wind of a big downward move expected on the dollar very shortly. Rachel volunteered how John Peng had mentioned to her on the Fourth of July outing about a major upcoming dollar slide and gold play, but that's when Frankie and Karen became strangely silent. After a few awkward seconds, Frankie said she would have to talk to Peng about it the next time she saw him, but Karen didn't even acknowledge she knew him. Rachel was about to blurt out why they were acting so strangely, but she decided to hold back.

This Peng thing is no coincidence; both Frankie and Karen are in on something they don't want me to know about. Or is Karen totally in the dark about Frankie's new profession . . . and her relationship with Peng?

Rachel tightened her laces on her pink jogging shoes and then got up and turned left at the stairs and started running south on Avenue B toward Sixth Street. She planned to take Sixth Street to the East River Promenade and then head down and back on it for a three-mile jaunt. She liked to jog early on weekend mornings, since she would encounter a lot of other joggers and walkers along the way and most of the people she would ordinarily worry about weren't up and about at that time.

She initially didn't see any cars as she crossed over Sixth Street, but then suddenly a black sedan came up to her and two men jumped out and pushed her into the car. Before she could even manage a scream, one of the men had a knife to her throat, terrifying her. The car quickly sped to FDR Drive, where it turned north along the East River before crossing over Upper Manhattan and Harlem and eventually linking with the Major Deegan Expressway. Rachel still didn't know where they were going, but she was glad she hadn't eaten anything for breakfast. As the car sped past Yonkers and into Westchester

County on the New York State Thruway, it finally dawned on her—*they're taking me to the Perry estate!* As they pulled up at the Perry compound and the Georgian-style mansion came into view, Rachel began to relax a bit—*at least I'll be getting out of this wretched car!* As they went inside, Rachel was directed to the oak-paneled study, where her father-in-law sat at the desk.

"Rachel, please have a seat. I am very sorry about what just happened." He handed her a soda and said, "Here, take this."

He looked away and then opened up to her in a low voice. "Rachel, what I most feared would happen did—the Dragon Family crossed us. They got the gold out of their site but then they pulled a fast one and intercepted *our* gold just as we were about to haul it off. My colleagues are very angry."

Perry turned back toward her, with a worried look. "I regret that we're going to play a nasty card . . . that involves you. I need you to do exactly what I demand, if we are to pull it off. Now, Rachel, it may get a little rough for you, and you may even get cut. And you're going to see me as you never have before. *The key is to act totally afraid the entire time.* Do you understand?"

Rachel nodded.

"What we're involved with here is a very high-stakes poker game . . . and our next move involves a bluff. We need to have them believe that *I am willing to kill my own daughter-in-law.*"

Rachel nodded nervously.

"One more thing. You could be in a physically uncomfortable position for several hours. But you have to go through with it, if I am going to be able to protect you . . . and me."

Rachel nodded her assent.

Perry shook his head. "That's not good enough, Rachel. I want you to look me in the eye—are you willing to go through with this to save both your life and mine?"

"Yes," she said in a trembling voice.

"Good. Then let's get this thing underway."

Perry kissed her on the cheek as he left the room. The two men who had kidnapped her came back into the room and tied her wrists and legs and put duct tape over her mouth. Rachel could control her breathing through her nose, but she couldn't control her panic. Then, they led her into the study, where Perry was sitting in front of a computer screen, talking to someone. Perry was talking in a voice that was more than angry—it was almost Satanic.

"Your Dragon Family doesn't know who they're dealing with. Nobody crosses or humiliates us Americans like that! We will do whatever it takes to hunt every one of you down—and I guarantee it will happen. But first, let me show you someone you've met recently."

Rachel was then brought in by one of the men, who dragged her by her hair while holding a knife to her head. The man at the other end of the Skype saw that Rachel was resisting, but her eyes had the fear of a caged animal. Then, Rachel turned toward the screen and was shocked to see Craig Brooke staring at her from the other end, with a very surprised and worried look.

Perry added. "Because you dared to mess with us, the ante's now been raised. You're going to give me all of your white maps—all one hundred and seventy-five of them—now!"

Brooke was alarmed seeing Rachel bound like that and taken aback at Perry's ultimatum. It was Saturday night in the Philippines; usually, he was out with friends. *Obviously, Perry knew I was at home; was he watching me the whole time?*

"Please," he replied, "I don't have any maps on me personally. And I don't think we have but about fifty all told, in any case." Rachel could see the panic in his eyes. She thought to herself, *I know now it's not all business with him . . . he really does care about me!*

"Well, you tell your friend Ben Fernandez to recount them and get them to me in a PDF right away . . . or your girlfriend here dies." The man holding Rachel grabbed her hair again and jerked her head backward, putting her neck in full view, with the knife hovering right over the skin.

"You wouldn't do that to your own daughter-in-law!"

"Ex-daughter-in-law . . . *who drove my son to suicide!*" Perry signaled to the man, who then ran the knife over her throat, causing a scarlet ring to form and Rachel to moan underneath the duct tape.

Rachel's thoughts again turned to panic. *He's lying about Jackson and me . . . or is he?*

Brooke was horrified. "Look, let me talk to him—we'll get you what you need. Just don't do anything . . . please!"

"You'd better get it fast, rajah boy! I'm calling back in thirty minutes."

The screen went blank and Rachel was let go and the tape removed for the time being. Perry and one of the men left the room, while the other one remained with her, watching her from across the room. She sensed there was at least one other armed man in the house, but she figured Patricia was out—Perry had no doubt arranged for that. Her mind was racing with all sorts of thoughts: *Why did I have to go out for my run this morning what if George isn't bluffing what will become of me who will tell my parents if I don't make it home for Thanksgiving where will they dump my body why didn't I just tell Brooke to shove it the first night please, Craig, don't let them kill me!* She regretted telling Karen nonchalantly that day at Caumsett, "If I die, I die." *What did I know about how it feels to die, anyways?*

Just as he had promised, Perry walked back into the room thirty minutes later. The second man returned as well, placing new duct tape over Rachel's mouth, which strangely enough didn't set off as much of a panic as the first time. *Perhaps my adrenaline is so exhausted I can't feel anything anymore.*

The Skype connection was re-established and she saw Brooke at the other end, along with her own image on the inset.

Perry spoke first. "So, what have you got for me?"

Brooke replied deliberately. "I talked to Don Benito. And he said he would give you all of the white maps in his possession." Brooke paused and took a deep breath. "But he told me point-blank that all the Family has is a total of fifty-three maps." What Brooke said was true, but what he didn't say was how Benito Fernandez didn't want to deal initially and only after Brooke's alternate pleading and anger that Rachel's life had been endangered by the Dragons' treachery did Don Benito make a couple of quick calls to Shiang and another high-ranking member of the Family.

Perry was obviously studying the situation and was not happy. Brooke was about to say something but realized he had better not. He tried to make eye contact with Rachel, but it was hopeless through the remote communication, where all one could do was look into the camera. But he could at least pray for her.

Perry finally turned toward the camera and said, "I'll be back soon . . . be damn sure you don't leave your computer." And then the screen went blank again. This time, when Perry left the room, no one else joined him and no one removed her duct tape.

In the other room, Perry presented his case in a hushed voice, although Rachel could make out most of the conversation. "Let me check a couple of maps out right now. If they seem okay, we'll do some tests over there in the next few days. We don't need them all, in any case, now that their operation's been completely exposed." For the first time, Rachel realized that Perry, though high up, wasn't really in charge. He wasn't anything like the lieutenant Brooke was, but his role now seemed to be more akin to a high-ranking general, maybe a chief of staff.

The voice on the other end was impassive. "Accept them but don't release her . . . she's obviously still worth something to them. And move your assets in place quickly over there."

When Perry returned, he nodded for one of the men to re-establish the connection. When Brooke's image came on the screen again, Perry sat next to Rachel and faced the camera. "Send me the PDF right away with all the images. We'll review them quickly to see if they're genuine . . . and then we'll do some verifying on the ground. Your girlfriend doesn't leave until everything checks out. And in case you didn't notice, we now know all the major players in your operation." Then pointing to Rachel's dragon necklace, Perry added, "And by the way, don't expect this little pendant here to save her if you double-cross us again." Rachel thought, *How did George know that was a gift from Craig?*

Perry turned off the connection and left the room again. Rachel was surprised she no longer felt panicked—more drained than anything else. About twenty minutes later—which seemed twice that long—he returned and checked his email. The images had been sent, all fifty-three. Perry wasn't totally surprised that most of the ones in the Family's possession were from Luzon; how they were obtained was anyone's guess. The cabal actually knew of a couple of the sites, so he could confirm that some of them at least were real. Perry then made a short text, "All data received." A few seconds later, another text came back reading "Good work."

Perry ordered the men to unbind Rachel and to remove the tape around her mouth. He began gently to clean up her throat wound, which was superficial and would heal without a scar, and he again apologized for what had transpired. "You did well, Rachel . . . I don't believe Brooke thought this was a bluff. Again, though, I am very sorry you had to be put through all of this—it was my mistake to ever let you get involved in the first place. And don't believe for a moment I ever thought you drove Jackson to suicide; on the contrary, you were the one thing that could have saved him, if it had been possible." Perry paused for a second and turned toward the men. "In a few minutes, these men will drive you to a new location in the countryside, where you'll be treated well. We'll know in a week or two if the maps check out. If they do, you'll still be able to make Thanksgiving with your parents and this will all be just a bad dream. In the meantime, you need to call Pacific and tell them you're not feeling well and that you plan to take the next few days off. And whatever else, *do not try to escape or talk to anyone about this.*"

"And if the maps don't check out?" Rachel asked.

Perry hesitated for a few seconds. "Then neither you nor I will have a lot to be thankful for at Thanksgiving . . . if we greet the turkey at all."

He then planted a kiss on the side of her forehead and left the room.

CHAPTER
16

Rachel had no idea where she was being taken as the car drove down the driveway, and lost in her grim thoughts she didn't notice that the person usually manning the gate entrance was not in the booth as she and the two men left the estate. She concluded that both Brooke and the Dragons—and even George Perry—did care about her, and that gave some solace. But she knew she was still in danger, even if the Dragon Family came through as promised.

As her car was waiting at the light at Bedford Street, two shots rang out from the car in front of hers. Rachel freaked out at the splattered blood all over her and thought she had been hit, but when she looked to her left and right she realized it was her captors who had been the targets. Both had massive wounds to the head, with part of their brains blasting through the holes in their skulls and landing on Rachel's leg. Rachel shrieked and wanted to flee as fast as she could but was paralyzed with fear. Then, two men opened the doors and grabbed her and pulled her from the car and pushed her into another one that sped off. Before she knew it, the car was heading south on the Saw Mill River Parkway. As they passed by Pleasantville, the car veered onto Route 117 and passed Sleepy Hollow before heading north to Ossining. She had no idea what was happening or where she was going until they stopped the car at a heliport, where a helicopter was sitting with its engines and rotors running. The two men who had rescued her quickly whisked her off into the chopper and drove off, just as the helicopter lifted off.

Rachel could tell from the sun angle and the blue tinge near the horizon that they were headed east-southeast, toward Long Island Sound. As they crossed over the wealthy suburbs of Westchester County, neither the pilot nor copilot said anything as they stared out the cockpit window. Soon they were over the sound, but the helicopter showed no signs of slowing or changing direction. *We're headed for the Atlantic Ocean—but where are they taking me?* She thought of the "disappeared"— the Argentinian leftists in the seventies and eighties who were flown out to sea and then pushed out of aircraft[106]—and began to suffer yet another panic attack. *Please, God, don't let them do that to me!*

The helicopter kept going farther out into the Atlantic. And just then, a large black hull started to appear, rising barely above the waves. Quickly, the chopper began to slow down and hover and then its rescue ladder was rolled out. Rachel started to breathe a little easier as her terror began to subside. *I'm being transferred to a submarine! How weird is this?*

Rachel was placed in a safety harness and the pilot told her to be careful when she went down the ladder, especially since she wasn't used to such turbulence. As she carefully made her way down the ladder, she could feel the ocean spray from the rotor wash whipping into her face. As she was about to reach the hull, one of the crew grabbed her and motioned for her to let go of the ladder. When she did so, he waved to the pilot and the helicopter quickly turned and headed back to shore, with the ladder dangling underneath. Rachel was quickly led down the hatch and into the captain's quarters. She had already realized

---

[106] See http://en.wikipedia.org/wiki/Death_flights

she wasn't on an American sub, but she was still startled when the captain started speaking to her in Mandarin.

"Miss Echon, I am Captain Cheng Wu. I welcome you on board the *Golden Dragon*, the first of our SC-class and currently the fastest submarine in the world."

Rachel seemed bewildered, so he tried to calm her down. "I know you've been through a lot in the past few hours, but I can assure you are totally safe now." He handed her a cup of tea. "We're going to stay here for a little longer, waiting for one more person."

"Where's here?"

"Fifty kilometers off the coast of Long Island, seventy-five meters above the continental shelf."

"And where are we headed?"

The captain smiled. "You'll find out soon enough. In the meantime, you need to rest. Please use the bunk in my room . . . it would be good to sleep a little. You can also use the shower to clean off." Then the captain looked at her blood-splattered sweats as he handed her one of the smaller petty officer's clean coveralls and said, "You can change into this afterward."

After Rachel was taken away from his estate, only Perry and a lightly armed security aide were still in the house. Perry started going through the maps on the computer and developing a plan to send in a new team of engineers, geologists, and private military contractors to at least three, maybe more, of the sites. The white maps would lead them to the general location and then, with the same modern imaging techniques employed by Pepe Santos for the Nueva Vizcaya site, Perry's team could determine the basic outline of the chambers and passageways and see if they corresponded to the red maps. There would be no immediate extraction, so the verification process could be completed in a matter of days, weeks at most. This time there would be no problem with the police, as the president had assured him that Filipino army troops would be on guard.

He knew that he had uncharacteristically screwed up. He hadn't taken all of the precautions and had violated Sun Tzu's first rule of war.[107] *I never should have underestimated the Dragons on their home turf.* But this time there would be no mistakes. He would make sure the Dragons would never get their hands on another ounce of Yamashita gold and that their recent victory would be short-lived. *They might be able to hide their loot for a while, but eventually they'll have to surface and sell—that's when we'll pounce.* And even if they had managed to get the gold into China—a distinct possibility, given Shiang's rank within the Family—he had the means to use the two carrier fleets in the Western Pacific to stir up trouble on the Spratly Islands, which would cause China massive headaches with the Filipinos. Hiding the Dragons' fifty billion in gold would hardly be worth the trouble to them.

What George Perry didn't know was that his guard at the gate was dead and that all of the extensive electronic security systems on his estate had been turned off. Had his lone remaining aide been monitoring the security systems in the basement, it would have been clear what was happening; but the long, tense session with Rachel necessitated a break. Silently, two assassins crept near the large window off the study and aimed their fifty-caliber Remingtons at the figures inside. Perry heard one shot crackle as it felled his security aide but not the second bullet, which traveled faster than its sound and exploded the

---

[107] The *Art of War*, generally but not universally ascribed to Sun Tzu, has as its principal theme, "If you know the enemy and know yourself, you need not fear the result of a hundred battles. If you know yourself but not the enemy, for every victory gained you will also suffer a defeat. If you know neither the enemy nor yourself, you will succumb in every battle." http://time.com/2801517/sun-tzus-art-of-war-how-ancient-strategy-can-lead-to-modern-success

back of his skull within a split second. Had he heard or felt it, Perry might have instantly realized that the bullet was his karma for all of the ones he had ordered around the world over the years.

The assassins quickly went to work. One deleted all of the email traffic and files from the Dragon Family and destroyed the hard drive on Perry's computer. The other quickly retrieved the code to Perry's vault underneath Manhattan Trust. They knew the location of the codes and the location of the red maps because of wireless video and audio devices adroitly and unsuspectingly placed in his room by "Monique" during one of her afternoon trysts with Perry. "Monique," in reality Frances Hinman Stewart, was acting under the guidance of the White Dragon Family, whose master tactician had been listening to all of George Oliver Perry's bedroom conversations during the previous several months, including the one where Perry revealed the "correction" made to the red map of "Many Monkeys".

Perry's death was variously attributed in the mainstream media to a bungled burglary attempt or a financial deal gone bad. Some who knew Perry's more nefarious role as a capo in the Bilderbergers speculated but did not openly claim it might be a politically motivated killing. But only a few anxious individuals running the Western financial and political establishment knew that the White Dragon Family was behind the assassination, because almost no one else knew that the White Dragon Family was even real. One of those who knew the truth was the head of the Federal Reserve and the other was her master—not the president of the United States of America.

It turned out that Perry's death was as charmed as his life, being mercilessly quick and sparing him the humiliation of dementia, the ravages of Parkinson's disease, and the torture of terminal cancer. His funeral the next week was attended by hundreds of dignitaries from around the world, from central bankers to former presidents, and because of his naval service, he received a full military burial in the Island Cemetery in Newport, alongside Oliver and Matthew Perry. In the middle of the eulogy given by the Fed chief, a message from the president was read, thanking Perry for his unsurpassed "dedication and vision in the cause of peace and freedom around the world."

Perry's vision was indeed prescient: Just as he had feared, he wasn't at the table to greet the turkey at Thanksgiving two weeks later.

CHAPTER

17

The two assassins quickly left the Perry estate, turning in the direction opposite to the police barricades in and around Bedford Street, where Perry's men still lay dead in the car. They quickly approached Mt. Kisco Road to the south.

The man who wasn't driving relayed Perry's access code to John Peng, who was waiting outside Manhattan Trust. As a legal representative of the large Shiang accounts quartered in Manhattan Trust, Peng already had access to the main vault, but to get into Perry's individual safe he needed the additional access code, which he now had. It had been more of a problem to fool the eye-scanner, but thanks to experts at Cybernalysis—a Shiang subsidiary—the biometrics databases from Manhattan Trust were hacked, thereby allowing for the reverse-engineering of Perry's 3-D iris template.[108] Now, Peng's biggest problem was time—he would have minutes at most once the vault was opened to retrieve the maps, exit the bank, and make it to the heliport.

He could feel the cold sweat on the back of his hand and on his forehead as he entered the code to Perry's safe. He was relieved as the handle on the vault began to turn. He quickly

---

[108] For more information on the ability to reverse-engineer iris markings: http://www.wired.com/2012/07/reverse-engineering-iris-scans/all

glanced inside—there were lots of papers, envelopes, bullion bars, and boxes of various sorts. He had to make a quick decision on where Perry would hide something as valuable as the maps, which was a problem since he didn't know if they'd be stored as printed maps, as original film, as a CD, or in multiple other ways. He started frantically sorting through everything—on top of everything else, his own life was on the line for, if caught, he would be arrested and undoubtedly tied to the Chappaqua assassinations. Then, he saw it—the sealed envelope with the large handwritten "YG" on it. He opened it and saw a note with instructions wrapped around a DVD whose case had the title "Yamashita Maps". *This has to be it!*

In the security room on the second floor of the Manhattan Trust Building, the guard monitoring the lower floors was fixated on the screen displaying the main lobby, where an irate customer—later identified as Jacques Delacroix—was apparently miffed and making threats because a large overseas funds transfer hadn't occurred properly. When that disturbance died down, the guard returned to monitoring the basement vault screens and noticed John Peng walking out at a brisker than normal pace and apparently coming from a novel direction in the vault. The security officer's suspicions were aroused and upon rewinding the tape he was astounded to see Peng from a different camera rummaging through what looked to be *George Perry's safe*. He then played the sequence again for his colleague and they both concurred—it was definitely time for the alarms! A massive clanging suddenly bellowed out everywhere in the building, and the doors to the outside were all shut down—but a split-second too late, as Peng had just exited the building onto the sidewalk.

Peng prided himself for his ability to function under stress; he was a classic "augmenter,"[109] which had once served him

---

[109]   According to sensation-seeking theory (Marvin Zuckerman, *Sensation-Seeking and Risky Behavior*, APA, 2007), "augmenters" are those who increase brain activity during arousing situations and are better able to

well as a helicopter pilot in the People's Liberation Army. But his pulse was now racing as he jumped into the black Lexus IS convertible as it raced through the streets of mid-town Manhattan. Peng figured his best chance would be to enter FDR Drive off Forty-Second Street and follow it all the way to the Skyport at Twenty-Fifth Street, as he knew it would be impossible for the police to block off the entire distance. As he was exiting FDR Drive, he could hear the sounds of squad cars less than a thousand meters behind. He ran the gate at the Skyport and pulled up right next to the same helicopter that had deposited Rachel on the submarine. The chopper had its engine idling and blade slowly rotating, although no one was inside, and Peng quickly climbed aboard and revved up the engine before releasing the brake. As he was lifting off, police cars were entering the Skyport from all directions. They fired some bullet rounds, but the Super Puma was already over the water and accelerating fast. It would only be minutes before he would intercept the submarine—too quick for any jets to scramble and reach him. *I'm going to make it . . . if only I can land it!*

On the Coast Guard cutter off Long Island, Ensign Martinez turned and said, "Commander, look at what the drone's picked up."

Lieutenant Commander Roberts came over and stared at the screen. "It's a sub . . . but it's *not ours*. Keep the drone hovering so I can study it." He looked even more closely at the screen. "It looks like one of the newer Chinese SC-class they've posted us about—look at the conical design."

"Conical?"

---

function under stress than are their counterparts ("reducers"), whose brain activity becomes inhibited during stress.

Roberts was still transfixed at the image. Almost as if he were talking to himself, he murmured, "It *has* to be the supercavitating one . . . but what's it doing here, so close to our waters?" He maintained his stare and then turned to Martinez. "What else do you have, Ensign?"

"There are two radar tracks from about thirty minutes ago—one to and one from the sub. From what we can tell, it looks like a helicopter left the helipad near Tarrytown, then hovered briefly over the sub before returning to the Skyport on the East River."

"And now . . . what's happening now?"

Martinez got up and went to another junior officer and briefly conversed with him before turning back to the commander, who had taken the ensign's chair and was still transfixed by the screen. "We're picking another radar track headed straight for the sub, sir; in fact, it should be there at any moment."

The lieutenant commander continued to fixate on the screen. "Holy shit, look at this, Ensign. A goddamned helo just landed right on a fucking Chinese SC sub . . . *and a man is getting out!*"

Lieutenant Commander Roberts slumped back in his chair and gazed at the ceiling, half-dazed. After a few moments, he turned back to Martinez and said, "I've got to talk with the captain . . . he'll never believe what just fucking happened."

Rachel heard the hatch close and could feel the submarine taking on ballast. She opened the door to the captain's room and was shocked to see John Peng conversing in animated Mandarin with the captain.

"What are you doing here, John?" she asked incredulously in English. "And *how* did you get here?"

Peng excused himself to the captain and then walked over to Rachel. "I'm escaping from the same bastards you are. And,

I came here the same way you did . . . except that my flight was one way." Seeing her bewilderment, he added, "I flew the helicopter out solo, with all of the cabal's red maps on me and the police right behind. Right now, the chopper's still floating in the ocean."

Rachel got fidgety. "I knew from the day we met something was up with you, John. At one point, I even thought you were working for Perry."

"That's what we wanted him to think. But I certainly won't be working for him in the future."

"Why's that?"

"Because he took a bullet to the head less than an hour ago in his study."

Rachel shrieked, "No!" and started shaking all over.

Peng was surprised by her reaction and kept his distance. "Look, I know it's a shock, Rachel, but I really thought you'd be glad . . . after what he did to you this morning."

Rachel recovered her composure and said angrily, "So, you knew about our Skype calls to Craig Brooke?"

"We knew everything that was going on in Perry's house over the past three months, thanks to your friend Frankie, who was working with us and had managed to bug his bedroom while he had her over."

Frankie . . . so she was part of all this after all! "But I thought you were just a client of hers."

"So she told you, didn't she?" Peng smiled and paused. "Yes, I was a client initially, until I realized what a real asset she could be to the Family. I could tell from their interactions at the Newport party, after you left, that Frankie was already a client of Perry's. I immediately contacted her after the party and, within a couple of weeks, Frankie was discreetly placing wireless cameras and listening devices in his bedroom for us when she visited him. Perry was blind-sided and never realized what she was up to."

Rachel replied sarcastically. "So, I bet you paid her well for her work, didn't you?"

"That's because Frankie took a lot of risks and so amazingly pulled it off. But if you'd ask her, I think you'd find Frankie didn't do it just for the money."

She replied sarcastically, "So I guess she did it for love, instead."

Peng seemed slightly surprised, even intrigued, at the thought, but let her comment pass. "No. She actually resisted at first and would never have worked with us if she'd have known Perry was going to get killed—which we didn't expect at the time, either. I eventually convinced her of our cause, but it would have been a lot harder if she hadn't already grown sick of the greed up and down Wall Street."

Peng could see that Rachel was still perturbed, so he switched to a more empathetic tack.

"Rachel, I'm sorry about George Perry, but I'm still surprised at your reaction. I know about the Stockholm Syndrome and all,[110] but from what I gathered, he nearly slit your throat this morning. We felt we had to move in and rescue you."

"It was all a bluff, John! He pretended and I pretended. He was mad at the Dragons because you crossed him and ran off with the gold. He was under a lot of pressure—I don't know from whom—to right things. Did you ever think what all of your schemes, and now his death, might be doing to me?"

"I'm really sorry, Rachel. But from what I understand, we killed him mainly in retaliation for his nearly having Pepe Santos killed off by altering the red map to remove a bomb placement symbol. We fortunately found out about it because we had Frankie's listening devices in place. Don't you realize your father-in-law was a monster?"

---

[110] "Stockholm syndrome" refers to the psychological phenomenon known as "capture bonding," where hostages begin to feel empathy toward their captors, even to the point of defending them. It was named after an actual hostage-taking in a Stockholm bank in 1973: http://en.wikipedia.org/wiki/Stockholm_syndrome

Rachel suddenly grew calm and looked down and away. In a soft voice, almost in tears, she replied, "I don't deny he may have done monstrous things—like a lot of powerful people all over the world, I might add. But he wasn't the head of it all—he was taking orders, too, from what I could tell—and he was no monster. He actually cared about his family and vowed to protect me. From the start, he didn't want me involved in any of this; in case you didn't know, it was *me* who came to him with the deal, not the other way. *He was a human being*, John . . . and now he's dead."

Peng reflected on her words. "Assuming you're right—up to a point—the fact remains that your father-in-law made a major mistake in underestimating the Family. He was brilliant at what he did, but he finally met his match in Ben Fernandez. You probably didn't realize it was Fernandez who orchestrated everything—your involvement, mine, Frankie's, Craig's, the rescue teams—"

"You mean the assassins. Did they include you, John?"

"No, I had nothing to do with his death. All I did was receive the codes to his Manhattan safe that were in the hidden bedroom location Frankie discovered and used them to remove the remaining red maps from his cache. I barely made it out of the bank and wouldn't have if it hadn't been for Jacques."

"Jacques Delacroix? He was in on this, too?"

"Sort of. I had been paying Jacques on the side to do a little research on the location of some Swiss gold stashes—he's a wizard when it comes to that stuff—and I basically asked him if he could do a little extra favor for me. In case you're wondering, though, Karen had nothing to do with any of this until you brought her in on it and started using her computer for messaging. Eventually, I brought both of them in on what was going on and they, even as we speak, are quickly covering both our tracks now that everything's heated up. But Frankie didn't know anything of your Dragon involvement."

"So what did Jacques do at the bank?"

"Oh, he posed as an irate customer and created a big scene that diverted the security cameras, just long enough for me to enter Perry's safe."

"And what do you think your life would have been worth if you hadn't made it out? I'm sure you did it all to please your uncle, but really, John?"

"Actually, I did it for a lot of reasons—yes, for my uncle, yes for the Dragons, but also for me. You don't know my personality, Rachel, how I thrive on risks and danger. I was able—with help, of course—to pull off the greatest single theft in the history of the world, if one can really call it that since the real theft of the gold occurred a long time ago by the Japanese and Americans. *You can't get any higher than that!*"

"But don't you fear that you'll be a target of the Bilderbergers, John. They know you were the major player in the operation."

"I don't think so. For one, no one can say I didn't open the safe legitimately—after all, I had the codes. And there is no way the cabal will pin the assassination on anyone in our group, including me, because it would be a major humiliation for them to acknowledge publicly their vulnerability to the Dragon Family and our theft of all the secret gold, right underneath their nose."

"But couldn't they retaliate clandestinely?"

"I'm not worried, Rachel, because our network runs a lot deeper than you might imagine. The last thing they want is for another big gun of theirs to follow in the footsteps of George Perry."

The conversation grew silent as Rachel pondered Peng's words. All of a sudden, Rachel recalled Peng driving up to Perry's Newport estate in the black Lexus convertible *Now I know where I had seen that car—Brooke drove me home in it that very first night!*

"So, the story Craig gave about finding my connections to Perry was all bullshit. It was you who brought him to me, after you learned I was his daughter-in-law. Who told you—Jacques?"

"Yes, shortly after I came to his firm, early in the year."

"So, instead of you approaching me, which you figured might not work, you had Craig sweet-talk me into this whole thing."

"Yes." Peng then looked down briefly and then turned to leave. But Rachel was still in the mood for questions.

"So, what's in store now . . . where are we headed?"

Peng turned back to face Rachel. "The *Golden Dragon* is headed for Caracas. We should be there in less than twenty-four hours, because of its advanced, supercavitating technology."

"What's that?"

"It's a special technology that creates an air bubble in front and thereby reduces friction and drag. As you know, because of water's greater density, it's much slower to travel in it than air, so regular submarines can only go about fifty knots. By creating a forward vapor cavity—along with its reduced-friction skin and conical design—the *Golden Dragon* can exceed that speed by many times over short periods and nearly double that speed over the long run."[111] Then he added, "Of course, even twenty-four hours can be a long time if one doesn't like closed spaces."

"Don't worry, John, I'm a lot smaller than you."

"Good. But just in case, Captain Wu has offered you his room if you'd like."

"He's already spoken to me about that." Then after a brief silence, Rachel continued in English. "So, John, what's going to happen once we arrive in Caracas?"

"We'll catch an overnight flight on the presidential plane and arrive in Shanghai the next morning. You'll be greeted by my uncle, Li Shiang, who you've met. I hope you thank him adequately. Whether you believe it or not, he used a lot of high

---

111 There are supercavitating torpedoes, but full supercavitation in submarines is only possible for short distances because of energy constraints, contrary to recent Chinese reports: http://time.com/3182422/chinese-supersonic-submarine

connections to arrange this whole Caribbean cruise to save your life . . . and mine."

"Of course, I might have just as easily ended up dead thanks to your uncle and all of your other White Dragon friends."

"On the contrary, Rachel, you were *psychologically dead* before Craig first encountered you. Don't you realize that our mission is what helped bring you back to life?"

She stared at him without speaking, then turned away. *Damn you, John Peng, why did you have to be so right again . . . not that you'll ever hear that coming from me.*

Since Rachel hadn't been on a submarine, everything was new to her. One particular novelty, the smells of machinery and unbathed men, was hardly pleasant. And she realized there weren't any tampons on board, so she figured she might have to improvise if her period started early. There was a laptop computer she could use, but all of the characters were in Mandarin, which she had not typed with before. So she basically just watched the young men as they went about their duties. Not having any connection to the military nor having ever considered joining it, she wondered what motivated the men to spend several months of the year in such cramped and difficult circumstances. She knew that, like the American military, the People's Liberation Army and its naval and aviation forces were largely voluntary. Did the submariners actually believe they were doing good for the world, or at least their patriotic duty? Or were they looking for new experiences and to move on after their service with skills that could make them more competitive in the Chinese workforce? *I wonder what they think of our sailors, situated in similar surroundings and poised to fire nuclear missiles at the major cities of China.*

She was starting to feel hungry, so she headed toward the galley. The cook was preparing for the next shift of thirty men and she offered her help, which he refused. But he did allow her to dish out her own spicy noodles and spring roll, which proved surprisingly tasty. When the crew arrived for their meal, many of them had not been told about the American woman on board and were quite surprised. They were even more surprised—and, in some cases even embarrassed, given their sexual banter—when Rachel greeted them in her fluent Mandarin.

Rachel decided not to linger and returned to the captain's quarters, where her mental exhaustion from the day's intense events led her to quickly fall asleep. When she awoke, there were still ten hours left on the voyage and they were passing a little to the east of San Salvador Island in the Bahamas, where Columbus first landed in the New World.[112] She could feel the warmth of the Caribbean waters, which elevated the inside temperature of the submarine. She also heard what the captain described as a pod of whales overhead at one point, and he even pointed out the sounds of nearby surface ships. She was surprised that the underwater environment was as noisy as it was.

Captain Wu told her they were going to skirt the Bahamas to the east and then traverse the Mona Passage between the Dominican Republic and Puerto Rico before heading due south past Aruba and Curacao and surfacing in Caracas. Rachel had never been to the Caribbean before and was imagining all of the colorful fish schooling about above the submarine. Jackson and Rachel had mulled going to Jamaica for their honeymoon but had opted instead for the Galapagos, which stirred Jackson's intellectual curiosity a bit more. The cruise and layover there at the five-star hotel in Puerto Ayora had been exquisite, and

---

[112] Columbus first named the island San Salvador in thanks for having reached the Indies—mistakenly, as it turned out. Until 1925, though, the island was known as Waitling Island. When it was confirmed that Waitling must have been Columbus' original San Salvador, it was rechristened to its original name.

she sometimes wondered afterward whether Jackson would have ever become so mentally unstable had he lived in such a relaxed environs year round.

After the captain retired to his quarters, his executive officer took Rachel on a tour of the boat. It was slightly more than one and a half times the length of a football field and about fifteen meters wide, but it seemed longer as Rachel had to avoid equipment and boxes in the aisles. Much of the food was still in boxes, as the submarine was still in the first half of its three-month deployment, having been resting just off Nantucket Island when the trouble started the previous morning. Rachel was impressed at how efficient the use of space was, with continuous rotation of men in and out of bunks, galleys, and repair and monitoring stations. She was surprised that the nuclear reactor powering the boat was right in its center, and she was further unnerved by the ballistic missiles lying about on the floor. She didn't realize that since this was still a shakeout cruise for the *Golden Dragon*, the missiles were fitted with dummy warheads.

After the tour, Rachel went through the small DVD library but didn't see any movies she especially liked. She decided to watch one of the few American movies in the set, *Independence Day*, which was dubbed into Mandarin. When the DVD finished, Peng came over to her and accompanied her to the galley to get a light snack of egg rolls, pastry, dried fruit, and tea. He then invited her to play backgammon with him. Even though it was a friendly board game, Rachel found it a little unnerving to be competing with Peng. She still felt a little uncomfortable around him and opened up to him about it after the first game ended.

"You know, John, when I first met you, I was a little wary. I didn't know where you were coming from."

Peng smiled. "So I take it you do now?"

"Do I? I'm still wondering if all of the stuff I've been involved in the past six months—that you've been involved in—is going to make the world any better."

"Our efforts are already having a major effect on the financial markets, to our advantage. The dollar and euro have steadily fallen as rumors of the huge gold recovery and its challenge to the hegemony of the Western currencies have been circulating around the world. But you're right to keep your distance from me, Rachel—I'm not someone who opens up much about my business. But you've met a lot of the Dragon Family and you know our purpose. Don't you think we've risked too much to go back on our word?"

"I certainly hope not . . . after what I've been through!"

"Look, there are more than enough powerful, wealthy men in the Family to make anyone suspicious of our motives. But you have to remember one thing, Rachel: George Perry and all of the rest of the Bilderberger elite running the show over most of the past century never suffered the helplessness and humiliation our leaders have due to all of the Western-backed transgressions—the coups, the financial bullying, the foreign troops on our soils, and the gunboat diplomacy, as when your aircraft carriers went right up against our shores.[113] Probably only one in ten thousand Americans remembers the Taiwan Straits incident, but do you think that few Americans would ever forget if Russian carriers paraded through the Long Island Sound? Rachel, every member of the Dragon Family—from the richest to the poorest, from the strongest to the weakest, from the lightest-skinned to the darkest—understands at a gut level what the average person all over Asia and even the rest of the developing world has felt. If the Dragons betray the people, we betray ourselves."

---

[113] In the Third Taiwan Straits Crisis in 1995, the American aircraft carriers USS *Independence* and USS *Nimitz* entered the Taiwan Straits in a show of force in defense of Taiwan that humiliated the Chinese: ppe.wiki.hci.edu.sg/file/view/ross3.pdf/209949578/ross3.pdf

Rachel continued to look away. *It all sounds so eloquent, yet . . . ?*

Peng continued on. "So you're still wary of me, Rachel . . . but what about the others? For instance, Li Shiang?" Rachel placed her two hands out flat and jigged them back and forth in roll, to indicate her ambivalent feelings.

"Ben Fernandez?" Rachel warily turned one hand thumbs-up, but then quickly began to jiggle the other hand, reflecting a little more positivity mixed with distrust.

"And Pepe?" Now Rachel turned both thumbs up.

"How about Craig?"

Rachel pulled her hands back and leaned back and frowned; then, she looked away again and replied coolly, "He told me at the start it was all business with him . . . and, in the end, I guess that's all it was."

She then turned back to Peng, and he stared at her for a couple of seconds.

"You're wrong about Craig, Rachel . . . *very wrong*," he said.

Rachel returned the stare to Peng for a few seconds. Then, without changing her expression, she rolled the dice to begin the next game. Deep down, though, she was smiling.

After the submarine surfaced at the Bolivarian Naval Port in Caracas just after noon the next day, Rachel and Peng were whisked off to the Presidential Palace. En route, they were told that they would be guests of the Venezuelan president for dinner that night. At the palace, Rachel was offered a choice of several evening dresses and shoes and a couple of outfits for the long flight the next day, and she chose an ankle-length yellow chiffon dress for dinner. It was only then that it dawned on her that she had no money and no passport or other identification. Fortunately, the Dragon Family prepared for everything and had contacted Karen shortly after Rachel had been kidnapped. Evidently, Karen used the extra key Rachel had given her to open the apartment and remove all of her valuables, which would be waiting for her in Shanghai when she arrived the next day. Other items would be boxed up and placed into storage, under the assumption that Rachel wouldn't be returning to New York any time soon.

That evening, Peng and Rachel were treated like foreign dignitaries. In addition to the president and his wife and daughter and son-in-law, there were several young couples from Brazil, Russia, and China, three key BRICS states. Although the dinner was largely apolitical, the Venezuelan president, in his toast to Peng and Rachel, stated that due to their valor the dawn of a new era was now at hand, in which the developing nations of the world would no longer be dependent on the Anglo-American-led financial monopoly. Rachel found it strange to be sitting next to Peng, her quasi-date for the evening. He was well rested and ebullient in the aftermath of his previous day's triumph and daring escape, and she had to admit that in his white suit he looked pretty dashing. *He'll be a big catch someday, as long as his wife doesn't put trustworthiness high on her list.* She found it even more bizarre that she had gone from jogging around the block in New York to nearly having her throat slit and catching the blood from two men's heads that got blown away next to her to climbing down from a helicopter into a supercavitating Chinese submarine in the Atlantic Ocean and then ending up half a world away in the tropics being hosted by the president of one of the largest nations of South America—all in the span of thirty-six hours. *Now those—or at least most of them—are stories for my grandchildren.*

CHAPTER
18

In lieu of the Venezuelan president's plane, Peng and Rachel headed to China on Shiang's executive jet. Its range did not permit the jet to fly nonstop over the Pacific, and Shiang could not trust the nations in between to refuel; so he decided to route it eastward to Moscow and from there onto Shanghai. Shiang's plane was outfitted with conference areas, communication stations, and several sleep rooms. Two attractive flight attendants catered to the whims of every one of its guests. Rachel wondered if George Perry's executive jet looked the same inside. Although Ben Fernandez may have been Perry's strategic opponent, Li Shiang was more his counterpart in the wealth and status arena.

After a leisurely breakfast, Rachel went over to one of the computers to check on Internet news. She realized she never had managed to contact Pacific Group and felt the need to do so, but she was the guest of Shiang now and needed to get his guidance on every move. Then she chuckled to herself, *What does it matter, anyhow—I'm never going back to work at Pacific.*

She started to think more about her situation. Although for the remainder of the trip she technically was a guest, in reality she was more like a prisoner, given her lack of money, passport and other identification, and employment. Though she should have been anxious about her future, she was on the contrary feeling almost euphoric now that she was temporarily freed from all responsibility to do anything or be anywhere.

When they landed at Sheremetyevo Airport in Moscow, she got out of the jet and into the executive waiting area. She could see that the sky was gray, with flurries in the air, although there was no snow on the ground. The gloomy atmosphere was in stark contrast to the tropical air and festivity of Caracas.

In less than ten hours, Shiang's jet would land at Shanghai's Pudong International Airport. All Rachel knew was when and where they would be arriving. She had no idea who would be there to greet her, although Peng had hinted that his uncle would meet them at the gate. After a long nap, Rachel woke and noticed Peng sitting near her, studying one of the red maps on the laptop screen.

"Do you mind if I have a look, John? I was wondering what these so-called red maps look like. After all, they almost put you in prison for life and me underground with no life!"

Peng passed the laptop to Rachel so she could get a closer look. "This evidently is the one for the cave you visited. Does it make any sense to you?"

"Not really. I can't understand the Japanese characters, and the overall layout seems . . . almost backward."

"That's because the direction of the little flag in the upper-left corner means you need to view the map in reverse, as if through a mirror." After the flight attendant retrieved a small mirror from her purse and Rachel placed it opposite the map, she was amazed at how the layout of the cave now corresponded to her mental image of it. The large room with the gold bars and the smaller one with the Golden Buddha were clearly marked, along with other rooms behind the concealed wall, one with a turtle next to it, signifying an explosive charge. She also saw what looked to be a booby trap not far from where she had been walking. *I hope it had already been dismantled before Craig took me into the cave.*

"So, I take it the Dragon Family knows how to interpret all of the symbols?"

"We know the basic code, although we will still need to be careful during the excavations."

Rachel was silent for a few seconds, then turned away from the screen and posed a question that had been puzzling her for a while. "So, John, I'm curious how you met Craig. Was it through the Dragons, or were you friends before?"

"Before. We met at Cambridge our first year and stayed close for two years thereafter. Even though he's white and I'm Chinese, we both had Asia in our blood and similar takes on the world. But he didn't like it at Cambridge and left after two years, whereas I finished my first-honors degree there. But we kept in touch over the years. I had heard about the Dragon Family coming together while I was at Cambridge and relayed it to Craig, who said he would in turn mention it to his father. His father had already been approached and was well aware of the historical realities, but when Craig spoke favorably of us, he became much more receptive. It was very important that Craig's father came on board, not because he has a lot of wealth anymore, but because of his historical standing and English roots. Most of the rest of his family shied away, preferring to maintain their allegiance to Britain."

"So, you're telling me everyone joined up out of lofty idealism . . . including you."

Peng smiled. "No, as I already told you, I'm not doing it just out of idealism, although I do believe in the Dragons' goals. Mainly, I joined because of family, Rachel. Before I was born, my father was removed from a high-ranking position in the Party in Yangzhou and was banished to the countryside. When he was 'rehabilitated,' so to speak, he found it hard to adapt to the dramatic changes in Chinese society that had occurred in the meantime. My mother's brother—Li Shiang—was already on his way to amassing a large fortune in shipping and commercial trade and he took me under his wing, making sure I went to a top international school run by the British in Shanghai and then onto Cambridge. My obligation to him is immense."

He paused, then added, "But you are partly correct about the others—there were, indeed, 'sweeteners' thrown in. For instance, Craig's father, like his grandfather Anthony, felt the British pressured Sarawak out of his family's control and gave it away to their ally, Malaysia. And, the sultan of Sulu was even angrier—he felt the British broke outright an agreement to lease North Borneo and basically stole it from his family.[114] Perhaps you've heard that the Malaysian government is very unpopular in Sarawak and Sabah provinces now, which is why they are both beset with growing independence movements.[115] What Putrajaya[116] doesn't know yet is that any attempts to put down the North Borneo independence movements by force will be met by an entire Chinese amphibious group—backed up by a carrier fleet, if needed."

"So, Shiang is going to get the Chinese government to put Craig's family and the sultan back in power?"

"Of course not. But they may recover some of their influence . . . and wealth."

"And what does China get out of it?"

---

[114] For a discussion of the different translations of the documents either ceding or leasing control of Sabah to a British trading company, see http://en.wikipedia.org/wiki/Sultanate_of_Sulu

[115] The burgeoning independence movements in Sabah and Sarawak are discussed in: http://www.themalaysianinsider.com/malaysia/article/do-sabah-and-sarawak-really-want-to-leave-malaysia; and http://www.sapp.org.my/constitution/130721_sarawak_independence.asp The claim of the sultan of Sulu (now deceased) to be the constitutional monarch of Sabah is described in http://world.time.com/2013/04/10/waging-war-at-the-court-of-the-sultan-of-sulu

[116] Putrajaya, a planned suburb of Kuala Lumpur, became the administrative capital of Malaysia in 1999.

"China will end up with an ally over the Spratly Islands and effective control of the eastern entrance to the Strait of Malacca."[117]

Rachel pondered Peng's last sentence for a moment and then it suddenly came to her. "Of course, it's all starting to make sense now," she said, smiling churlishly. "All of this dates back to the Philippines communist rebellion of the seventies, which China supported.[118] Fernandez allied with the Chinese then and continued to serve as an agent for them throughout the decades, right? His jumpstarting of the Dragon Family—why couldn't I see this Chinese power play all along? So much for all of Fernandez' 'idealism'!"

Peng smiled. "Good girl, Rachel, you've indeed figured it out . . . mostly. But as I mentioned before, don't underestimate Fernandez. He's a complex and brilliant and, up to a point, idealistic man. And the Dragons are not just a Chinese front, even though Fernandez' brainchild, the Asian Monetary Fund, eventually was incarnated by the Chinese.[119] But in the end, it's about who has the biggest gorilla in the room. Without the Chinese, everyone would still fear the Americans."

Rachel then changed the subject to another question that had been bothering her. "So, how did you know that Craig knew that I wrote the book?"

---

[117] A summary of the strategic importance of the strait to China is contained in: http://www.academia.edu/1931497/The_Strait_of_Malacca_as_one_of_the_most_important_geopolitical_regions_for_the_Peoples_Republic_of_China. The Spratly Islands in the South China Sea closest to Sabah Province in North Borneo are a source of dispute among various nations, in part because of their strategic location and potential hydrocarbon wealth: http://www.bbc.com/news/world-asia-pacific-13748349 See also footnote #98.

[118] See footnote #91.

[119] The Asian Infrastructure Investment Bank, under the aegis of China, was officially launched in October of 2014: http://en.wikipedia.org/wiki/Asian_Infrastructure_Investment_Bank

"One day I was with Jacques at his condo and I was poking around and I saw your book—I mean, I didn't know it was your book at first, but it had the Imperial label, and I knew Craig was a marketing exec there. And I read the jacket cover and got interested—you know, I'm another one totally convinced about your government's role in September 11ᵗʰ, but that's a whole other story—and I noticed that on the title page was the inscription 'To my best friend, Krew.' That's when I picked up your connection to the book, even though I later found out you didn't write it."

"And I thought I had covered my tracks pretty well."

"Because you never thought a guy like me sleuthing around your best friend's apartment could be good friends with your publisher."

The conversation died away, and then a few minutes later Peng struck it up again.

"So, Rachel, since you're asking a lot of questions, let me ask you one."

"Sure. Well, maybe."

"Don't worry, it doesn't involve you. It involves your friend Frankie. Do you think your friend Frankie could ever be tamed?"

Rachel smiled. *Isn't that a hoot—he has the hots for Frankie!*

"Well . . . I'm not sure. If you asked me back when we were roommates in college, I would have given you an emphatic 'no'. She was *really* wild back then. I think she's still pretty free-spirited, but I do sense some changes in her."

"How do you mean?"

Well, I'm certainly not going to tell him she makes love differently to me than she used to!

"She's searching for something more than the sex and money and drugs. I really think she's looking for a relationship and wouldn't be as dismissive of a long-term one now as much as she used to be. But John, do you really think you could go from being a client of hers to an honest lover? As her ex-roommate in college, I have to warn you there's a big difference between the fantasy and reality of Frankie."

"Rachel, I stopped being a client the minute Frankie started working for us. I dealt with her as a real person after that. And I really admire her for what she did for us. It took a lot of verve . . . and intelligence."

"Yeah, there's no question that, especially when it comes to emotional intelligence, Frankie's well into the genius range."

Peng placed his chin in this hand and looked up and to the right, pondering Rachel's words.

Rachel decided to break the silence. "John, if you can pull off the heist of the century and land a helicopter solo on a submarine, you don't need me to go after Frankie. But don't be under any illusions—you may be able to rein her in a bit, but you'll never completely control her. But I don't think you really want to."

"You're right." He paused, before adding with an impish look, "So, are you ready to be my friend now?"

She smiled. "Sure, John, I'm willing to be your friend. Just don't ask me to be your lover."

"I'm not asking you to be my lover, Rachel . . . although you did look sensational last night."

About an hour before their descent, the flight attendants told Peng and Rachel that Li Shiang and his wife and some "special friends" would meet them at the airport and that they should shower and change into autumn clothes. Rachel had received slacks and a sweater outfit in Caracas, and she figured that would be warm enough, at least to get to the restaurant.

Shiang's jet pulled up to a special gate at Pudong International. Greeting them were Shiang and his wife and one of his assistants, who gave Rachel a bouquet of roses; in return, Rachel dutifully thanked Shiang for her rescue. Then, Rachel could hardly believe her eyes—standing off to the right were Frankie and Karen! She went right to them and gave them both big hugs.

It was off to the Szechuan restaurant in two separate limousines, one taking Shiang and his wife and assistant and Peng and the other taking the young American women. At first, the girls talked excitedly about what had transpired, with Rachel telling of her kidnapping, her time on the submarine, and the dinner with the Venezuelan president. But then the conversation quickly turned sour when Frankie reminded Rachel of Perry's death.

"So, you heard that George Perry was assassinated, right?"

"Yes, I did. And, it really hit me hard. I know he and his friends did a lot of bad stuff, and Jackson was pretty much estranged from him, but he was always polite to me."

Frankie then chimed in. "So, how do you think I feel, Rachel? I go from sharing his bed to unwittingly setting him up for a hit."

Rachel turned to Karen and then asked Frankie, "Does Karen know?"

Frankie replied, "Yeah, Karen knows everything now."

They were all silent for a little while, but then Karen lightened it up a bit. "You know, it may not have been pretty, but we managed to screw all those bastards on Wall Street. And if we're lucky, half of them will jump out of their windows. Dartmouth used to produce the guys who fucked Main Street to save Wall Street.[120] Now, it's produced the 'Big Green' gals who brought Wall Street down!"

"And to think neither of you would have even dared go to one of those 'Occupy Wall Street' rallies without your Louis Vuittons!"

---

[120] Two Dartmouth graduates—Henry "Hank" Paulson '68, as treasury secretary, and Timothy Geithner '75, as chairman of the New York Federal Reserve and then Paulson's successor at treasury—were instrumental in the controversial bailout of the big Wall Street banks after the financial meltdown in 2008 (see Johnson & Kwak, 2010, *op cit.* chap. 6)

"Yeah, you go, girl," said Frankie, laughingly. Then she looked around and said, "Hey, where's the bubbly? I thought all these things had refrigerated bars in them."

Karen said, "Ah, don't bother. After lunch, when we drag Rachel here back to the room, we're gonna empty the liquor bar big-time!"

The lunch with Shiang was fairly sedate, although Rachel could tell he was in good spirits. And why not? His Dragons had pulled off a stunning upset and, as his nephew had intimated, he had probably personally made tens of millions in the process by betting against the dollar as it fell hard in the last several days. Shiang didn't make a speech at lunch but did say a few words at the end, thanking all four of them for their "noble efforts" on behalf of the Dragon Family. He presented Karen, Frankie, and Rachel each with diamond earrings set in gold, while he gave his nephew a watch with the same twenty-four-karat gold.

Rachel was watching the interactions during the lunch and noticed that Peng was gazing at Frankie a lot more than the others. If she noticed it, Frankie didn't let on. *Is Frankie just playing hard to get or is she uncharacteristically dense today? Something has changed in her!*

As the lunch was concluding, Shiang conferred with Rachel briefly about her plans. He told her she would stay in the same hotel as the other girls but that he had arranged for her to take another flight on his plane to Manila the next day, where other Dragon members would greet her, along with some of her relatives. He indicated it would be too soon to go back to America but that, if needed, she could work for one of his enterprises "somewhere in Asia".

Before they all left, Peng came over and gave a brief hug and kiss to Karen, a big smile and longer hug to Rachel, and a more extended embrace to Frankie. Then, the limousine drove the three of them back to the Intercontinental Hotel where, as Karen had promised, they opened up the liquor cabinet and fridge. During the course of the long afternoon spent gossiping, they talked about the reality that they might not be able to go back to the States for a long time, if ever. Karen indicated she was headed for Sydney the next day, where she would soon rendezvous with Jacques, who had already been offered a job with one of the trading companies there but had flown to France in the interim to take care of some family matters. "You know, we have a few friends down there who are into yachting big time, so we should be back on the water in no time."

Frankie also indicated she had a friend in Sydney and would leave on the same flight as Karen. She had an offer from Li Shiang to work for one of his companies in Australia, and she indicated her wild days and escorting were going to be a thing of the past.

"You know why I'm going to get my act together?"

Karen gave her a deadpan look. "Could it be that you're about to turn twenty-nine and you almost got yourself killed in this latest little escapade of yours?"

"Nope. It's because of our little hike up Moose Mountain homecoming weekend. I know you saw me huffing and puffing after the first half-mile or so. It was then that it finally dawned on me that my bod may still look good on the outside but on the inside I'm wasting away."

"So, what would you do in Sydney?" Rachel asked.

"Oh, if I don't take the Shiang job, I'd probably go back to financials and start hunting for some really adventurous guy with money . . . who would like someone who really knows what she's doing in bed. I figure I've got only a couple more years before my wrinkles and cellulite start popping out, although I could remove them once I get the next installment of my trust."

Karen then asked, "So, Frankie, you're telling us you could turn from a royal slut into a 'stand-by-your-man' woman overnight?"

"Oh, it may take a few months of 'sex-addicts anonymous'— and the right guy."

Rachel then chimed in, "If you haven't found Mr. Right within a year, come see me—I know exactly the man for you."

Frankie laughed. "Oh, don't tell me John Peng. True, he's good-looking and has a lot of money and has just about everything else I would want, but I don't trust him one bit."

"That's why you're made for each other—he doesn't trust you, either. But he asked me if I thought he could ever tame you."

Frankie smiled and even blushed slightly. "Really, he said that?" *Frankie never blushes—she's clearly interested in Peng!*

Frankie then quickly turned the tables on Rachel. "So, what about this fellow you mentioned, the guy who got you into this whole mess? What's his name again?"

"Craig Brooke."

Karen said, "I don't believe he even exists, Rachel. Show us a photo."

Rachel took out her smartphone, which was among the few things Karen had brought over from her apartment, and pulled up the photo of her and Brooke at the Dragon Family reception in Baguio.

"Wow," Frankie said, "he's really cute, Rachel."

Despite the drinks, Rachel was still in no mood to get started talking about her romantic interest, even to her best friends, so she lied. "Yeah, Frankie, but John just told me on the way over that he thought Craig's gay."

"Well, you're just going to have to do something about that, Freckles."

Karen took out another couple of miniature bourbons and handed them to Frankie and Rachel. "You can start by downing another one of these, Rach."

CHAPTER
19

Rachel looked out the window as the high-rises of Manila grew larger during the jet's descent. She kept wondering who would meet her at the airport. Would it be Don Ignacio again, Ben Fernandez . . . or even Craig Brooke?

Although Rachel understood the new impending reality of her life at a cognitive level, it was only on the trip from Beijing that she actually *felt* the dislocation and uncertainty. Her elation on the plane from Caracas had transformed itself into a mild angst as she wondered what she would do now, where she would live, and where her income would come from. Would she be indebted, even captive, to the Family for her livelihood in the future? And when would she ever get to see her family again? *Family . . . God, I forgot all about Thanksgiving next week. What am I going to do, call Mom from Manila and tell her I'm going to be AWOL for the holiday?*

Part of her didn't even want to get off the plane. *Maybe I should have stayed in China. I could have worked at Pacific's office in Shanghai or used my experience and Mandarin in some other capacity. But that's a pretty stupid idea . . . what would I do with no money or place to live?*

As she entered the terminal, she saw only Fernandez waiting for her. The lack of a gathering actually calmed her, as she knew that Fernandez would get her situated and then get down to business.

"Welcome back, Rachel," he said as he shook her hand. "You must be exhausted after all of the stress and travel."

"Yes, definitely."

"That's why I'm going to talk to you about everything that's happened, after you've managed to rest up in your hotel room. But I do want to give you something as a token of the Dragon Family's thanks and also with the realization that you're going to need something to get by on in the next couple of months. Please don't refuse—it's not a payment for services, because we know you would never have gone through it all for the money."

Rachel accepted but didn't open the envelope, which she later found out had five hundred thousand Philippine pesos in it, equivalent to about ten thousand American dollars.

Fernandez then told her he was going to leave but that before he did, he wanted her to meet a "special person". And just as he was exiting, she saw him shaking the hands of someone who was coming from behind a post. It was her father! Overwhelmed with joy and unable to control the emotions that had been suppressed for days, Rachel broke down in tears.

"Daddy, Daddy," she sobbed as he put his arms around her. "You don't know how I've missed you and Mom. At one point, I didn't know if I'd ever see you all again."

After they shared their long embrace, her dad said, "C'mon, honey, let's sit down and talk a bit before I take you to the hotel." Then, after sitting down, he stared at her. "Look at you! What the hell have you been doing behind our backs?"

Rachel tried to smile. "Oh, I can't begin to tell you all that's happened. I'm so happy you were able to be here . . . but I wish Mom and Christina were here as well, so we could celebrate Thanksgiving."

"Now, that's an interesting idea. I think I'll call them and tell them to get on the next flight to Manila."

"What do you mean?"

"Rachel, we're all going to celebrate Thanksgiving here . . . at the hacienda. All of us, plus Lola and Aunt Isabel and her family, we'll all be there."

"Really?"

"And that's not all. I took your advice and am coming back here to Luzon to live . . . permanently, perhaps."

"How can you do that?"

"Well, look at it this way. America's not necessarily safe for us for the near term . . . and it may be difficult for everyone, what with the financial collapse that seems imminent. Texas Instruments has arranged for me to help manage the tech center in Baguio, beginning early next year. So I expect to take it."

"And what about Mom and Christina?"

"I'm sorry to say but your grandmother has really gone downhill and is now in hospice. Mom will stay with her in Austin until the end, so she'll finish out the academic year there. Since she's now eligible for early retirement, your mom will then join me over here. And Christina will finish her master's this year, so she'll probably join us here, too—at least for a while."

"And I thought only my life was going to be uprooted. Little did I know."

"Rachel, to be honest, some of this might have happened even without all of your doings. Your plea to me to visit Lola last June finally made it clear that I was being selfish for distancing myself all these years. Why should I blame her for Miguel's death? After all, it wasn't about her. And now I better understand what it's like to have a child a long way away as you're getting older."

"So, can I stay with you, while I sort things out? I actually was impressed with Baguio and would enjoy living there for a while. And, you'll love it with all of the streams for fishing and even golf courses nearby . . . if you are willing to play in the rain half the year."

"You don't have to remind me about the Baguio rains. But Rachel honey, I'd love to have you stay with me, as long as you want. We could use months to catch up on things, and I'll even teach you to fly fish if you want. But let's go back to the hotel now."

Rachel and her father were both smiling as they headed to the Marriott, the same hotel she had stayed in five months earlier. When they got out, her dad gave her the key to the room and told her she needed to rest and then they'd do some shopping and go to dinner, just the two of them. They would stay another night in Manila before driving to Rosales over the weekend. As he left, her father mentioned that he had just met a "fine young man who said he knew you and would try to give you a call while you're in Manila."

"You're not talking about Craig Brooke, are you?"

Her father merely smiled and then drove off.

Brooke didn't end up calling her because he was sitting right in the lobby when she arrived. He got up to meet her and managed to sneak up behind her while she was at the front desk.

"Rachel, it's good to see you again." When she turned around with a surprised look, he went to kiss her on the cheek, and when she didn't object he continued on.

"I just wanted to let you know that you have a right to be mad at me because I haven't been totally truthful with you."

"Oh, really?"

"You know what I said about it 'being all business'? Well, it wasn't . . . at least not after your trip here."

"And you think you're telling me something I don't already know?"

"So, John told you about my feelings?"

"Sort of. But the way I really know is because your eyes gave away your panic when the knife was at my throat."

At the mention of her hostage experience, Brooke winced and turned away.

But Rachel wasn't going to let him off the hook. "So, it may have been more than business for you, but why do you think it was anything more than that for me, Craig?"

When he didn't respond, Rachel told him with a stern face to come back to her. Then she went right up to him and planted a big kiss on him and then broke into a broad smile. Brooke immediately wrapped his arms around her and gave her an even longer kiss.

After they broke off, Rachel opened up. "Craig, I felt something the very first night you left me off at my Brooklyn apartment. It wasn't love or anything, just an intense, almost suffocating loneliness I hadn't experienced since Jackson's death. But what really got my feelings in gear was when you turned back to Rosales so I could see my grandmother. Do you know how many men would have done that?"

"I don't know, but I'm glad I did it. I guess it's because I was already in love with you at that point."

"But you know that same loneliness came back to me at the airport after you dropped me off. For a couple of months, I tried to put you out of my mind because I thought that was it, but I was conflicted . . . and I kept fantasizing about you." She paused. "And now you're here for me, in the flesh."

Craig smiled at her and kissed her lightly on the cheek again. "Speaking of reality, I'm wondering what your plans are for the near future. Are you going to join your father in Baguio?"

"I am. And you have a standing invite to visit . . . or join me."

"I would love to, Rachel . . . I really would. There are a lot of universities in Baguio, and with my master's degree and publishing experience, I'm sure I could manage to find something up there, although it probably wouldn't bring in much."

"I don't care. We wouldn't need a lot of money—ha, ha! But couldn't you go to work for the Family in Baguio? I was amazed that first night how much you knew about economic and political history."

"I could, but I now realize that I'm really not cut out for all of this intrigue—especially after seeing you almost get your throat cut. As you can probably surmise, this game is going to go on for a while, with the possibility of more retaliations. Deep down, I'm more of a romantic."

"Speaking of romantic, weren't you supposed to take me the next time I was here to a dinner on the Baywalk, to see the sunset over Manila Bay?"

"I didn't actually say I'd include dinner, but I'll be glad to throw that in as well. How about tomorrow night, if you're free."

"I'll make sure I'm free . . . there's no way I'm going to miss out this time." She gave him another long embrace and, noticing his arousal, she kidded him, "But don't expect to get anything afterward—I'm starting my period."

He winced slightly as he deadpanned, "Now, that's *really* romantic!" Then he smiled at her and said, "In case you hadn't noticed, Rachel, I'm very patient. I figure there'll be plenty of time for lovemaking in Baguio. But since I'm also a believer in transcendence, perhaps I could get some astral sex in the meantime?"

She laughed and said, "Show me the way, Spiritual Boy!" Then he responded with an even tighter embrace and they engaged in a more passionate kiss. *Maybe I will end up after all having grandchildren to tell my stories—our stories—to.*

Printed in the United States
By Bookmasters